Stories from Three Brothers

DAVID GEORGE | BUD GEORGE | MICHAEL GEORGE

Stories From Three Brothers
Copyright © 2020 **David George, Bud George, Michael George**

All rights reserved. No part of this book may be used or reproduced by any means, graphic, electronic, or mechanical, including photocopying, recording, taping or by information storage and retrieval system without the written permission of the author except in the case of brief quotations embodied in critical articles and reviews.

Stratton Press Publishing
831 N Tatnall Street Suite M #188,
Wilmington, DE 19801
www.stratton-press.com
1-888-323-7009

Because of the dynamic nature of the Internet, any web addresses or links contained in this book may have changed since publication and may no longer be valid. The views expressed in the work are solely those of the author and do not necessarily reflect the views of the publisher, and the publisher hereby disclaims any responsibility for them.

ISBN (Paperback): 978-1-64895-186-2
ISBN (Hardback): 978-1-64895-188-6
ISBN (Ebook): 978-1-64895-187-9

Printed in the United States of America

Dedicated to

Bill and Laverne George
For good or bad, they raised all three of us

THE LAST SEASON

Bud George

About this story

A long time ago, Bud and I were talking about writing. I told him about an idea I had for a story, its plot, and its ending. A fair amount of time went by, and I still hadn't written it, so Bud did. I thought then, and still think, that he did a great job writing it. I liked the story so well that when I got an idea for a novel, I stole his story and used it, with some changes, as the first chapter of my novel *Why A Refuge*.

I chose this story to start this book, first, because it's a damn good story.

My second reason, because of this story behind the story.

Bud's a great guy, and so far as I know, my stealing his story never upset him any more than his stealing my idea ever upset me. We simply shared, and that's partly what brothers are for. We, the three of us, in one way or the other and off and on, have shared a lifetime.

—Michael

*****

I bought my ticket, stuffed my rig and bag in a bus station locker with a bent door, and found an all-night chili joint two blocks later. I ordered a bowl and added a layer of crushed red pepper to get rid of the hospital taste in my mouth.

The good, strong coffee made me think of home, the old man, and the five years of letters I should have wrote.

The day I left, he put a twenty-dollar bill in my shirt pocket and told me the door was open. There would be room for me if I didn't get rich off rodeo.

I was eighty-six cents from being broke and out of smokes when I climbed up the bus steps and sat in the first seat behind the driver to avoid the long walk back to the only other seat.

That little fuzzy red-haired leprechaun of a driver made it look easy. Pushing a big flexible diesel through the late-night traffic. When we rolled onto the freeway with the bus running a steady seventy, the leprechaun pulled out a crumpled pack of Marlboros from his shirt pocket, lit one, and handed the pack to me. He said he'd noticed my bucking rig and asked me how my season had been. I told him it was my last one.

He let me off on the highway, and I walked into the sunrise up the mile long road that ran past the old man's place. There was an auction sign with that day's date nailed to the mailbox post.

I went up the driveway and saw an old green Chevy one-ton with a dent in the door and Texas plates parked next to the pole shed. The man sitting on the ground with his back against the front wheel was my uncle Roy. I set my bag on the truck hood and sat down beside him to watch the sun finish coming up. I asked him what he was doing way up here.

"I come to buy a saddle," he said and asked me if I'd had breakfast. I shook my head no, and he handed me the pint he was working on.

Roy was one of the old man's brothers, and he helped raise me when he was around. He never stayed in one place long, but he came back to work for the old man off and on. Most people didn't think they got along because they fought and disagreed about everything in public, but I never saw them that way when they were alone. They would talk quietly for hours while working or just sitting around at night, smoking and drinking coffee.

Roy gave me my first horse, an old, soured, ex-rodeo bronc. He said I could have the damn thing if I could ride it. I worked for near a week to get him saddled, and then he threw me every day for a month. But I rode him.

There was a good-sized crowd on hand when we walked inside the shed to watch the auctioneer do his stuff. The old man walked over and shook my hand and said it was good to see me.

We watched the auctioneer sell off the hand tools and spare parts, and then came the dusty old stock saddle, the same one I sold to a dealer to help finance my first rodeo season. Roy was the highest bidder at seventy-five dollars.

It was late in the afternoon, and bidding had started on the land and buildings when I saw Brad's big Lincoln coming up the driveway. He was the third brother. He made a lot of money in business and the stock market. Just before I left home, he started in politics.

Brad and Roy never got along. Just too different, I guess. Roy was a drifter and didn't give a damn about money or what anyone thought of him. He was easygoing, and some thought lazy, but I worked with him. I knew it wasn't true. Brad was always in a hurry; he never had time to sit and bullshit. His clothes were expensive and always looked new. I never saw him get his hands dirty.

Roy and I stepped into the kitchen as the old man was counting bills into Brad's hand. Roy turned and slammed the door—hard—leaving.

I stayed and said hello to Brad. When he left, I talked to the old man for a while. He told me Brad had been holding the note on the place. Brad had offered him more time on it, but the old man said no. It was due, and that was it. The only way he could pay Brad and his other creditors was to sell everything. He was flat broke now.

I'd picked up my bag, left the bucking rig on the hood of Roy's truck, and was halfway to the highway when Roy stopped his truck next to me. The old man was with him.

"Get in, boy!" he ordered.

I did. Then I told him I was broke and couldn't even buy a meal.

"Fuck it," Roy said. "We'll eat when we get to Texas."

MATTIE JONES
Michael George

The hot summer sun tortured the delicate skin on Mattie Jones's face as she waited for the bus, making her wonder why she'd been foolish enough to go out on a day with a temperature above ninety degrees. From now on, she told herself, she'd stay home on days like this.

When the bus finally arrived, all the seats were taken. She found it difficult to hold herself up and onto her packages at the same time. Then two black teenagers left their seats and motioned for her and another elderly lady to sit down.

Mattie let the other lady sit down first before gratefully taking her seat. She looked at the two boys, smiled, and said, "Thank you very much." They returned her smile and nodded.

She thought it strange that they didn't speak until they started talking with their hands and realized they were both deaf.

When the bus got close to her stop, Mattie noticed a large group of young men on the sidewalk. They were white, and all of them were wearing the same color shirts, all with the sleeves torn off. The tallest man in the group noticed the deaf boys, who were rapidly signing to each other, and pointed excitedly at them. She didn't think much about it until two of the boys from the sidewalk boarded the bus a few blocks later, after chasing it in an old van.

They got on without paying their fares, hurrying to the back where the deaf boys stood. The bus driver ignored them, deciding that the fares they didn't pay weren't worth the hassle it would take to collect them. He quickly regretted his decision.

The boys from the sidewalk jumped the deaf boys as soon as they reached them, talking to them as they did.

"We seen yer signals," said the tall man who'd first seen them, then looking at his friend, "didn't we, Darryl?"

"You damn right we did, Sherman," Darryl agreed. "And we don't like none of you Red Rascals on our turf. Ain't too smart of you to be a ridin' by, makin' them secret signals. Now you got to pay."

The deaf boys were confused by the newcomers' actions, then terrified when they pulled out their knives.

"Cut 'em good," Sherman said, "poke their eyes out."

One of the deaf boys went down immediately, with knife wounds in his stomach and chest. The second boy stood longer, with Sherman holding him up as Darryl cut his face and tried to poke out his eyes.

Mattie was the only one on the bus to make any attempt to stop the attack. She couldn't move as fast as she wanted to when she charged the boys with the knives, swinging her full shopping bag at them and screaming as loud as she could. Her voice alerted the bus driver to what was happening, and he slammed on the brakes, knocking Mattie and both the gang members to the floor of the bus.

A wild brawl followed, with Sherman and Darryl fighting to escape. The driver did his best to stop them, getting stabbed twice in the arm for his efforts. They knocked Mattie down when she made a second effort to stop them, kicking her as they left the bus. The rest of the passengers sat watching, doing nothing except avoiding the chaos.

When the police came, they questioned almost everyone on the bus. They tried to ignore Mattie. She was the only one who could give them an accurate description of the attackers, but they believed she was just a little old lady with a very vivid imagination because she said she tried to fight off the attackers and that both of them had swastikas tattooed to their left shoulders. Or possibly she was senile since she was extremely excited when she tried to talk to them. Why else would anyone as old as she was get so excited?

Mattie was upset and angry when she got home. Just because she was old, there was no excuse for the police to treat her the way they had. She also felt that there must be something she could do. It was time for the news, so she decided to watch it first, to see if there was anything on about the injured boys.

The weather started the newscast. A storm watch had been issued for the southern half of Minnesota, and already, tornado and severe thunderstorm warnings had been given for counties west of Minneapolis. The forecaster said the storms were heading northeast, and he named the counties in the storms' path. The weather warnings were interrupted for a few minutes of news. The incident on the bus, and the boys who were hurt, were only given a few lines.

No one was arrested for the crime, even though one of the deaf boys died and the other lost most of the sight in his left eye. He was blinded in his right eye.

A few days later, Mattie decided to go grocery shopping. She hadn't gone out since the incident on the bus and hadn't paid any attention to the weather outside, so she was surprised by the dark clouds filling the sky. She slipped and fell off her front steps when she focused her attention on them.

She bruised her right hip and elbow. It was only because she landed on soft grass that she didn't break anything. After she got back on her feet, she realized a light drizzle was starting, but decided to walk to the three short blocks to the store anyway.

The pain from the new bruise on her hip bothered her when she started out. By the time she finished shopping and was on her way home, she was in agony. The weight of the bag she carried pulled her slight frame to one side as she trudged through the now heavy rain. All she had in the bag was a stalk of celery, a medium-size onion, a quart of milk, and a pound of hamburger. Her sore hip made it feel like a sack of rocks. In her other hand, she carried a small handbag with ten dollars in it. The only cash she had until she could get to the bank and make a withdrawal.

She walked with her head down, trying to watch her step and not fall again, and didn't see the two young men approaching her. They were beside her before she heard them. Moving fast, they knocked her down and grabbed her handbag and groceries. She still got a good look at their faces. Familiar faces. They were Darryl and Sherman, the men on the bus with the knives.

The fall knocked the wind out of her, so it took her several minutes to regain her feet. No one in the passing cars paid any attention to her.

She walked the remaining two blocks home before calling the police. It took them two hours to get there. When she explained what happened, they made it no secret that she had spoiled the tranquility of their day with her petty problem.

"A lousy ten dollars," the older middle-aged cop asked, "is all you lost?"

"It was all the cash I had," Mattie explained. "They were the hoodlums who stabbed the poor deaf boys on the bus. Do you think I'll be able to get the money back? You should know who they are. I don't mind losing the old handbag. I have another one I can use."

She didn't like to throw anything away and had several old purses.

"Well now, lady…Mattie," the older cop answered, "it is Mattie, isn't it?"

"Yes, that's right. My name is Mattie. Mattie Jones."

"Good. Now, Mattie," he said, forcing a smile, "it ain't likely we'll ever get your money back. Even if we do catch them muggers. Which, considering muggers and gangs are a dime a dozen in this neighborhood, ain't very likely either."

"I told you who they are. They're the men who stabbed those poor boys on the bus. Their names are Darryl and Sherman."

"You didn't tell us anything. Those men who did the stabbing on the bus haven't been accurately identified or caught."

"They certainly were identified. The problem is, you people don't listen. So what am I going to do now? Are you sure you can't catch them? How can I go out with those hoodlums roaming the streets?"

"Look, Mattie," the cop said, showing his exasperation with her, "in this city, we get a hell of a lot of calls like yours every day. There ain't no way we can catch all the muggers. Even if we did, some shyster lawyer would get them off and out on the street again, quicker than you can believe."

"What will I do? How am I supposed to go out? They might remember me from the bus."

"Mattie, I don't know what you're going to do. All I can do is tell you to be more careful in the future. Don't carry all your money with you when you go out. And don't go out at night."

"I never go out at night. It wasn't dark when I was out. It was over two hours ago."

"All the same, be more careful in the future."

"What will I do now?"

The older cop answered with a shrug and they left.

"What she ought to do," the second cop, a young black man, said on the way to their car, "is move into one of those homes for old folks. That's where she belongs. This isn't her neighborhood anyway."

Mattie stood at her front door, watching the police car until it was out of sight, glad she'd finally decided to give up the house she'd lived in for over forty years. The cop was right; it wasn't *her* neighborhood any longer.

Supper that night was a can of mixed vegetables. She didn't feel like cooking nor did she feel like cleaning up the mess she'd make if she did.

Two days later, she made a nervous trip to the bank, withdrawing enough cash to get through the next week. She knew she should open a checking account, but hated all the nonsense of writing checks, balancing accounts, and paying fees. With money in her savings account, the bank paid her. Besides, since she didn't drive or have a driver's license, too many places wouldn't accept her checks. Most clerks didn't recognize her identification, when almost everyone else had a driver's license.

She walked to the grocery store, after her trip to the bank, and was a block from home when the two muggers jumped her again. She banged her knee on the hard sidewalk when they pushed her down and had a difficult time getting up. The empty-handed walk the rest of the way home seemed harder than walking did while she was loaded down with groceries.

She was disappointed when the police came to her house. It was the same two cops who came the first time.

"Do you mean to tell me," the older cop said, "you let those guys mug you again?"

"Yes," Mattie answered, "and I think they're doing it to get even for what I did on the bus."

Why didn't the police understand?

"Sure, they did," the cop said disgustedly. He didn't believe she did anything on the bus, other than try to stay out of the way, the same as everyone else. "Last time, they got a lousy ten bucks and some hamburger. Such a great haul, they jump you again the first time you go out? You call that getting even?"

"Why else would they do it?" She was puzzled. Why were the police acting as if she had done something wrong? "They didn't get any money this time. I had it in my pocket instead of my handbag."

"I don't know, Mattie. I guess we'll see what we can do. You're going to have to be more careful from now on."

With that, they turned and left her.

"There are a lot of places she could go," the younger cop said, getting into the car. "Why does she have to stay here? Ain't no one in the neighborhood who wants her kind around."

Mattie knew she was in serious trouble. With the attitude of police, they weren't going to help her. She tried to make another trip to the store for food and was jumped again.

She called the police. Again, they left abruptly. They wouldn't listen to her. What could she do? She was alone, at the mercy of the hoodlums. The police weren't going to help.

Her children were gone, living out of state, and her husband, Charlie, was long dead. Life was so mean sometimes. Charlie shouldn't have died. Not so close to retirement, with his health so good. If only that cable hadn't broken. All those years of digging wells without an accident, then a fault in a cable and he had to have his head in the way. Couldn't even leave the coffin open at his funeral.

They could have traveled or moved closer to their daughter. Something. It was all gone, and there was nothing left of him. Only some personal things and old drilling equipment in the garage.

And…a small pistol of his. Maybe she should carry it from now on. It might be enough to scare those horrible criminals who were making her life so miserable.

Mattie went out to the garage. Searching through it, she came across a wooden box with the word *danger* written across its top. It was full of dynamite percussion caps. A strange thing to find. Leaving something so dangerous around wasn't like her husband. There were enough explosives in the box to level the garage, her house, and several of her neighbor's. She would have to get rid of them in the near future before something set them off. All her husband ever used to set them off, when he was dynamiting a well, was a small electrical spark.

The gun was more important right now, so she left the box of caps where they were and continued her search. She found the gun in a small cardboard box at the bottom of a pile of old clothes. The twenty-two revolver was rusty, but seemed to work. She took the gun and some shells in the house with her.

She felt a little better when she went to bed that night.

With it tucked in the waistband of her skirt when she went shopping that afternoon, she had a little more confidence than she'd had in the past. Darryl and Sherman were high on the drugs they were selling, so they didn't realize what way she was going when they jumped her, still on the way to the store. She struggled, and it surprised them so much she managed to pull the gun.

"Now get away from me," she demanded.

"Will you look at this old broad?" Sherman said, laughing. "She's got a gun. Ten bucks says she ain't got the guts to use it."

"That might be a hard bet to win," said Darryl.

"Only for you," Sherman answered, reaching for Mattie's gun. He lost the bet when she pulled the trigger. The gun misfired. "You should have taken the bet," he said, laughing and taking the gun away from her. "You'd have won." He slapped Mattie across the face. "Now give me your money, you old bitch."

"I don't have any," she said, trying to hide her fear.

"Give me the purse." He yanked it out of her hands and looked through it. "Where's your money? You hiding it?"

"No, everything I have is in there."

"Listen, bitch," the mugger said, knocking her down, "next time, you'd better have some money. And if you want to stay alive, you won't call the cops again."

Mattie's terror finally took hold. She screamed so loud the already drug-dulled men became even more confused and ran. Too afraid to think, she went home and called the police.

"You know, Mattie," the older cop said when they got there, "down at the station we're beginning to wonder if you ain't letting your imagination run away with you a bit. When people claim they're jumped as often as you do, well, they're generally exaggerating the whole deal. Or else maybe provoking it. Pulling a gun was a really stupid thing to do. You probably don't even know who you pointed it at. Another stupid thing to do is to waste a police officer's time. If you don't realize how valuable our time is, you'd better start knowing it. We can't keep coming over here because you were scared by a shadow or got lonesome or some other idiotic thing."

"I didn't mean to take so much of your time," Mattie said, close to tears. "It's just that I don't know what to do. I'm an old woman. I don't have any way to fight back. All I can do is call you. What else can I do? They said they would kill me if I don't have money next time. What should I do?"

"Maybe you shouldn't live here all alone."

"Where would I go?" she asked, even though she knew what their answer would be.

"Isn't there someone you can live with?"

"No, there's no one."

"Well, I'm truly sorry about that. The thing is though, you're going to have to do something. We have too many legitimate calls to answer, to spend so much time here."

"But I..."

Not interested in hearing any more from her, they left.

"You should have told her to move into a home somewhere," the younger cop said on the way to the car. "Way things are, there's a lot of *young*, hardworking people, who belong in this neighborhood, that could use a house like hers."

Mattie just stood there, wondering why a black man didn't know better than to be so bigoted.

Watching the weather change from rain to ice and then to howling, blowing snow made Mattie even more depressed. She already felt as though she'd had her chance to do something about the muggers, and that she'd messed it up. She knew now that she should have checked the gun before she went out with it, to be sure it'd fire. It was probably the ammunition that failed. It certainly was old enough. Old, just like she was. Like everything around her. And like her, none of it worked quite right anymore. It all seemed so senseless now. She'd even worried about how to get rid of those dynamite percussion caps out in the garage. They probably wouldn't have the power of a firecracker. Not after all those years, sitting out in the garage.

Or would they? Was there a chance they still had their power? They might. It was worth checking. She sure didn't have anything lose by checking them. Not the way things were going.

The thought that they might still work was too exciting to wait until it stopped snowing. She bundled up and fought her way through the snow drifts to the garage.

As she rested from her ordeal in the snow, she looked around the garage and soon realized there were a lot of things stored in it that she'd never looked at.

She spent the rest of the afternoon digging through the garage. Most of what she found, she decided to throw away. The dynamite caps and the two cases of dynamite she found, she decided to keep. If they still worked.

As long as they'd lasted this long, stored in the garage, she saw no reason why they wouldn't last a little longer.

Late in the afternoon, she brought a handful of the caps into the house with her. After a lengthy rest, she examined them carefully. They appeared to be in perfect condition. This time, though, she was going to be sure.

Maybe she didn't know much about guns, but she did know explosives. It wasn't for nothing she'd worked alongside her husband all those early years, while they struggled so hard to get his business going.

She took a few caps down the basement and set two of them off in the old coal cellar. Both were more powerful than she expected or dared hope they would be. They made quite a mess when they knocked loose ancient coal dust, but that was the last thing she was worried about. She was also mildly surprised that none of her neighbors heard them go off. Or if they had, that they hadn't called the police. Then again, her neighbors did tend to ignore most of what went on in the neighborhood. They probably assumed the sound was just another murder.

Back upstairs, Mattie used her long-ago acquired knowledge to build a powerful, compact bomb. She rigged an old egg timer on the bomb for a timing device, then fit it into one of her many old handbags. Anyone who took it away from her would set off the timer and, one minute later, the bomb. That should discourage them from bothering her again. *If*, that is, they were still alive.

For the first time in months, Mattie felt something other than fear when she left the house. It was still snowing lightly and most of the sidewalks weren't shoveled, so she was forced to walk in the street. Traffic was still light and was no problem. It was only difficult to walk.

She didn't really expect Darryl and Sherman to bother her on such a miserable day, but if they did, she hoped they'd try to mug her on the way to the store, the way they did the last time. That way, her groceries wouldn't be ruined. Either way though, if they did mug her, she was determined to follow her plan. They'd get her handbag and all of its contents.

Her excitement grew as she walked, trying to remember what to do. Above all, she must remember to scream. She wanted them well away from her when it exploded. If that failed, she would try to run, even though she knew she wasn't likely to get far enough away. Anything was better than letting them continue to terrorize her.

She was near the store when they jumped her, taking her off guard. They were high on drugs again and immediately grabbed her handbag. They did it so suddenly, they shocked her. She started to scream without thinking about it. They were even more disoriented than she was and took off running.

She was inside the store, and they were a couple of blocks away when the bomb went off. She was almost done with her shopping by the time the police arrived.

Two police cars and an ambulance were there when she went by on her way home. Her two cops were there and the older one was talking to someone who pointed at her. He called her over. She smiled when she got close enough to see the blood spread quite widely over the top of the fresh snow. It was pretty obvious that there were two less hoodlums in the city of Minneapolis to terrorize or even hassle her.

"This man tells me," the cop said, "you might know something about what happened here. There's two dead men, so if you do, you'd better tell me."

Mattie shrugged, letting her smile change to a frown. "What would I know?"

"I don't know, Mattie, but this man said you screamed right before the explosion occurred. Was it you who screamed?"

"Probably. Those muggers tried to rob me again, just like they've been doing all along. They didn't get anything from me this time because I wasn't carrying anything. They ran when I screamed. After that, I heard a loud noise. I don't know where it came from. Do you think they were the ones who got killed?"

"I don't know who they were. They were too much of a mess to tell. Why did you ignore the explosion?"

"That's a silly question that you ought to know the answer to, Officer," Mattie said, smiling again. "It was you who said I shouldn't be bothering you police anymore. I can't very well pay attention to things like that and still not bother you, now can I?"

"That's not exactly what I meant."

"You sure could have fooled me." She started to walk away, then after a few steps stopped, turned, and said, "If I think of anything I should bother you with, about what happened, I'll call you."

"Yeah, you do that, Mattie."

"Kind of a waste of time, ain't it," the younger cop said, "talking to that senile old broad."

Mattie went home, content to be a senile old broad. The old handbag she took out of her closet was a comfort too. Almost as comforting as knowing how dead Darryl and Sherman were.

She fell asleep that night with no sense of guilt, instead, considering all her options for the future. Even the police might suspect her if she eliminated more of the city's trash. Then again…

How Billy and I Saved Bobby Z's Career When We Were Still in High School

David George

I hitchhiked from Miami to Minneapolis. It took me five days. "The cities swept about me like dead leaves, leaves that were brightly colored but torn away from the branches," in the words of Laura's brother Tom from Tennessee William's *The Glass Menagerie*. I had just returned from two years abroad, and I was now a stranger in a strange land. Reverse culture shock set in immediately, exacerbated by the odd creatures who offered me rides.

A plump, heavy-jowled, middle-aged fellow insisted on giving me a lecture on birth control. The problem, he insisted, was that birth control blocked the sperm, making orgasms impossible.

"What do you mean?" I asked incredulously.

"Well, 'cause when the sperm meets the egg then ya got an orgasm, see?"

I stopped asking questions.

As I stood under a street light late at night in a small town in Georgia, a gent behind the wheel of a beat-up old pickup, wearing coveralls and a dirty t-shirt—I figured he was a local farmer—asked me where I was headed. Minneapolis. The farmer paused, looked his would-be rider up and down, and asked, "How'd ya like to get dropped off in the middle of the woods?"

My experience with gays in the world of theater, in both Minneapolis and abroad, had made me comfortable with those of diverse sexual orientations. But a closeted Georgia red dirt farmer? I thanked him but declined his offer.

An old man in a beat-up 1949 Hudson picked me up in Kentucky. As far as I could tell, the man had neither teeth nor dentures. He was dressed like an old-time ranch hand. In the middle of his story about how he had won the old Hudson in a poker game, I fell asleep. When I awoke, we were parked on the side of the highway.

"What's going on?" I asked.

The old cowboy's toothless response: "I'm dying."

"My god," I exclaimed, "let me drive you to the hospital."

The cowhand looked carefully at me, closed one eye, squinted the other, and to my consternation inquired, "You have a driver's license?"

After an hour or so of back-and-forth, I succeeded in convincing him and drove him to a hospital.

One rainy night in Wisconsin, I was offered a ride in a hotrod—a '32 deuce—chock full of liquored up teenagers. The driver pushed the hotrod up to 90, drifting back and forth across the two-lane blacktop. I asked him to pull over so I could take the wheel, and when that didn't work, I threatened to kick his ass. My status was elevated from supplicant passenger to the man in charge.

My last ride took me into the Twin Cities. The vehicle was a large high-powered Chrysler and the driver an obese fellow, in his fifties I imagined. The Chrysler flew along the highway, the speedometer marking 120 mph. The driver casually informed me that he hated "cunts"—meaning women, I supposed—but that he loved speed and the power it gave him. "Over women?" the passenger pondered. The fellow went on to declare that he knew speed one day would spell his doom and they would slop him up from the highway with a sponge. My silent entreaty was "Please not today."

There were long silences during my hitchhiking, standing alone on the highway with my thumb out and monotonous rides in cars with strangers when conversation had played itself out. The silences gave me time to think my way back to life in my home country. Incidents from my childhood and adolescence slowly began to take shape. It was a process of reconstruction and of fantasy. I couldn't resist tinkering with the past. One such incident was series of encounters with a folk singer, Bobby Z, that took place during my last year in high school.

Everything I had to read for my high school classes was boring: *The Good Earth*, *The Red Badge of Courage*, *Main Street*, Emily Dickinson's poems. Well, perhaps not boring, but tame. Much too tame. Ah, but the Beats, that was a thrill ride, like taking a 30-mph curve at 80. In a stolen car. Kerouac's *On the Road* inspired hitchhiking trips across the country. Much to my parents' dismay. One day I came to my high school biology class with a book of Allen Ginsberg's poems. I showed one of my favorites to the girl next to me who was dissecting a frog. When she read, "America Go Fuck Yourself with Your Atom Bomb," she dropped her frog mutilation tools, raced to the teacher's desk, spoke with him while pointing at me, led him back to my position at the dissection counter. He demanded to see the disgraceful verse and then sent me down to the principal's office. I knew what awaited me there.

The principal's favorite method of punishing boys with criminal tendencies was to make them drop their drawers and whack their bare butts using a paddle with holes drilled in it to increase the effect. He also took "special" students on motorcycles rides and "very special" kids on weekend camping trips. The principal's paddle treatment was my second encounter with a pedophile. Why did I subject myself to such treatment? Why was such treatment even allowed? That is the question. Whether tis nobler in the mind to suffer… Shakespeare had no answers for me.

But back to Ginsberg. "Howl" was my favorite poem. I made myriad attempts to imitate the poet, based on a stint as a juvenile delinquent earlier in my adolescence: "Variations on the theme of Ginsberg's 'Howl.' I saw the dead minds of my generation destroyed by violence clueless heedless hot-wiring JDs racing through the darkness of urban streets looking for an angry fight unhip teen angels bleeding…" I never did become a poet.

I had one friend in high school, Billy, who was into the Beats even more than I was. And he was hip to the local Beat scene, centered in Dinky Town, the commercial strip bordering the University of Minnesota. The epicenter was a coffee house known as the 10 O'Clock Scholar, where local folk musicians, including Bobby Z, had evening gigs.

Some of the folk artists, though they never reached Olympian heights, nevertheless became local legends: "Spider" John Koerner, Tony Glover, and Dave Ray. Billy dragged me along to parties where the local Beats talked about poetry and Bobby Z and other folk musicians played. Bobby was a freshman at the U of M and my contact with him was short-lived, though it was my good fortune in subsequent years to meet up occasionally with Dave Ray—RIP—and John Koerner.

My most memorable encounter with Bobby Z took place one afternoon at the Scholar. Bobby asked Billy and me to join him for coffee to discuss an urgent matter. Seated around a cigarette-scarred table with our mugs of bitter coffee—no cafe latte or macchiato in those days—Billy began the conversation.

"So what's up, Bobby?"

"What's up is I think I gotta marry this girl."

"Marry what girl? And why?" Billy inquired.

"Her name is Johanna. The deal is, I slept with her last night. What does a gentleman do in a situation like that? You marry her. It's the honorable thing to do."

Billy's rejoinder was "Is this a put-on? Gentleman? Well, your lordship…you just slept with her. It's not like she's pregnant or anything."

Billy was more sophisticated than I. My thought was *I'm just a high school kid*. Bobby Z, though still local, was a bigger-than-life folk/Beat artist. Besides, he was a grown-up with a grown-up dilemma. Though only a year older than me, to me, Bobby Z was a full-fledged adult. Did I even belong in the conversation? I tried to join in, to be noticed, with "Hey, you guys read Ginsberg's poem 'Father Death Blues'?"

Bobby and Billy ignored me.

Bobby: "But she could be pregnant."

Billy chimed in again: "You can't know that. Besides, marrying a girl 'cause you slept with her…that is so square."

Bobby responded: "I know times are changing, but I guess I'm still a little old-fashioned."

"Why don't you ask Woody Guthrie?" I ventured a joke. Woody Guthrie was Bobby's idol. My joke fell flat.

"Even if she is pregnant," Billy added, "you could just split. A rolling stone gathers no moss."

Bobby paused for a moment, then looked at Billy: "A rolling stone. I like it. But what if she really is pregnant and shows up at my pad in the middle of the night with the bad news?"

Billy: "Just say, go away from my door."

"Or my window" was my contribution.

Bobby: "My window? Makes her sound like some kinda peeping Tomasina. But just blowing her off, that's not my thing. I don't know what the answer is. It's like something floating around in the air…"

"Blowin' in the breeze," Billy interjected.

Bobby: "In the…whatever. Part of me feels protective of her, like a girl. But the growed-up part of me cares about her…sorta like a woman. I don't know. Sometimes a just feel like a man of constant…"

"Bumbed out?" I asked.

Bobby: "Constant…constant…there's a French word. Chagrin?"

Me: "There's a Ferlinghetti poem…"

Bobby cut me off: "I like chagrin. Maybe I'll write a song with the title, 'A Man of Constant Chagrin.'"

Billy responded, "You're a freshman in college. How much constant chagrin you have to deal with?"

A wistful look on his face, Bobby took a sip of his rancid coffee, looked around the Scholar with its collection of battered and mismatched tables and chairs, and then turned back to us. "Sometimes I wake up and have this one too many mornings kind of feeling."

"What's that mean?" I inquired.

"It means I feel old at nineteen. I wanna be young forever."

Billy scoffed: "Maybe you just got the homesick blues."

"I'm from the north country. And good riddance to that. Homesick ain't my problem. My problem is…"

"Your problem is this girl you slept with who think you gotta marry," Billy finished Bobby's thought.

"Why shouldn't I marry her? Give me one good reason."

Billy and I talked over each other in a staccato dialogue: "You got your whole life ahead of you." "You wanna career as a musician." "Good luck with that if you get tied down." "You won't be the guitar man. You'll end up as a tambourine boy."

I was gaining confidence, beginning to feel I belonged in the conversation, so I offered, "Ginsberg's Kaddish starts out, 'Strange now to think of you, gone without corsets and eyes, while I walk on…'"

Bobby extended his arm, palm up to silence me, and leaned toward Billy. "Hold on a minute. What's that…tambourine…something?"

Billy gave me a satisfied smile and responded to Bobby Z, "It's what my granpa used to say when I caused a ruckus. He was from the old country. He used to say things like, 'now you settle down, tambourine boy. Stop yingle yangle. You're going shake house down.'"

Bobby Z became thoughtful again. "I like that. I don't wanna settle down, I wanna be a tambourine boy and shake things up. I'll just tell Johanna I'm headin' down the highway."

"On the Road. Just like Kerouac." I retorted and was again ignored.

Billy: "So you've decided not to marry her?"

"All I really wanna do is play music. I wanna be free. I wanna meet Woody Guthrie in person. I wanna end up at the Newport Folk Festival."

Billy laughed. "Sure. Just like every other folkie around here."

"You'll see. Don't think twice about that."

Billy again: "When you make it to Newport, let us know. We'll hitchhike out there to check out your act."

As things turned out, Billy and I hitchhiked in the opposite direction, out to San Francisco to immerse ourselves in the Beat culture during the summer after our freshman year in college. By that time, however, the Beat scene had morphed into the Hippie zeitgeist. But that's a story for another time. Bobby Z disappeared, and we never learned where he ended up. But for years, we joked about how we talked him out of a premature marriage and thus saved his career. That is, if he had a musical career.

And now, on my rides from Miami to Minneapolis, I remembered Bobby Z at age nineteen. Innocent, humble, imagining he was about to embark on an epic journey. I still wondered why Bobby asked us, two high school kids, to talk about an apparently existential quandary. Because we were too young to judge? Because the older and wiser folks in Bobby's circle would have considered his predicament absurd and uncool?

Whatever the reason, the brief encounter left me with an amusing tale to ponder and pass the time on my hitchhiking trip home.

Decker Brown's Beaver Cat

Michael George

It was a bright, clear morning when Decker Brown left his cabin for his daily rounds on his trap line. The sky held a deep blue, without the hint of a cloud, but the light breeze made the fifty degrees seem less than it was.

Decker wore gloves and a cap, and before he reached the woods, he turned up the collar on his lined, hip-length denim jacket.

Once in the woods, the scent of pine needles was strong in the spring air. Snow still hung here and there in small patches and covered the ground under the pine trees. Last fall's dead oak leaves, that still hung on the trees, chattered among themselves in the breeze.

Decker's new neighbor was working in his yard, and Decker waved to him as he neared the first beaver dam of the day. The neighbor didn't notice Decker and failed to return the wave.

"So don't wave back, you stupid idiot," Decker complained loudly, just not loud enough for his neighbor to hear. But Decker didn't care who heard him, because he hated people in general and his neighbors in particular.

Decker loved trapping, and it was with a great deal of satisfaction that he discovered a large male beaver in the first trap he checked. It was doubly satisfying in fact, because when he examined the dead animal, he found that it was a fine pelt. More important though, the beaver had one front foot missing, so Decker knew he caught one who previously escaped his trap.

The second trap at the dam was empty, and Decker moved on to the beaver's lodge further up the small creek. The lodge was built at the edge of the creek, and it rose up several feet higher than the creek banks. Because of that and because the creek banks were muddy and most of the ice was gone from the creek, it was difficult to get down and around to the front of the lodge where the traps were set. Decker held on to a short bush growing near the lodge as he slid down the creek bank.

"Pssst, pssst, pssst!" growled a giant white tomcat Decker found freshly caught in one of the traps, set and staked out in front of the beaver lodge.

"Well, I'll be dogged," said Decker when he saw the cat. "Would you just look at what we got here?"

The cat was caught by a hind foot, and it managed to pull itself up and onto the side of the beaver lodge. Tenaciously, it clung there, its claws digging deep in the mud and wood as the full weight of the trap and the old bricks tied to it strained to pull the cat into the cold creek water.

Decker grasped the cat behind the neck and lifted it further from the water. The cat relaxed as Decker freed its foot from the large steel-jawed trap. But as he set it down to examine the mangled foot, the cat unfurled the long claws on its front paws and swiped viciously across the back of Decker's hand. The claws went in deep, and Decker fell back against the side of the beaver lodge as he jumped in pain.

"Pssst, pssst, pssst!" The cat spit angrily as Decker sucked on the rapid flow of blood coming from his hand.

Then Decker reached for the ungrateful beast, hoping to catch it and smash out its brains against the nearest tree stump. Even though it only had three good legs, the cat still had amazing speed and agility. It leaped high in the air and see off into the woods.

"You'd best run, cat!" Decker threatened as he vigorously shook his injured hand to ease the pain. "For if I ever set eyes on you again, it'll be the last of you."

Decker mentally cursed the cat as he wrapped his dirty handkerchief around his hand to stop the flow of blood. He continued cursing as he made the rest of his morning rounds on his trap line. The cat occupied his mind so strong that he failed to notice that he was being followed.

By noon, he was weighted down from three more beavers and a pheasant that he set a special trap for.

He always completed his morning rounds near a lake with a shelter he built there. He started a fire within a ring of stones he laid out for a fireplace. While the wood burned itself down to hot coals, he cleaned the pheasant. As he did, he decided he would have to stop trapping any birds until fall because the way the entrails smelled, it was getting too warm. Just a slightly higher temperature and the whole bird would have been spoiled.

When it was cleaned, Decker put the pheasant on a handmade spit over the fire and turned it slowly. He didn't hurry. He always took the time necessary to cook the pheasant, rabbit, or squirrel he found in one of his traps on his morning rounds. He relaxed while it cooked, chewing on a piece of hard candy, and smoking a long thin cigar.

Decker found it relaxing to smoke a cigar before lunch, and on this day, it had the added effect of helping to dull the pain in his badly scratched hand.

He had trouble holding the bird when it was cooked. His hand throbbed as he ate, and it was getting too stiff to use effectively.

"That dirty rotten cat," Decker swore out loud to himself. "It had best never come around again. 'Cause if it does, I'll make some short work out of it."

Over and over, he let the image of the white cat with the black spot on the top of its head pass through his mind. All through the afternoon, he entertained thoughts of revenge against the cat who hadn't been grateful when he freed it from the trap. Never mind whose trap it was that mangled the cat's foot.

On a normal day, while eating, Decker would have stopped to watch the muskrat swimming across the lake. Or the crows perched in the trees behind him, waiting for him to leave so they could clean up the scraps he left behind. But on this day, his painful hand irritated him so much that he even failed to notice the new growth, which was so much a part of the fast approaching spring.

He was totally disgusted when his hand continued to ache throughout the day. He decided to quit early. He knew he could check the remaining traps the following day. He was fairly sure the remaining beaver ponds were trapped out anyway.

His cabin was a welcome site as it came into view. The small building was an eyesore to his neighbors, but to him, it was a thing of beauty. He built it with his own hands. Even though hadn't ever gotten around to finishing the outside, inside it was finished admirably.

The kitchen was furnished with hand-built cabinets that rivaled those found in any suburban rambler. It had a center cooking island with built-in cooktop and a microwave oven. The double stainless-steel sink was set into a Formica countertop. The refrigerator was large enough to accommodate a family of ten. The floor was covered with hand-cut quarry tile and the ceiling was wood, with real, natural wood beams. As was the entire cabin, the walls were sheet rocked and painted white.

The living room was simpler. The same wood and beams covered the ceiling as the kitchen. The floor was oak and partially covered with a bear skin rug. A stone fireplace filled one end of the room, and it was furnished with a couch, an old end table with a shadeless lamp, and an extra-large television.

The bathroom opened onto the living room at the opposite end from the fireplace, and the bedroom was a sleeping loft off to one side of the room.

He didn't feel like cooking with his hand throbbing the way it was, so he microwaved some curried rabbit from the night before. He drank several glasses of chilled Chablis with the meal. He went to bed shortly after eating without washing his supper dishes. His hand aggravated him so much he even skipped watching the news.

It took him over an hour to fall asleep. He was just falling into the first pain-riddled stages of it when he heard the noise.

Ka-thunk...tic ka-thunk...tic ka-thunk...tic it went, on and on, back and forth over the roof. On through his dreams, and then the lank, slippery haze of first awakening. And finally, through the awareness of pain, getting dressed, and going outside to see what was on the roof.

The white tomcat moved back and forth over the roof's ridge, dragging its torn foot behind it. It stopped to stare at Decker with one blue eye and one yellow eye. Both eyes shown a bright translucent red as they picked up the faint light of the moon.

Decker picked up a convenient rock and threw it at the cat. The rock missed and the cat disappeared on the other side of the roof. He went back inside and to bed. Sleep was just slipping over him when he heard it again. *Ka-thunk…tic ka-thunk…tic,* the cat was back on the roof.

"You no-good devil!" he screamed at the cat. "If you think I'm going to stand for this, you'd best think about it some more!"

He took his twelve-gauge, semi-automatic shotgun with him outside. The cat was perched on the brick chimney. He emptied the shotgun at the cat as fast as he could fire, but the cat was gone the instant he shouldered the gun. He only managed to knock several bricks loose.

He quickly reloaded and ran to the other side of the house, hoping to find the cat there. As he rounded the corner of the house, he was sure he saw the cat sitting on a living room window ledge. Without bothering to aim, he shot at it. He knew without looking, from the sound that followed the gunshot, there wasn't much left of his television.

It was a dejected but still furious Decker who finally gave up and went inside to go to bed. He purposely left the lights off as he walked through the living room, so he didn't see the destruction there.

Sleep took longer this time, as he cursed his traps, cursed himself, and most of all, cursed the three-legged white tomcat. The cat gave Decker enough time to fall into a deep sleep, and the clock was on the morning side of the night when the familiar *ka-thunck…tic* of the cat on the roof woke him instantly. Without bothering to dress, the naked Decker crashed out of the cabin with his loaded shotgun. The cat was on the chimney again and seemed to be smiling at Decker this time.

Decker fired so wildly that he not only blew more of the chimney apart, but also shot several holes in the roof. When he gave up and went inside, he heard the cat, "pssst, pssst," and he was sure it was laughing at him.

Three more times Decker went out after the cat, missing it each time with his wild shooting until the chimney was nearly gone and the roof was punctured with holes. By then, Decker was sleeping with his gun and had even fired through the roof from his bed, showering himself with chunks of wood, sheetrock, and insulation.

The last time the cat woke him, it came through a hole in the roof and sat on Decker's feet. Without thinking, he shot at it from a prone position as he woke up. Of course, he missed the cat again. And even though he felt very little pain, he knew he didn't have much of a foot left.

"Pssst, pssst, pssst," the cat said as it leaped from the bed, to a dresser, and then out through a hole in the roof.

Ka-thunck...tic, ka-thunk...tic, came the sound of the cat on its way off the roof, while Decker lay bleeding from his foot and wondering if he would ever walk another trap line or set another trap.

A Grandpa Summer Day

Michael George

The creek ran narrow, deep in the woods, far from the sand burrs and high weeds. Tall hills kept cows and a tired old percheron away from road traffic and the river. Wild strawberries and huge thorn-riddled patches of black raspberries grew there. A giant, calloused, and wrinkled old hand took the boy's small city-soft hand and swung him across the silver clean creek, from a rock to a rock on the other side. The boy followed his grandpa along animal paths to find and bring home the cows for milking. The boy didn't feel the light chill in the early-morning late-spring air, as he took two quick steps to match each stride of his slow-moving grandpa.

They found the cows in the meadow at the end of the valley pasture. Though Grandpa cursed them, his words were kind and coaxing as they drove the cows home. Dew wet pants clung to the boy's legs, and the sun was chasing the hill shadows away when they tied the eight swayback cows into their proper places in the barn. The boy fed the cows loose hay from the loft, using a three-tined fork, as Grandpa readied his milk pail and three-legged stool for the milking.

At breakfast, boiled coffee with thick sweet cream was set before them in heavy mugs. The boy helped himself to a giant slice of fried brown ham and two eggs, soft in the middle and crisp on the bottom. He put a large slab of butter on the hot biscuit he took from the bowl in the middle of the table. Black raspberries, coated with sugar and soaking in warm milk, fresh from the morning milking, filled him and finished the meal. His grandmother dropped her lined face into a smile while she bobbed her grey head in appreciation of his appetite.

The constant *ka-chug, ka-chug* of the ancient green tractor and the *clackity-click* of the sickle bar stopped the bird song and insect hum of the still early morning. Tractor exhaust filling his lungs and the endlessly falling meadow grass made the boy sleepy, as he rode the once-upon-a-time horse-drawn mower.

Grasshoppers flew in varied patterns before him, tickled the bare flesh of his face, and clung with tiny unseen fingers to his clothes. The flit, jump, and turn of butterflies teased his eyes.

He struggled with the foot pedal that raised the sickle bar over dirt ponds left by woodchucks and gophers. A hen pheasant waited too long to leave the nest of eggs she was protecting. Grandpa stopped the tractor to clean out her legs, jamming the mower.

The black dog and the yellow-brown dog, who were their companions in the field, made a breakfast of the dying bird, when she landed a few hundred feet behind the tractor and mower. The boy noted the concern for the dead bird in the grandpa's face. The boy shuddered as he thought of dying.

The day was hot by dinnertime. Grandmother served it out in the screen porch, which stretched along one side of the yellow brick house. Plates of cold, sliced ring bologna, and cheeses, yellow and white, were placed between already buttered biscuits. Iced coffee, rich with cream and sugar, washed them down. A salad of leaf lettuce and radishes from the garden, soaked in vinegar and oil, followed. A bowl of black raspberries was, again, dessert.

The boy knew the day would be long when Grandpa decided the hay mowed the day before was ready to bring in. Sweat and fine particles of hay and dust covered the boy's arms and shirtless back. Long wooden poles with this steel spikes through them, brought hay in never-ending piles from the ground to the wooden wheeled hay rack. The boy's breath heaved and choked as he tried to pack down the hay as fast as his powerful grandpa, who pushed it from the front of the hay rack to the back with his pitch fork in quick and easy motions. A red checkered scarf covered Grandmother's head as she drove the tractor pulling the loader and wagon.

Cold well water ran freely from the pipe coming out of the ground near the barn. The boy drank deeply before he let it run over his head and down his back. *Refreshed, he watched Grandpa attach the sling to the hook at the end the rope running on pulleys up into the haymow. It was carefully laid out on the bed of the hayrack before it was loaded.* With Grandpa's signal, Grandmother pulled up the rope and hay, hooked to the tractor at the other end of the barn. When the hay reached its correct position in the haymow, one end of the sling was released and the hay dropped free. Another drink of cold well water, and they returned to the field for more hay.

Grandpa left the boy swimming in the pool made by the creek where it rolled around a small hill. The water cooled the boy and washed the hay and dust from his back and out of his nose. His body shone clean when Grandpa returned with the cows and the old horse. The boy shivered with excitement when Grandpa picked him up and put him on the back of the horse. He rode all the way to the barn.

Grandpa laughed at his intent expression as he tried to hold the milk pail between his legs and make both his hands squeeze milk from the cow he sat under. His hands and arms ached from the effort. The pail was no more than a quarter full when the great tail came crashing into his face, knocking him down to the straw-covered floor. The boy wanted to cry as he was picked up, but soon, he was laughing along with Grandpa at the mess he made.

The boy ate mounds of mashed potatoes covered with thick dark gravy and slices of roast pork. Fresh cooked peas from the garden were soaked in butter and black pepper. He drank milk and just managed to eat all of his apple pie. A visit from a neighbor to watch the new television followed soon after supper. The boy fell asleep on the couch. He was carried in Grandpa's arms upstairs to bed. There, he dreamed of tomorrow and another Grandpa summer day.

Doreen and Blackie

Bud George

I am gonna get knocked on my ass again. I hate football. This is (theoretically) touch football, gym class. But the animal across from me is some kinda "A" team star jock strap asshole, and he takes this silly bullshit game seriously. And he drools.

So what could I do? I stepped aside, stuck my foot out and gave the back of his head a shove. He landed hard on his face.

I dropped back, way back, into the lilac bushes through the chain-link fence (I'd cut a hole early in the year with a pair of bolt cutters from metal shop. The shop teacher said don't even ask to borrow tools, so I didn't.)

I found my cigarettes and matches up under the bridge, sat, lit one, and thought about what the animal would do to me when he caught me (if he knew or remembered). Most of these guys have left and right marked on their hands so they can figure out which way to run during the big game.

The next day, I dropped back through the fence before the big game started. I found a girl smoking a cigarette, one of my cigarettes.

"This is how you go out for football?" she asked.

"I hate football," I said.

"Sit and have a smoke," she said, handing my pack of cigarettes and matches to me.

She was small and pretty. I thought most girls were pretty, but most girls didn't talk to me or offer smokes, even my smokes. Her name was Doreen. She was Blackie's girl. Blackie was way bigger than me, a sports hero, and he drooled when the game got intense. Over the next few weeks, we met, smoked, and talked. I asked her about Blackie.

She said, "I help him with homework."

The weather was getting colder. Walking to school one morning, I found a blanket in the backseat of an unlocked Hudson. Since no one was using it, I brought it along with me and stashed it under the bridge with my cigarettes and candy bars. Doreen liked the blanket and the candy bars and the cigarettes.

It was cooler, still football season, so we rolled up in the blanket and talked and did a bit of exploring, quite a bit.

I hate football, but maybe football season's okay. By the end of football season, it was too cold, even with the blanket, smokes, and candy bars. I saw her now and then in the school halls, sometimes with Blackie, but I usually ducked out of sight.

Spring finally came, nice outdoors. One day, as I walked the school hall, she grabbed my arm. She pulled me against the wall behind her locker door and put her hand in my pocket.

This was okay with me. God, she smelled good. Peppermint gum, perfume, and cigarettes.

"Hey," she asked, "you going out for baseball this year?"

Rocky .05
Bud George

He's gonna beat the crap out of me. Wrong guy James? Supposed to fight Jimmy. This guy James is way older than me. Probably fourteen or fifteen and he's got muscles, and I think a mustache, maybe. Jimmy's easy. I make a farting noise, he laughs, and I slug him. I'm gonna slug him for missing this match if I live through it.

Shit! My mother's in the audience. What's she gonna think when I get pounded for three rounds.

So we touch gloves and the referee says leave your glasses off. Well, I think it's better if I can't see this guy too clear anyway. Maybe it won't hurt as bad.

Three rounds later, I was still on my feet, sorta, but pretty dizzy, and my nose was dripping blood on my green boxing trunks. He won. I found my way to the locker room and pulled my jeans on over my bloody boxing trunks and sat down to clear my head.

James comes in, big smile, comes over to me and says, "You okay, kid?"

He holds out his hand. I think he's offering to help me up, so I stand up fast. He, having only offered to shake hands, wasn't ready. I bumped his nose hard with the top of my head, knocked him on his ass on the concrete floor, and bloodied his nose, turning his red and white striped trunks all red.

I sat for a few minutes until my nose bleed stopped. Then I put my glasses on, tried hard to only smile and not exactly laugh, went over to James, the champ, and said, "You okay, kid?"

I did not offer to shake hands.

Hang Lost

David George

A soldier armed with a machine gun paced sluggishly back and forth in the heavy air, pausing occasionally to admire a *piranha*, a streetwalker in hotpants and plastic boots who patrolled the opposite sidewalk, humming this year's Carnival tunes. The clatter of African drums tumbled out of a *macumba* temple a few blocks away. VW Beatles and Fiats rattled along the narrow side street. The anemic breeze from Ipanema Beach did little to relieve the heat, but I would take what I could get this late February night in the *Cidade Maravilhosa*, the Enchanted City of Rio de Janeiro.

My two companions and I were the only customers in a small bar named—after the popular song—*Garota de Ipanema*, Girl from Ipanema. It specialized in a sugar-cane brandy called *cachaça*, doughy meat pastries, demitasses of rancid coffee laced with sugar, and live music. But the tiny stage was empty tonight, with no musicians in sight. Was the soldier with the machine gun outside frightening people away? I asked myself.

Norris Wysockey's slender hand—not to mention his long blond hair—shook as he gulped down a shot. I shuddered.

"Take it easy, man. Mixing hooch with grass. You're gonna end up…"

"Dope and booze ain't the problem. I mean, that voodoo crap you two dragged me off to tonight. I didn't leave Chicago to come all the way down here for…satanic cults."

Renata Amaral scowled at Norris. "Voodoo crap? Satanic cults? Macumba come from Africa, baby, the Holy Land."

"Holy? All those people jumping around and shaking. Having epileptic fits." Norris tried to steady his hand as he downed another snort. "That woman in the veil. Stumbling all over. Waving that sword. On the ground that kid was lying, you know, I thought she was gonna gut, I mean, human sacrifice…"

"Earth calling Norris," I intoned. "You smoke too much weed. She was possessed by a spirit. That's the whole point of the ritual. It was a curing ceremony. For the little boy."

"They ever heard of doctors in this…Possessed? What the hell's that? And that guy you called the pie something…"

"*Pai de santo*," Renata said. "He the priest."

"Priest? Witch doctor's more like it. Lighting gunpowder in his hand, dousing candles on his tongue…A *filho da puta* he calls me. Means son-of-a-whore, right? What kinda…"

"He was possessed by Exu, the trickster," I explained.

"Trickster shmickster. By the devil. That asshole was trying to jerk my chain. That pie dude's voice sounded like the frigging Exorcist."

"*Exorcista* film. You gringos perverted. The little girl with that *crucifixo*…"

"Norris, you blew your chance to talk to a real god. You had a hot line to heaven."

"Do you actually believe…heaven? Hell's more like it. Not just the voodoo stuff…Like yesterday. The bus I'm riding. The driver's going down the street flat out. He takes his hands off the wheel. And steers with his knees. I guess he's showing off to some chicks sitting in front. I'm freaked, you know. The lives of thirty people this cat's endangering. Guess what the other passengers are doing? Shuckin' and jivin' and cheering him on! "

"Well, you know how it goes. The big stars here are either soccer players or Formula One drivers. The guy's just keeping in practice until he gets his big break."

"Oh, such a comedian you are."

"That's a step up from being called a CIA agent."

"Say again?" Norris asked nervously.

"Well, you know Alex," Renata answered, "he look the part. He big and strong, he talk good Portuguese, he wear jeans like a typical student, he hang out at the clubs, tell everybody he here to study Brazilian music. Just the right cover for a CIA agent. My friends say, keep away from that *americano*, he CIA. But I trust Alex. My *santo* say trust him."

"Your what?"

"My *santo*. My *orixá*."

"My oreesh what…?

"What she means, Norris, is the *Macumba* god she's got a personal connection with."

"Oh, so now she talks to these voodoo gods?"

"Renata, who you think Norris's *santo* is? The god of disease?"

"Oh no, his *orixá* the god of love." She smiled brightly at Norris.

"Yeah, yeah, pulling my chain again…Alex is spoze to be showing me the ropes, not yanking…Anyway, what's with this CIA agent business? You look like all the other grad student types. Swarming all over this place."

"Well, when I first came to Rio from Minnesota with a Fulbright grant, that's what I thought I would be. Graduate student, that is. I signed up at the USP, you know, São Paulo U, where they offered a program on Brazilian music. 'Cept instead of music, what I ended up hearing were gunshots from a gang of thugs. They belonged to this paramilitary group, get this, they called themselves the Communist Hunting Command."

"Name sounds kinda fascist," Norris interjected.

"You got that right. Boy, they were for sure the generals' little darlings. They attacked a group of students at the USP they considered too far left, anti-Catholic… Anyway, one kid took a bullet in the head, some had acid thrown in their faces. I can still see this scene playing over and over in my mind, it's like a…celluloid face, I don't know if it's a boy or a girl, it's smoking, melting…"

"Acid? Face melting? Freaky."

"Then, the building where I studied was firebombed and gutted."

"So's that when you joined the CIA?"

"Right. What I did, I got my ass out of there and never went back to the USP. There didn't seem to be much point in studying music anymore. I mean, I still really dig it…"

"Come on, Renata, our boy Alex here is CIA, ain't it so?"

"I tell you what Alex is…"

"Getting back to my story, Norris, what happened at the USP was just the start for Brazil. The shit really hit the fan when the military declared a state of siege…"

"What's state of siege mean?"

"It means no more congress, total censorship, protestors shot on sight, people disappearing into the military dungeons. Then they're tortured, executed…"

"Executed? You mean like the electric chair?"

"I mean, like shotgun blast to the back of the head, getting chucked into the ocean from a helicopter…"

"Okay, okay! Enough already. I don't need to hear more of this crap. You're blowing my mind, and it ain't in a good way…"

"You no want to learn what going on? How you say…See no evil, hear no evil…"

"What the hell, might as well go on with your grisly tale. But I'm still waiting for you to fill me in on your CIA mission."

"Why not? My assignment is to assassinate you, Norris."

"So funny I forgot to laugh."

"If the DOPPS ever find out what Alex really doing…Put him on the parrot perch real fast."

Norris looked at Renata, then leaned toward me and asked in a conspiratorial voice, "Who's the dopes? What're they doing to the parrots?"

"You know," I answered. "The D O double P S. The gestapo. They tie you to the parrot perch. Hang you upside down from a pole. Attach wires to your genitals. A little electroshock therapy to put you in the mood for a chat."

Norris sighed. "Wild and crazy. Voodoo, CIA, gestapo, torture. So what kinda trip you on, Renata? Robbing banks for the revolution?"

"I work in theater. Dancer. Actor. How you say? Starving *artista*."

"And Renata's also helping me with my new research project."
"On what? Starving artists?"
"On the urban guerrilla underground."
"Alex, you sure good idea telling Norris about this?"
"Norris is cool, don't worry. I can tell it like it is."

I looked at my two friends. What a contrast, I mused. Norris, pale complexion, thin, almost delicate, he looked vulnerable in his t-shirt and shorts. Renata, wiry, solid in her dark blue dancer tights, white blouse, red sash, *Macumba* talisman, short-cropped black hair, cafe-au-lait complexion. I pondered the irony or symmetry? Renata had taken him under her wing, then I had taken Norris under my…

"Hey, order me another *cachaça*, will ya?"

I placed a hand over his glass. "Go easy. You're gonna get blind."

"The hell with it. I'll order myself. Hey, waiter, *cachaça*. More." After Norris was served, he put away another belt. He shivered and returned to his Cassandra mode. "Oh man, it's all so weird. I got this feeling something terrible's gonna happen to me in this shithole. I can't get a handle…"

"Hey, baby," Renata chimed in, "there only one way to survive in a shithole."

"I'm sorry, I didn't mean…"

"You wanna survive, you gotta…ah…*deixar cair*…hang lost."

"Hang loose."

"Yeah, baby."

Silence perched on the small table; I traced my fingertips over a cigarette advertisement imprinted on its tin surface: *Charme Com Filtro*. I looked around the room: the barman, bored, rubbing the counter with a rag, Norris staring into his glass, Renata looking at Norris with a faint smile on her face. Not for the first time, I wondered who his *orixá* might be. Exu of the underworld, Xangô god of thunder, Oxumaré lord of the rainbow. My rumination was cut short when a man in soiled pants and ripped shirt staggered through the antique swinging doors. Drunks, it occurred to me, weren't a common sight in Rio. Without hesitation, he wobbled over to our table, sat down.

"Hey, buddy, buy me a drink."

His voice sounded cold sober. The barman appeared instantly and waved a dirty rag in his face.

"Split. Don't bother the customers."

The interloper didn't argue. He stood up and walked briskly away but he paused at entrance long enough to thrust up his forearm in the banana gesture, as in slide a banana up yours. I watched him through the window: he approached the soldier on the sidewalk, gestured animatedly while looking our way, then walked off.

"What was that all about?" I asked Renata, when Norris ordered another *cachaça*. She shrugged her shoulders and turned to our companion.

"Hey, baby, you travel all way here just to drink up our rum?"

"This poison you call rum? I'm in the Peace Corps."

"Piss Corpse!"

"Corps, not corpse."

"You here to save us from poverty, *comunismo*, or bad breath?"

"Community development."

"You gonna save us from community development?"

"Get off my case. Hands-on stuff I'm doing. Self-sufficiency, see? Setting up co-ops. Credit unions. Literacy. Breaking dependency. Grass roots we're talking here. Not some US imperialist caca. You get what I'm saying?"

Renata and I, in near perfect synchronization, stood up, applauded, plopped down in our chairs, leaned closer to Norris, and stared wide-eyed at him.

"Hey, knock it off." Norris softened his tone. "Okay, okay. So a month I been here and I ain't done diddly. Sittin' on the dock of the bay, so to speak. On the beach. Getting horny."

"What getting horny mean?"

"What Norris means is he's living like a monk, but he'd like to be Don Juan."

"Cute blond like him. Got hands like in an El Greco painting. He remind of a poet."

"Thanks. Actually, I do write some poetry…Okay, I get it, joke's on me again. You two about ready to give me a break?"

I wasn't certain if I heard the surf on the beach, the breeze, or the electric fan overhead. I shifted my position in the wicker chair. My hand wandered to the tabletop and came to rest on my notebook.

Norris took notice. "So what's in that little book you keep fondling?"

"Notes from the underground, old buddy. It's all that's left of the revolutionary inner circle."

"What do you mean, 'all that's left'?"

"What Alex mean is they just a few left. Most of them, if they not in exile or jail, they dead."

"Oh shit," Norris looked around nervously. "You nuts carrying that around with you?"

"You'd be surprised what's in these notes. All those wild revolutionaries are more interested in literature than in Marx. And the only reason they even considered talking to me is they think I can give them special insights into their heroes, Beats like Ginsberg and Ferlinghetti. I'm even helping one of them with a translation of Kerouac's *On the Road*."

Renata interrupted, "There more to it than that. These guys know their time up. They hope people like David be their…how you say? *Cronistas*."

"Chroniclers."

"Yeah," Norris interjected, "but how you know who's who? Who's them dopes guys, who's CIA, who's setting who up? Can of worms…Hey, what's that noise?"

My attention suddenly strayed to the hills above ringing with the shouts of dancers and the syncopated uproar of drums, bells, whistles, tambourines. "It's rehearsal for the carnival parade, man. Wanna head up there later?"

"I've had enough adventure for one night."

"This is different. You would not believe the tricky samba footwork. They got some cool moves would amaze you."

"Yeah," Renata chimed in. "And that percussion band you hearing got like a hundred African instruments. It look like chaos, but come *Carnaval* time, all those people be dancing in perfect rhythm down the whole parade route. They wearing these heavy costumes no matter how hot it get. They just hang lost."

"That's the ticket. Hang lost. The hell with revolutionaries and dictators. Here we are in Rio, Carnival's only a week away. Let's celebrate. Lemme buy you a drink." I called out an order to the barman. "Norris, you're gonna love this. Something better for your stomach. Condensed milk, peanuts, and *cachaça*."

"Alcoholic peanut butter?"

"That's the spirit. Look at that, Renata, *senhor* culture shock here is actually smiling."

"Aw, screw you both. Hey, dig this…"

Renata stopped him, raising the fingers of her right hand, thrusting her palm abruptly forward. Somebody had just strolled into the bar, and it wasn't the girl from Ipanema. It was two policemen; they were wearing masks, one depicting a skull, the other a leering devil—or Exu the trickster? My first thought was, the masks were for Carnival. My second thought was, they were for hiding the cops' identities. The jig was up, they were finally going to arrest me. Or Renata. Were there more police outside? What about the soldier? I didn't dare look through the window. The tall, bony mulatto in the skull mask was strapped to a machine gun. It had worked around to his back and hung horizontally over his buttocks. The other cop, in the devil mask, was a fat redhead. An automatic pistol in a frayed black leather holster dangled inward down the slope of his belly and bounced off his crotch. The cops were trying, loud and off-key, to harmonize an old Carnival tune. It included a lyric about a longhair—"could he be a? could he be a?"—to which the shouted answer was always, "*bicha*!" meaning "faggot." Each with an arm draped over the other's shoulder, they tottered to the bar chanting, "*Bicha, bicha*." I picked up my notes, slipped them inside my shirt, and whispered, "You got your passport, Norris?"

"No. Damn. I'm holding too. We gonna get hassled?"

"Everybody hang lost," Renata said in a casual voice as she kept an eye on the cops.

The policemen were having a chug-a-lug contest. They had to lift up their masks to drink, but since their backs were turned, we couldn't see the cops' faces. The redheaded devil won the first round. They ordered two more water glasses of *cachaça*. They raised them to their lips, but Skull changed his mind and threw his drink, glass and all, over his shoulder. It smashed against the wall. The devil cop snorted into his glass, and they both cackled. The barman served up more *cachaça*. Fat Devil poured his on the floor; bony Skull took up the challenge and tossed his drink in the barman's face. They guffawed. The barman kept a straight face. Business as usual. Devil looked at the trio's table, tapped his partner on the shoulder. They stomped over, looking Renata up and down. Skull snapped a command: "*Documentos!*" Renata showed her national ID card, which the cops grudgingly accepted. Norris quivered with fear. "*Documentos!*" Renata tried to explain that Norris was an American citizen, that he'd left his passport, they stopped her with a sharp "*silêncio!*" They threw Norris against the wall, frisked him, found the marijuana. They demanded to know if Norris was a pusher. When he failed to respond, Devil backhanded him across the mouth. Blood spattered down the front of his Chicago Cubs t-shirt. "*Comunista! Subversivo!*" Skull tried to kick Norris in the crotch but missed by a wide margin. Norris doubled over anyway. The cat is learning fast, I thought.

"Let's piss on this *bicha*'s face," said Devil to Skull. They dragged Norris toward the bathroom. Renata dug her fingers in my arm, growled in my ear:

"*Vamos dar uma porrada neles.*"

"How we gonna kick their ass? They got guns!"

"They having too much fun to notice us. We move fast, we got them. You take the skinny one. Let's go!"

I nearly sank to my knees under the weight of dread. Bile crawled up my throat. I'd boxed Golden Gloves as a teenager, but here I was facing heavy artillery.

"Oh, shit. Here goes…"

I jumped out of my chair, tripped, grabbed the table to keep from falling. I regained my balance and ran to the bathroom, where Renata was already maneuvering around behind the cops who were busy trying to force Norris's head into a urinal. I moved in close to Skull, spun him around. I bounced a left off his nose—dented his mask but it stayed put—then missed with a right. The cop tugged at the machine gun strap. I landed a roundhouse right on his cheek;

in my mind's eye, I saw him hit the floor and the machine gun go off. But Skull staggered against the wall and wouldn't go down. Both hands on the machine gun barrel, he pulled it to his side. I grabbed his arms, tried to pin them against the wall.

"Norris, goddamn it, help me!"

Someone pulled me off, pushed me backward. I stumbled and fell. I saw Renata move in front of Skull. She arched a leg clad in dancer tights high in a beautiful chorus girl kick. Her sandal caught Skull under the chin, straightening him up. He slid down the wall, then lay twitching on the floor. I realized I was sitting on top of Fat Devil, who didn't move. I stood up; the three of us stared at each other. Renata bent over, ripped off the cops' masks.

"Carnival souvenirs."

She held them out to Norris, offering an exultant smile. He shook his head, compressing his bloody lips. Renata dropped the masks, removed her sash, wiped off the blood. She turned, walked quickly out of the bathroom, followed by her companions. We looked at the barman, who gave us the thumbs-up sign.

Norris tried to shout, "Let's get the hell out of here!" It sounded like retching.

Then we were gone, flying through the swinging doors out to the street. The soldier and the piranha had disappeared. Three fugitives headed toward the beach.

"Okay, now we walk. In case any more policemans around. Hang lost."

And so we walked, as I tried to contain my panic. We zigzagged through the Ipanema district past covered fruit stalls and sleeping forms in doorways. We finally reached *Avenida Atlântica* on Copacabana Beach. Big waves crashed in the darkness beyond. Five minutes went by on my watch, several hours on the agony clock. I observed *Macumba* candles burning in the sand, offerings to Iemanjá, goddess of the sea. Would she come to our aid? Did I even believe in such things?

We managed to flag down a VW taxi and clambered in back, I gave directions. As the taxi moved along the beach, I pondered the burning candles. Had Iemanjá really come to our rescue? When the driver turned into the tunnel leading to Botafogo Beach, Norris broke the silence.

"Wow, tonight you saved our butts, Renata. That scene back in the bar was awesome. You do karate? You put those fuzz down like a coupla lead sinkers."

"That not karatê, man. That *capoeira*. It come from Angola in slave times. Now we do it like dance. But *capoeira* come in handy when other cat in no mood to samba."

I instructed the driver to turn left at Vermelha Beach. In a few moments, we would reach the Urca district, in the shadow of Sugar Loaf Mountain. My right hand was starting to ache.

"So what we gonna do now?" Norris asked. "I mean, we have to lie low for a while or split to another city or what?"

"No, baby. Those policemans drunk and we knock them up good. They not gonna remember too much details. Besides, they got to have good excuse for we kick their ass. So they say there ten of us. Ten *subversivos*, two meters tall."

Renata sat in Norris's lap and put her arms around him. Now what? I imagined Norris thinking.

"Maybe I'm losing my marbles, but Rio I think I could get to like. Who needs Chicago? Hang loose, that's where it's at."

The VW rattled up *Avenida São Sebastião*, the cobblestone street that led to my apartment, featuring one of Rio's most spectacular views: across Guanabara Bay stood Corcovado Mountain topped by its colossal Christ statue, his arms outstretched, offering welcome to visitors and solace to residents. And now, I reflected, the three companions were heading toward the embrace of the Rio Christ? Guided there by sacred *Macumba* chants? I would need some time to answer those questions. Two things I was sure of: I nearly got my ass shot off but I was still here in one piece, and it was time to share with Norris the best collection of Brazilian tapes and records this side of Guanabara Bay. After we'd pulled up in front of my building and paid the fare, the driver wanted to know if the passengers were Americans.

"Hell no," I told him, "we're musicians, just here for Carnival, drummers from...Timbuctú."

SOME NICE DRY OAK

Bud George

The sound of the oven timer and the telephone brought her back to the kitchen. She was watching huge snowflakes falling slowly, straight down, covering the bird feeder outside the window. She picked up the phone, and using her shoulder, she held it to her ear, leaving both hands free. Her hello was punctuated by the crash of breaking glass.

"Damnit!"

"Margaret, this is your mother. What happened?"

"Oh, hi, Mom, happy Thanksgiving. I just knocked a glass off the kitchen counter." She turned the timer off, opened the oven door, and placed three pies on a rack to cool.

"Margaret, your pa is sick." Her mother's voice weakened to little more than a whisper. "He's real sick. Dr. Johnson said there's little hope."

"Where in hell are you now, Mom?"

"Don't swear!" The voice firm now. "We're at the hospital."

"Mom, I'll come. Lewiston?"

"Yes."

"Tell Pa I'll be there, tell him I'm coming, tell him…"

"Yes…goodbye."

She stood with the phone still on her shoulder, not hearing the receiver's steady buzz, and watched the snowflakes pile higher on the bird feeder.

"Maggie, what's the matter?" asked her husband, his voice thickened by the Thanksgiving drinks and laughter. He loved having guests, his family especially.

She quickly hung up the phone. "My father is in the hospital."

"I'm sorry." His smile faded.

"We'll have dinner, then I'll leave. He's in the Lewiston hospital, I'm going up there."

The dinner went smoothly, but she was quiet and ate little. She'd have eaten little even without the phone call, with her appetite dulled by the long day of food preparation. After dinner, as her husband's sisters took over the cleanup chores and the men returned to comfortable chairs and another drink, she brought a suitcase from storage, then returned it and chose instead an old knapsack. She packed it carelessly with a few clothes and a toothbrush. She dressed in jeans, a sweater, and warm boots, said her goodbyes, kissed her husband's cheek lightly, and left.

She threaded the pickup smoothly through heavy Thanksgiving evening city traffic. The snow, deep enough now to make travel difficult for most cars, was no obstacle for the pickup with its standard transmission and limited-slip rear end. Her father taught her how to drive when she was twelve, in an older pickup, and she smiled thinking about it. It was much older, but not very different from the one she was driving now. He had slowly and carefully explained the controls and the entire engine and driveline to her, then rode the length of the farm road and back with her once. After that, he let her drive alone and only rarely gave her a bit of advice about bad weather driving or how to handle an emergency.

Out of the city freeway traffic was very light. She found a truck stop open ten minutes out of the city, where she bought coffee in two foam cups with covers and cigarettes. She enjoyed the feeling of solitude, driving alone, sipping coffee, and smoking a cigarette, with the heater fan and wipers providing a nice background to the country music on the radio. She reached Lewiston hospital, a one hundred and six mile drive, in a little over three hours.

She hugged her mother in the brightly lit hospital corridor.

"I'm so glad you've come, Margaret," her dry-eyed mother said.

"Can we see him now?" Margaret asked, her eyes tearing now, almost crying.

"He's sleeping now." She stepped back, giving Margaret a small half-smile.

They entered his room. He was a big man, too tall for the hospital bed, so the sheet didn't cover his pale feet. *He looks so old and thin*, Margaret thought, standing next to the bed, her hand on his, crying softly. "I'm here, Pa. I love you, Pa."

"He insists on going home tomorrow. Dr. Johnson agreed to it. He said there isn't anything they can do for him. He didn't want to go to the hospital at all. You know how stubborn he can be." Her mother smiled as if remembering some past happier time.

Traveling was difficult when they left the hospital, even for the pickup. Several times, the drifts were deep enough to stop them completely, but Margaret backed up, and slipping the clutch, eased the pickup through them.

Her mother made tea when they reached the farm, and they sat in the linoleum floored living room. Margaret felt relaxed and at home. The place hadn't changed at all in the twenty years since she'd left. Her two or three a year visits always relaxed her. She liked to visit alone to be released from the pressures and obligations she felt toward her husband and children. She dozed in the rocking chair, and her mother covered her with a warm homemade quilt.

When she woke up, her neck was stiff, but she felt rested. Her mother was in the kitchen, turning bacon, and wonderful smelling coffee was bubbling in the percolator on the old-fashioned wood cooking stove. They ate, and over coffee, her mother said, "I called the hospital. They'll bring him home as soon as the roads are clear."

Later, Margaret put on one of her father's old work jackets, far too large for her, but warm, and went out to the tool shed. She found an old grain shovel and used it to clear a path to the house, to the wood pile, and to the barn. She filled the kitchen wood box and sat down at the table again with her mother. She told Margaret of the church doings over the past few months and a little local gossip.

They sat quietly for a while.

"I guess I'll have to move to town," her mother said, breaking the quiet.

Margaret went outside again and started the old Case tractor, using jumper cables from her pickup. She checked the hydraulic system and added fluid from a rusty can she found in the tool shed. She cleared the driveway and the farm yard using the tractor's front end loader. The she parked the tractor in its original place and was walking back to the house when the ambulance entered the driveway. Her father was sitting up in the front seat next to the driver.

"Hi, Pa," she said while opening the right side door of the ambulance.

"Hey, Moe, good to see you." He smiled. He was the only one to call her Moe. It was his pet name for her. She liked the sound of it now; it reassured her and gave her hope.

With the driver on one side of him and her on the other, they helped him into the house. He sat in a straight back kitchen chair and thanked the driver. After the driver left, he said weakly, "Help me to bed."

They did, and he fell asleep almost immediately.

Friday night, Moe slept on the couch, again covered by the warm homemade quilt. Saturday she awoke to the good breakfast smells. She looked in the bedroom and found the bed empty. She ran into the kitchen.

"Ma, where the hell is Pa?"

"Don't swear! He's out in his workshop."

"For Christ's sake, he shouldn't be up!"

"Don't swear. Go tell him breakfast is ready."

When she entered the workshop, it was a warm place smelling of pine, with sawdust covering all the windows and most of the tools.

"Breakfast is ready, Pa."

"Goddamn pine ain't worth a shit," he answered. "I'll be in, in a minute."

Through Saturday, he worked in spurts, frequently coming in for coffee and to rest. Moe looked in on him in the shop several times during the day. That evening, she discovered what his project was. *A pine coffin.*

Saturday night and Sunday morning, she tossed and turned under the warm quilt, finally reaching sleep with the first light of morning. When she woke up, her mother was washing dishes.

"He's outside," she said.

Moe rushed out the door, not stopping for a coat or gloves. She had to talk to him, to comfort him, to make her peace. Time was running out. He was at the wood pile, splitting kindling wood.

"Hey, Moe," he said as she approached him. "You slept late."

"Yes, Pa, I slept late." She looked at the neatly piled wood he was making. All clean, new pine.

"Goddamn pine ain't worth a shit," he complained. "Maybe in the spring, I'll get some nice, dry oak. *Build it right.*"

Lexicology

David George

By the summer of my seventh year, I was an avid reader and word collector. Grandma showered me with books, new words tumbled from the pages. Synonyms led down endlessly forking paths. Spring was sudden movement of a cat, sparkling water, bright new season.

One rainy June day, Momma entered the room where my sister Eloise, the oldest, and my big brother Eric were teaching me to play Scrabble. Momma's eyes were red, her hands shaking. My first thought raced toward Dad, training that summer with the National Guard. She fastened her eyes on me.

"There's something I have to tell you, Jimbo. Your friend Chucky's in the hospital. He may not be coming home."

"Chucky Digatano?" Eric interrupted. "He get hit by a car?"

"He has polio."

She pronounced this new word in a tone invoking the most dreadful term I knew: tornado, the woeful funnel cloud that swept across the Minnesota plains where we lived.

"What's polio, Momma?"

"It's a disease, sweetheart. Another word for it is infantile paralysis." She struggled to steady her voice. "Way out here, we hoped the epidemic wouldn't get to us."

Disease I understood. We children knew well the bane of measles, mumps, chicken pox. But none of those had given Momma this haunted look.

"Is he in an iron lung?" Eloise asked.

"Yes, I'm afraid he is."

"Is he gonna be in a wheelchair?" Eric's eyes shone with excitement.

"That's the best we can hope for."

These novel words hinted at a menace invading our own neighborhood, not lurking beyond the horizon like a tornado. Polio? Infantile paralysis? Epidemic? Wheelchair? Iron lung? I imagined Chucky attacked by a robot from the science fiction stories I'd read.

The following week, Grandma led us on our annual trek to the Aquatennial Festival in Minneapolis, in spite of warnings from Uncle Calvin and Aunt Bea that it might be a risky venture what with the epidemic in full swing. But Momma said we couldn't hide from the world, so off we went to Minnesota's celebration of its brief summer, a festival with a grand parade, puppet shows for kids, boat races, food stands offering the delights of snow cones and corn dogs.

Eloise's birthday soon followed. After her party, she ran out to play with her new baton, the one present she had wished for with all her might; she always talked about becoming a cheerleader when she reached high school age. Eloise went to the small park on the corner to play with the baton. She became frustrated because she couldn't catch it when she threw it in the air. She couldn't lift her head up to see it, her chin just wouldn't go up. She came home crying and told Momma she didn't want to play with her baton anymore and she didn't care if she ever became a cheerleader. Momma seemed to panic when Eloise came down with a fever, complained of pain in her back and legs. The doctor swept into our house, hovered over my sister, spoke to Momma in a muffled voice. Other men appeared; they took Eloise away.

When Eloise went to the hospital, another infectious word penetrated my collection: quarantine. Now out of reach was the hidden treasure that until then had awaited on the outskirts of town: a stream filled with croaking bullfrogs, pinching crayfish, snapping turtles, fields from which thunderous clouds of pheasants might emerge at the adventurer's very next step. Now Eric and I were forbidden to leave the confines of our yard. Momma or Grandma kept vigil. Eloise's illness allowed Dad to plead hardship. He was released from National Guard duty, which for Eric and me meant a third warden. A tennis shoe placed on sidewalk's edge drew shouts across our exploratory bow.

"Jimbo! Eric! Stay right where you are!"

At night when everyone in the house was asleep, Eric would dare me to sneak out with him to explore the neighborhood, but my head was filled with dark-cloaked "polio-men" and iron-lunged robots. The neighborhood, however, lurked just beyond reach during the day when other kids came to stare at us, quarantined, exotic animals locked in a zoo.

As we grew older, Eloise recounted bits and pieces of her experience:

The first thing I remember is waking up and thinking it was still my birthday. They told me I was in the hospital and I had polio. Soon I was transferred to Fort Snelling in St. Paul. Polio patients were housed in the military barracks, totally isolated from the outside world. After two weeks, I was moved to the Kenny Institute in Minneapolis for therapy. I didn't have any complications like paralysis or difficulty breathing so I became the "poster girl" that Sister Kenny used to teach parents how to use appropriate exercise to make sure polio patients recovered properly. Most the other kids in my wards were sicker, several had to be fitted with braces because they couldn't walk by themselves, some went home in wheelchairs, some in iron lungs never made it home at all. As to long-term effects, one leg was shorter and it was a struggle to walk normally because I didn't want anyone seeing me limp, my pelvis is crooked and I have severe scoliosis which makes my back really ugly. And that also has contributed to my arthritis. I am lucky too…polio can have a rebound effect after as many as fifty years. However, Dr. Walsh had me take the oral vaccine when it came out, and I really think that is the reason I have not had any recurrence of the disease. Another odd thing I remember about that period: the first ADULT movie I ever saw was the one about Sister Kenny that starred Rosalind Russell which mother took me before my eleventh birthday.

In early August, my sister Eloise came home, not in a wheelchair but supported by Momma, Dad, and Grandma. Everyone acted like she was back from the wars, which elicited no small measure of envy from Eric and me.

The third week of August, I became feverish, felt pain in my legs. The doctor came knocking again, examined me.

"I'm not certain. We'll have to wait and see. Besides, the hospital's full this summer."

He returned each day for a week. The fever and pain subsided. But I was too weak to attend Chucky's funeral. I missed the first two weeks of school in September, an occurrence I did not regret. I suffered no apparent effects from my brush with polio. However, when I grew older, x-rays revealed that I had suffered a mild case of the disease. And like my sister Eloise, I, too, have one leg shorter than the other, scoliosis, and arthritis. But I think of kids like Chucky who died, those who ended up in wheelchairs, and I mourn for them while I give thanks for my own good fortune.

After the polio vaccine was discovered, the disease receded from consciousness and then from memory. The scourge from my childhood is unknown to new generations. Eloise, Eric, and I grew up, had families of our own. We, too, worry about our children. Other epidemics have swept across the land. And other more ominous diseases may yet appear on the horizon. But my lexicon is forever infected with polio, infantile paralysis, iron lung.

THE SECRET FORT

David George

1 *Eostara brought forth brightly colored eggs and green apples. As March begat April, Persephone distributed spring's multitude of gifts. Flora tended her fields of newborns: crocus, violet, iris, lily, larkspur, dandelion. In May, Pan pursued Syringa, who escaped his entreaties by transforming herself into a lilac bush. Faeries and sprites sang and danced into the light of June. There were rumors of Spring-Heeled Jack lurking, but the Morrigan vowed to curse those who brought harm to children.*

2 Ingemar's face was sprinkled with freckles, he wore his light brown hair in a buzz cut, and in spite of his frail appearance, he was wiry and quick. At eight, he was the youngest member of his baseball team by two years. His speed in the outfield and productive bat had merited him special consideration by the older kids who, in other circumstances, would have taunted a younger boy from a troubled family. Today's game, the first of the summer, was tied one to one. Ingemar had singled in his team's only run and had tracked down a fly ball that looked like a sure extra base hit. Something was not quite right, though. Ingemar noticed a man watching him. He was tall, athletic, but not like a baseball player. More like a weight lifter. Ingemar tried to guess his age, but to him twenty, thirty, forty… he hadn't a clue. The man seemed to move around the park as the boy shifted positions during the game. If it was Ingemar's turn at bat, the stranger would be standing behind the backstop. If he sat on the bench between innings and looked back, he would see the man staring at him. If he played leftfielder, the man would be standing behind the outfield fence. Finally, when he chased a fly ball that sailed over the fence and ended the game, he found himself face to face with the stranger.

"Good try, kid. Almost caught that one."

"Oh, thanks, mister. But I missed it by a mile."

"Listen, kid, I live over on Djevel Street. Me and my Aunt Eva moved in a couple months ago. That green house on the corner by Lyndale. Know which one I mean? You would not believe the special collection of stuff I got there. Ain't never showed it to none of the punks in the neighborhood. But I can tell the way you play ball you ain't like them other snot noses. Kinda kid would appreciate my collection."

"Sure, thanks, mister. Gotta go, game's over."

When he returned to the infield where his team members were rehashing the game, Johann, the pitcher, smirked at him.

"Got something going with Harry the Fairy?"

"What?" Ingemar was puzzled.

Anders, the catcher, chimed in, "Harry Skallemort, the Norwegian Fairy. He invite you over to see his collection?"

All Ingemar could think of responding was "Sorry I didn't catch that homerun ball, fellas."

Johann patted him on the back. "Ain't nobody coulda caught that ball. You did good today. We got a game with that team from South Minneapolis next Saturday. See you then."

The boys disbanded. As Ingemar walked off the darkening field, he thought someone was following him. When he looked around, he noticed a figure duck behind a tree. He looked back several more times but saw no one. Ingemar did not go straight home. He couldn't resist his usual impulse to wade into the Theodore Wirth Park bogs in search of frogs. He knew early evening was prime frog catching time; he had been hunting them since age five.

It all began one night on Uncle Calvin's farm, when Ingemar and his cousin Carl sneaked out to go frog hunting. Carl, who was ten, had been pestering Ingemar to join him on the hunt, and finally, Ingemar had relented. Carl's hunting gear consisted of a flashlight, a pitchfork, and a gunnysack. On the first night of hunting, they squeezed through the window of their second-floor room, hung from the edge of the tarpaper roof, dropped to the wet grass, listened for signs of adults. They heard peepers in the trees, bullfrogs in the slough, creaking blades high on the windmill. The boys crept past the barn. When a cow shifted in its stanchion, they stood frozen, then ran toward the pasture into the bright moonlight, leaving concealment behind. They had to cross cornfields, a narrow patch of woods, slither through a barbed-wire fence, wade into a swamp on the edge of the farm. Carol shone the light along the edge of the swamp until he spotted a frog. He handed the sack and the flashlight to Ingemar and told him to keep it focused on the prey. He raised the pitchfork and plunged it downward, impaling the creature. The frog emitted a sound Ingemar had not expected, a wail that sounded like a baby's cry. Carl deposited the animal, still alive in the sack. They caught several more frogs that night. Carl had assigned to Ingemar the task of securing the bag filled with crying, squirming swamp dwellers. Ingemar had been satisfied with the adventure and the thrill of the hunt but had not developed Carl's taste for killing. In his subsequent frog-hunting quest, his method was simple. Spot a frog with his flashlight, grab it with his hands, feel it squirm beneath his fingers, then release it. But the baby's cry often echoed in his mind.*

He heard a splash behind him; someone was lurking in the cattails. This was the first time he had seen another person in the swamp at night.

"Hello! Who's there?"

There was no answer; he ran toward home.

Ingemar's grandma was making potato sausage when the boy burst through the back door of the small ramshackle cottage.

"Gramma Alma!"

"My lord! Your pants are all muddy. You were down in the swamp again hunting frogs, ja?"

"Yes, Mom-Mom."

"I tell you how many times, Ingemar Grodason? Keep out of the moras."

"Gramma, know those Norwegians moved in over on Djevel Street? How come they call that guy Harry the Fairy?"

"How you like I wash your smutsig mouth out with soap? Who make that kind of nasty talk about a nice man? I'll have you know, Ingemar, the Skallemorts are a decent Lutheran family. Hush. We all have our troubles. You dasn't try to be better than other folk, young man. And no more nasty talk."

Family? Ingemar thought Harry had said it was just he and his aunt Eva. The boy was also puzzled by his grandmother's bitter complaints of "nasty talk."

Ingemar's grandfather Olle, soused most of the time, had taught him to repeat, "He's a dirty little Norska with his shirt tail out, his barn door open, and his wiener hanging out," when he was five. The old man incurred his wife's displeasure as he regaled Ingemar and his two brothers with bawdy songs, offered clandestine sips from a flask of aquavit he carried in his hip pocket. Every time the old man asked him to recite one of his salty jests in front of his drinking buddies, his grandma blew a gasket.

Grandma Alma didn't understand that grandpa's intent during those three bitter years had been to provide his grandsons what he referred to as "yuks and yokes." The three brothers had become orphaned when their parents' car, on a return trip from Uncle Calvin's farm, sailed off the road, floated through the gentle air of a southern Minnesota June evening, and came to rest in peace against an elm tree. Ingemar's oldest brother always insisted, "It was the ol' man's fault. He was stinkin' drunk."

But Ingemar had his own secret story. Their father had plunged in flames to glory as a fighter pilot in Vietnam. Although he knew it wouldn't make sense to anyone else, in his story, his mother was riding in the airplane with his father when it went down.

In the days following the baseball game, Ingemar, in an acute state of inquisitiveness, kept asking himself why they would call a Norwegian a fairy, why the word ticked the old lady off. He thought of fairy tales he had read: Cinderella's fairy godmother. Peter Pan and Tinkerbell. Rumplestiltskin? Spinning straw into gold but no fairies.

Thumbelina's boyfriend. Was he a fairy? If so, he certainly wasn't big and strong like Harry Skallemort. He wasn't Norwegian, was he?

He approached his brother Erik in the backyard tinkering with his bicycle.

"Erik, I was just wondering about that Harry the Fairy guy."

"Why? He offer you two-bits to play drop the soap?"

Ingemar always had the feeling his thirteen-year-old brother was trying to confuse him, he was wary of traps. "Two-bits for what? I mean..."

Too late.

"You don't know shit from shinola, you little punk. Git outa here."

The Frog Prince. No, that's witches.

Maybe the oldest brother would be more helpful. He found him in his usual spot, in the weeds that covered the empty lot next to their house, where he did "speriments" with insects. He was currently tending a nest of daddy-long-leg spiders. Ingemar's interest in his brother's hobby had increased to the point he considered giving up frog hunting. Although he couldn't explain it to himself, he was fascinated watching the eggs turn to babies and then to adults. Ingemar stopped at the edge of the clearing where the spiders' nest was located.

"Hjalmar, how come they call that Norska fella Harry the Fairy?"

"You keep away from that creep. He tries to pull anything you let me know, I'll kick his ass."

How a scrawny fourteen-year-old was going to beat up a muscular man like Harry Skallemort was a mystery.

Turned Pinocchio into a real boy. Magic wand. Magic! Was that it? Could Harry do magic tricks? Ingemar didn't believe magic really existed. He stopped believing in Santa Claus when he was five. The teacher whacked him on the hand with her ruler when he tried to explain it all to the other kids. Magic tricks? Bet that's the special stuff he was talking about at the game. Got a collection of magic tricks. Only one way to find out. Take Harry up on his invitation.

It was easy to go wandering around the neighborhood in North Minneapolis on a summer night when Grandpa was on a binge.

Grandma Alma couldn't keep track of three rambunctious grandsons. *No, how no way*, Ingemar repeated to himself as he walked the three blocks to Djevel Street. June bugs buzzed, gypsy moths circled around streetlights. He stopped in front of the Skallemort house, waiting nervously, trying to decide if he should knock on the door. He hesitated for a moment, noticed the yard light was on, then went around back. Harry was sitting on rickety stairs that led to a dilapidated screened-in porch. He was wearing a tight black t-shirt, the sleeves ripped off, dirty sweat pants, legs cut short. He was a redhead, his hair plastered down. Leathery skin. He looked like a lazy lizard, slow-moving but fast and powerful when he wanted to be. The lizard hissed, "Looking for something? Hey, you're the kid I saw at the ball field. Come to check out my collection, didja?"

"Guess so."

"Say, ain't you one of them Grodasons? Blockhead Swedes. Your old man's a drunk."

"Ain't not."

"Sure, whatever." The man paused to roll a cigarette, light it, take a deep puff, as Ingemar shifted uncomfortably in his ragged tennis shoes. "What's your name?"

"Ingemar."

"So you wanna see my collection, Ingemar blockhead?"

"Can you do magic tricks?"

"Sure, you betcha. Collection, magic, you name it. Us Norwegians don't usually have no truck with you Svenska blockheads. But maybe I'll make an exception. Just this one time. Considering you got the knack. For baseball, I mean. Look, I got this secret fort. It's an underground fort. Nobody knows about it. Got all kinds of magic stuff down there. I'll show it to you. And my collection, too. Maybe."

"A secret fort? Really? Me?"

Harry stood up and stretched, his muscles bulging, the veins on his arms and legs popping out.

"Maybe not. Nah, you might tell somebody. Got hidden treasure down there."

"I wouldn't tell a soul. Gramma Alma's always saying you can't get a thing outa me."

"Wouldn't tell a soul? Well, I guess." He moved his face close to Ingemar's, looking into his eyes. "But I gotta blindfold you before I take you there. Otherwise, it wouldn't be a secret no more. Would it, lingon-berry? You gotta promise to keep your trap shut about the fort."

"I promise. Honest Injun. Won't tell nobody. Really."

"'Cause if you rat, something real bad's gonna happen to you. Understand, lutefisk breath?" He flicked his cigarette toward Ingemar, missing his face by a few inches. The man's tone was menacing, but Ingemar was certain this would be his only chance to explore a secret underground fort. "Wait here."

Harry went into the house, returning quickly with what looked like a dishtowel. He wrapped it around Ingemar's head, covered his face, tied it. The musty-smelling towel made breathing difficult.

"See anything? Don't bullshit me now."

"Nothing. Cross my heart and hope to die."

"Okay now. The fort's a long ways from here. It's in a place nobody could ever find it."

Ingemar felt himself spun around several times. Dizzy, stumbling, he was led about in circles. They stopped. Ingemar was certain they were still in the Skallemorts' yard. He heard a creaking sound, a trap door being raised. He smelled fresh earth, something sour that reminded him of swamp water, then an acrid burning stink. Light from below filtered through the towel.

"Okay now, sit down. Stick your legs out. Feel the ladder? Climb down real slow. I'll hold you. Don't want no blockhead falling into my fort and breaking shit."

Climbing down the ladder, Ingemar felt cobwebs brush against his face. Once inside, his feet on solid ground, he heard the trap door close with a hollow thud that seemed to resonate through his body. Harry removed the blindfold. A lantern cast flickering, twisted shadows. The strong smell of the kerosene made Ingemar gag; he feared he was about to throw up. The fort was even larger than the boy had imagined, nearly the size of the family two-room "shack," as his oldest brother Hjalmar insisted on calling their home, to Grandma Alma's dismay. The fort had dirt floor and walls, propped up by two-by-fours. A second room contained a crude bunk covered by a greasy army blanket. Planks set on bricks served as shelves, piled high with stacks of magazines. Ingemar looked closely—there were comic books, drawn in black and white.

"Go ahead, take a look. Bet you never seen nothing like it."

Ingemar picked out a copy of "Popeye." He opened it. Popeye, his member hanging out, was chasing Olive Oyl. He caught her, inhaled a can of spinach, his thing got huge.

"Why's Popeye stabbing her with his…Golly, where'd you get this?"

"Wait'll you see the other stuff I got." A lower shelf held tools, boxes of nails, objects Ingemar didn't recognize at first. On closer inspection, they were wood carvings. He lifted one up.

"This looks like a wiener."

"You're a wiener, dickhead. Shut up and do what I tell you. See this notebook? I'm writing everything down. If you don't watch out, I'm gonna show it to your brothers."

"Write what down? I didn't do nothing."

"That's what you think. You was looking at dirty comics and playing with that prick. I'm writing it down right now." He scribbled in the notebook.

"I think I wanna go home now. Thanks for showing me the fort."

Harry put an arm around Ingemar's shoulder, smiled brightly. "Hey, you hear the one about Swedes' yellow hair? How come so many you Svenskas got yellow hair? From pissing outa basement windows."

Harry Skallemort snorted as he laughed. It reminded Ingemar of the pigs on his uncle Calvin's farm. The stench of the kerosene was stronger. Ingemar was certain that if he vomited in the secret fort, Harry would be very angry with him.

"Okay now. Lemme show you something, blockhead. Guess I better call you a wiener from now on." He picked up a carving from the shelf, unbuckled his belt. "How much you wanna bet I can shove this up my butt and it won't hurt?"

A moth flew into the kerosene lamp, which sputtered faintly.

"I think my folks are prob'ly getting worried. It's kinda late."

"Your old man's too plastered all the time to give a rat's ass where you are. Worried my ass. Hey, wanna see my tattoo?"

Harry turned toward Ingemar, pointed to the inside of his left thigh. On it was a tattoo depicting a grinning skull with the words "Death Head" beneath it.

"What's that?"

"That's my name."

"I don't get it."

"You don't get much of anything, do you, blockhead?"

"Where dja get that tattoo?"

"Prison. Everybody gets tattoos in prison. I put mine where only special people get to see it."

Ingemar recoiled at the word *prison*. Had Harry murdered someone? The smell of kerosene again made his stomach heave.

"Prison?" Ingemar asked in a tremulous voice.

"They said I was diddlin' little girls and boys. It was bullshit. Never touched them brats. Hey, how 'bout my treasure? Wanna see some?"

"Spoze."

Something was scratching inside the walls. A mole?

"Close your eyes and don't move."

When Ingemar complied, Harry quickly pulled down the boy's pants. He charged toward the ladder. Harry blocked his way.

"Please, Mr. Skallemort, let me go home."

"What's this Mr. Skallemort crap? Name's Harry. Okay now. I'm writing all this in the notebook." He scribbled furiously. "Go ahead, read it. Says how you was going around with your pants down. Want your brothers to see that?"

"Please, Mr. Skallemort, I mean, Harry."

He picked up the notebook, scrawled with the pencil. The scraping sound persisted. Frogs? Was that how they disappeared? Digging underground?

"Guess your brothers are gonna love to see this."

"I wanna go home."

"You do what I tell you or your brothers are gonna find out you're some kinda queer."

Harry stood up, silhouetted by the lamp. A dump truck rumbled down Djevel Street, the fort shook, a thin cloud of sparkling dust enveloped the man.

"Harry…the Fairy…"

"What the fuck did you say?"

"Harry the Fairy. That's what the kids on the ball team call you."

He slapped Ingemar's face. "Call me that again I'll break your neck. Get down on that bed."

"No. I wanna go home."

"I wanna go home, I wanna go home. Goddamn queer Swede."

A few inches from his face, a large black and yellow spider slid down a thread. Ingemar wished ardently that the spider would attack Harry Skallemort. He imagined the spider spinning her web tightly around the man until she squeezed the air out of him, covering his mouth until he could no longer say blockhead, dingle berry, lutefisk breath. She would wrap his hands so he could not write in his notebook or touch Ingemar ever again. Harry would be tied securely to the smelly bed, trapped forever in his underground stink hole, crying like a baby, like a frog stuck with a pitchfork. The pain the boy now felt would be the spider stinging the man over and over again, poisoning his body the way Ingemar was now poisoned. He believed fervently the spider was watching over him, witness to his ordeal.

Later, Ingemar submitted numbly as Harry repeated the ritual in reverse: tied on the dishtowel, led him up the ladder, closed the trapdoor, walked about in circles, spun him around, removed the blindfold.

"Don't you dare tell no one about my fort, dingle berry. I got all this stuff wrote down. Git!"

Ingemar ran all the way to the swamp. The night was filled with hisses, harsh cries. The boy took off his soiled clothes, waded into the water, rinsed off his jeans. He put them back on soaking wet, then headed to the nearest street lamp. He held his shorts up to the light; they were stained red. He walked down an alley, tossed them in a trashcan. When he got home, only Hjalmar was up and about.

"Where the hell you been? It's eleven o'clock."

"Down by the swamp. Where the folks?"

"Aw, Mom-Mom's out checking out those skid row bars. Trying to find Granpa. Say, you're a mess. Been frog hunting?"

"Yeah, but I didn't catch any."

"Well, you better put your clothes in the wash before the old lady sees you. Jeez, you look terrible. Been in a fight?"

"Got stuck in some muck. Thought I wasn't gonna make it out."

Three days passed while Ingemar stuck close to home. He even stayed away from the swamp. The image of the spider he had seen in Harry Skallemort's fort burned ceaselessly in his mind. At ten o'clock on a bright morning, as his grandmother was mixing lefse dough and Ingemar was lying on the sofa reading *Stuart Little*, Harry rode his bicycle up to the front porch.

"Hey, Ingemar," he yelled, "come out here a minute. I wanna talk to you."

The boy scrambled up the ladder to the attic where he and his brothers slept.

"Ingemar, Harry Skallemort's here for you."

"Tell 'em I can't come out right now, Mom-Mom. I'm reading."

"Always buried in those books. You dasn't be rude. When folk come over, we act polite, ja? And when they're good Lutherans like the Skallemorts we always think of the golden rule, like the Bible says."

He climbed down. Grandma Alma didn't notice his gallows walk to the front door.

"What's up, Mr…Harry?"

"Come here, I got something to show you." He held a book of matches in the palm of his hand. On it was a drawing of a naked woman, on all fours, her back arched, her tongue pressed between her teeth. "How much you gimme for these matches, blockhead?"

"Don't want 'em."

Harry pulled out a notepad, the doomsday book. "I know somebody'd like to see this. How much allowance you get a week?"

"Six bits."

"Six bits, that'll do." He stuck the matches in Ingemar's shirt pocket. "Six bits a week, you get a new book of matches. See you around, lutefisk breath."

Ingemar remained motionless, mute. A cat crossed the yard, stopped at the edge of the porch. Looking up at him was Misty, his smoky gray kitten. Misty, he thought, the amazing jumping cat. A grasshopper flew above the kitten. She leaped high, turned a somersault as if launched from a trapeze, snapped her jaws shut on the insect, landed softly, contentedly munched her prey, all the while watching Ingemar with her soft blue eyes. *But Misty got kilt last year. Smushed by a bus.* The boy jumped off the porch and scurried from the yard. Faintly, he heard his grandmother calling after him. He ran ahead blindly, crossing streets, cutting through yards, scrambling over fences, tearing his shirt and pants. By the time he reached the swamp, he was bleeding from several cuts. He tunneled through a stand of cattails, perched on a grassy hummock out of the mire. He huddled there through the morning and afternoon. Voices, which he recognized as his brothers', called his name. At one point, he heard nearby footsteps. By nightfall, human voices had disappeared. Then over the swamp, an alien silence descended. Ingemar strained to hear a familiar croak, peep, or buzz. Over the cattails, a silvery web gradually took shape, forming a screen before him. Two figures became visible, his mother and father, riding silently in an airplane. They turned to Ingemar and smiled. A gust of wind shook the web and the airplane fell from the screen. The smell of kerosene drifted through the cattails. The web dissolved, Ingemar heard a splash, dimly saw a boat moving toward him. A lantern strung above it shone on Harry Skallemort, who strained at the oars in a steady rocking motion and stared across the water at the boy.

3 The summer of his eighth year might have been a dreaded time for Ingemar because he had to spend nearly his entire vacation on Uncle Calvin's farm. For reasons never explained clearly, he was often sent to the farm for a week, a month at harvest time, now the whole summer. The farm had always meant for him heavy, dirty, sometimes sickening work. He preferred being in the city, playing baseball with his teammates, hanging out at the swamp. This year, however, the farm seemed like salvation. Back home, after spending the night in the swamp, assaulted by visions of his dead parents and Harry Skallemort, he had been found. He spent another week hiding in the attic, refusing to speak. In desperation, his grandparents sent him to Uncle Calvin's farm. For Ingemar, it was a refuge from Harry, who could never find him on a small farm in Southern Minnesota. And if somehow he were to appear, magically, Ingemar imagined all the lethal farm instruments he could use to defend himself, after which he could feed Harry to the pigs.

Ingemar threw himself feverishly into the farm work, milking cows by hand at dawn, picking and shucking corn, slopping out the pigsty, joining a bucket brigade to empty the cesspool. He tried to breathe through his nose, but particles of fecal matter kept finding their way into his mouth. As a reward, Uncle Calvin taught him to drive the old Ferguson tractor. He plowed a field, raked hay, pulled the wagon where the bales were piled. He loved the smell of the hayloft, the haze that filtered the sunlight creating dust streams of pale gold. Ingemar tended a nest of baby spiders in the hayloft, feeding them flies he picked from the strands of sticky flypaper hanging from the rafters of the barn. In spite of his cousin Carl's entreaties, he no longer joined in the frog hunts. Waking up at five in the morning, walking into the newly born day was always a moment of transport. Time would stop. Ingemar could not distinguish himself from the air, the frail light, the damp grass beneath his bare feet. Then the engines would start up: tractors, combines, threshing machines, mowers, balers. It was as if the farm's heart had begun to beat, a thrilling race was about to begin: rake and bale the hay before rain could spoil it, cut and thresh the wheat, pick the corn before the crows finished it off, dig out the potatoes before the gophers got them, keep the cows out of the alfalfa fields so they wouldn't eat themselves to death, pick pails-full of black raspberries in the woods while warding off clouds of mosquitoes and avoiding the thorns which tore at clothing and skin.

There were farm chores he could never accustom himself to, especially the butchering. Running after chickens, holding them squawking over a stone, Aunt Ruby severing their necks with an ax, blood spurting, the chickens flopping about headless as if making a last desperate attempt to take flight from death. Butchering pigs was not quite so bad; he hated the huge sows that were capable of killing a boy Ingemar's size if he got too close to her piglets. He watched dumbfounded when Aunt Ruby and Uncle Calvin threw into the pigpen the carcass of a cow that had committed alfalfa suicide. The pigs descended on the carcass, tore it to shreds, reducing it to clean white bones in a few short minutes. Ingemar fantasized the creature being dismembered was Harry Skallemort.

4 Late August, return to home. Ingemar Grodason kept his own counsel, his own lookout. If he heard someone come into the yard, he made a quick exit through the back door, concealed himself in the outhouse. He avoided Djevel Street, the dreaded location of Harry Skallemort's secret fort. He took circuitous routes to school, arrived early, left late.

Ingemar's reappearance at Sinclair Lewis Elementary after the events of the past summer made him feel like a frog in the desert. During recess, he climbed an elm tree at the edge of the playground and sat alone until the bell rang. He daydreamed hour after hour and stayed after school to finish work he had failed to do in class. He stared at the words or numbers on the page, unable to focus. Finally, his teacher sent him down to the office.

Ingemar sat facing Miss Silva, the counselor. He noticed she had warm brown eyes; most of the people he knew had blue or green eyes. Her hair was unusual as well, black and shiny, cut short for a woman, he thought. And she seemed very young compared to the other adults at the school. Miss Silva started asking him questions:

"I understand you're not doing your school work, Ingemar. Can you tell me why that is?"

"Dunno."

"Your teacher tells me you don't play with the other children. Is that true?"

"Guess so."

He looked away from her and focused on a strange painting on the wall. It depicted a group of dark-skinned people dancing, the men in baggy white pants and shirts, the women wearing colorful dresses, an orange wall covered with large white flowers behind the dancers. He noticed that Miss Silva, too, dressed oddly. She wore a white blouse, a light brown jacket—it almost looked like a man's— and pants. He had never seen a woman in pants at the school before.

"They tell me you're quite a baseball player."

"Not anymore."

She did something that startled him. She leaned forward and took his hand. "Tell me something, Ingemar, do you like to read?"

"Not really." He tried to stop the tears that welled up in his eyes.

"Well, your test scores indicate you read far above grade level. You must be reading something."

"Well, sometimes I do."

"What do you read? Can you tell me that?" He averted his gaze. "Fairy tales?"

"No!" He pulled his hand away from hers.

"Adventure stories?"

"A little. About monsters. Spacemen. Stuff like that."

He forced himself to look at her but then regretted it. He was sure she knew he was lying. He hadn't read anything for months.

"I understand you spent last summer on a farm. Did you ever read a story about a farm, like *Charlotte's Web*?"

"Dunno."

"It's by the same author who wrote *Stuart Little*. Have you ever heard of that book?"

"Started it once. Stopped reading it. Stupid."

His lips began to quiver; he remembered the day Harry Skallemort showed up at his house on a bicycle.

"*Charlotte's Web* is a really wonderful story. Like to give it a try? I think there are some things in that book that might help us. What do you think?"

She took his hand in hers once again; he did not resist.

And so Miss Silva and Ingemar embarked on a journey through E.B. White's book about Wilbur the pig, slated for execution, and Charlotte the spider's plan to save him with a tale she spins called "Some Pig." As they read the book aloud together, Ingemar suspected Miss Silva was trying to get him to identify with Wilbur, but he continued to dislike pigs. The one he admired, her clever plot, her power, was Charlotte, the guardian spider. Still, he begrudgingly acknowledged Wilbur's determination to keep going. And the special friendship between the spider and the pig moved him. Maybe someday he could have friends again, although he wasn't so sure about that. He always looked forward to his meetings with Miss Silva. The thought had come to him that his mother was probably like her when she was alive. Not that there was any physical resemblance, but something about her eyes, they seemed to look right into him, not in a mean way, a sort of smiling way. And the sessions with the counselor rekindled his love of reading.

Ingemar began to write stories. He showed one to Miss Silva, about the great swamp war that stopped only when the queen of the spiders promised the king of the frogs she would get rid of the enemy who had been poisoning all the swamp's creatures. The story ended this way: *The spider queen was not the itsy bitsy kind but big as pig. She snuck into Harry the Fairy's secret fort, then busted up all his nasty stuff, then waited for him to climb down the ladder, then jumped him and stung him all over, then wrapped him up tight in a giant silk web and left him in his stink hole forever, then went back to the swamp to tell the frog king their enemy would never bother them again, then she went to take care of her babies.* She told Ingemar she liked it very much. She looked at him silently. A question formed in his mind for the first time: *Does she understand?*

5 *The Minnesota summer sprites had conjured autumn. The leaves, laden with pixie dust, turned from leprechaun green to orange, red, auburn, then fey and brown they fell. In late November, by the time the first snowflakes sparkled in the air and Jack Frost brushed the window panes, Ingemar was almost ready to believe that Harry Skallemort had vanished. Magically.*

To Say Goodbye

Michael George

He sat on the couch, with his feet tucked under him, in the living room of the quiet, late night house. His left hand held the last of too many beers, his right, a cigarette. His eyes were tired and sore and his voice scratched from hours of talking.

She stood in shadows cast by memories of yesterdays. She bent and kissed him. He trembled, returning it.

"I love you," she said.

"And I you," he answered.

It ended as a pale blue light brought morning.

*****

The soup was good…it was hot and filled with meat and beans and peas. It was made from the barmaid's hands. He filled his mouth, savoring it, while meeting her eyes across the table. Resting his spoon, he touched her hand. She smiled. He was warmed yet chilled and afraid.

"The soup is good," she said.

"Yes, it is," he agreed.

Her brow furrowed with concern. "Is something wrong?" she asked.

His hand shook when he raised his spoon. The soup it held returned to the bowl.

"What is it?" she again asked.

"It's tomorrow because I remember yesterday."

She sipped from the glass next to her, savoring the cold beer as it entered her mouth and slipped down her throat. She asked no more.

* * * * *

He arrived first, tasting the apprehension in the air from the snow coming, as he opened the ancient oak door of the cabin. It was filled inside with the scent of the last fire and the massive barn timbers flowing along the ceiling.

He quickly built a fire in the old cast-iron stove. Smoke rose easily up the chimney, then was lost in small swirls in the sky. He watched the road as the snow began. A sense of joy filled him as he watched her car roll down the last hill.

She shivered coming inside, and he warmed her with his arms. He knew again the excitement and comfort of holding her. As they undressed and folded back the quilts, the blowing snow howled through the screens on the porch. They heard a chipmunk scurry for cover under the floor. He felt the joy of her laughter when an out of season gosling called for its mother.

Slowly, they made love with a quiet intensity, while down in the ditches, the cattails bent low in the lusty wind.

* * * * *

Talk filled the crowded room, overcoming the music. Smoke burned his eyes. He left his corner, squeezing through and past arms and hands filled with scotch and other conversation helpers. The frozen porch of pine and fir groaned as he stepped out. He leaned against the house, watching silver-grey shadows cast by the moon, onto misshapen drifts of snow. He was chilled before she joined him.

"It took so long," she said, "because he was watching closely."

"Where is he now?" he asked.

"Talking to someone else."

"Good." He kissed her.

She warmed him with her touch, but he was quickly chilled when she slipped away. She returned to the house. He stayed outside for a while, hoping his car would start in the morning.

*****

April pushed its stagnant water in swift currents overinflated riverbanks. Sand bags filled the shoulders of the road. They blocked a freeway lane crossing the bridge over the muddy river. Traffic moved in snappy, fast-changing lines, while small cars practiced precision driving techniques with trucks.

Her head rested on his shoulder, easing the tension he felt from the too-hot spring sun, and a schedule complaining she might be late.

"I'm sorry there wasn't time," she said. "It was a fun day, I had fun today anyway."

"It was," he agreed, wondering how she would explain the smell of the horses if she was late.

"Next time," she said when they arrived at her car, "we'll take the time."

Then she left him alone with the fly who invaded the car back at the riding stable.

*****

Biscuits from Betty Crocker and meat and cheese from the delicatessen on the corner filled them before they merged together on today's bed.

Later, they sat in the middle of the bed without clothes. They shared a bag of cheese popcorn and the last cup of strong black coffee he brought along in his battered steel thermos bottle.

"It's funny," she said, "how things like this can taste so good."

He smiled, studying her naked body. "Yes, some things can taste wonderful."

She laughed. "Oh you!" She jabbed him gently in the ribs.

She set the empty coffee cup on the dresser near the bed. He gently took her with him as he lay down on the bed again. A long, deep kiss began their celebration of the morning being so far away.

* * * * *

They went out and played in songs of a different nightmare. He watched them spread the picnic lunch over the blanket serving as a table. Imported cheese and fancy sliced meats were scattered among long loaves of french bread and bottles of wine.

His stomach tightened, watching her talk and laugh with the other one. Pain began in his neck, crept around, and seized his forehead. He dipped his hand in the cold creek water, letting his eyes focus on lazy cows dancing over the short brown pasture. The afternoon sky turned red and rain came to end the nightmare.

* * * * *

Long rows of bananas and watermelon, with greens piled high among tomatoes and squash began their day. He held her hand while walking past the stands of fresh food smells and farmers. He found pleasure watching her marvel over such a place in the middle of her city.

They bought caramel apples to eat. For her, two pair of earrings, from a stand in the row at the end where they sold trinkets and old memories. As they left the place, before they got in the car, she kissed him. She filled him with her own building excitement.

* * * * *

Mist filled the world, catching the quiet places. They stopped along Main Street to pet a dog minding the front seat of a pickup truck. A small cafe fed them cheeseburgers and milk in tall glasses.

Later, highways were left behind and forgotten as muddy gravel roads became their dream. They stopped near a stand of pines. In the distance, oaks held the fires of autumn, even through the rain.

She carried a blanket and spread it under a pine with low branches and long wet needles. They made love in their clothes with eyes and hands, then slept in the soundless rain, away from bad promises and another's expectations.

*****

Piles of straw cushioned their backs, warming them. The bright October sun outside cut through the brisk, early morning chill. He sipped the wine and handed her the bottle. When she finished it, he touched her. She pushed his hand away.

"Please don't," she said.

"Why not?" he asked.

"That was the last time. It's too late for us."

His heart stopped as he searched her averted eyes. Does she mean for today or forever? He wondered.

She stood, turning away as she dressed. He remained motionless, unspeaking, until she finished. She turned to him, her mouth open as if to speak, but left him without words.

"Are you sure?" he asked her back, noticing how her hair sparkled in the sun, with the slight movement of her head. Then he knew how long forever is and the wrong way to say goodbye.

FOR A CUP OF COFFEE
Michael George

She held her head out the car window, trying in vain to see the road ahead. A strong wind drove the wet snow so hard it stung her eyes, even though she wore glasses. She wanted to stop and clean the ice off the windshield wipers, but was afraid if she did, she would get stuck.

Wet snow covered the highways to a depth of six inches, and in open areas, drifts were growing rapidly. Because the snow was wet, the drifts packed down hard.

Even though the weather was as bad as it was, Peggy Maynard was close to home and confident she'd make it there without any serious trouble.

She was sure that the worst that could happen was having to walk the last mile of country road after she left the highway. She hadn't seen a snowplow for the last fifteen miles, and if they weren't plowing the highway, they wouldn't be plowing the back roads. So she was fairly certain she'd be walking at least some of it.

It could prove to be a long and difficult walk, but not *that* long and difficult. Not bad enough to be called a damn fool. That's what her husband, Curtis, called her that morning. He was always doing things like that.

He just wouldn't let go and give her the freedom she wanted, needed, and deserved. As far as he was concerned, he knew everything. She knew very little. Especially about things like this. He always worried about a little snow. He didn't have faith in her driving ability. She drove in snow before, and she was driving in it now, without problems. She was almost home.

She hoped, this time, he would get it through his thick head that she was perfectly capable of dealing with situations like this. She was tired of arguing about it with him, the way they did in the morning.

Curtis started the argument before they were out of bed.

"I think you should stay home today, Peggy," he said as soon as she opened her eyes. "There's some real lousy weather outside already, and according to the radio, it's going to get a lot worse. They're expecting a blizzard before it's over. Travel advisories have been out state wide for a couple of hours already."

"Oh, hell, Curtis, they put those advisories out every time it snows. They don't mean much."

"Maybe not, but the fog is thick and it's raining like hell. If the rain turns to snow, it's going to be awful damn slippery, so I think you should stay home. They can get along at your office without you for one day."

"You're going to work, Curtis, aren't you?"

"Yes, but…"

"But nothing! My job is as important as yours. I'm going to work."

"It's a hell of a lot different for me than you."

"Why, because you're a man?"

"Hell no. It's the fifty miles you drive, compared to the five I drive, that concerns me."

"I doubt it. You just don't give me credit for being a good driver. Too bad. I'm going to work. We do need the money too."

"You know you can call in sick and get paid for the day, if money is really your reason for going."

"It's this way, Curtis, I am going to work. I'm so damn tired of you trying to tell me to stay home every time it snows. We aren't living in the dark ages. It isn't going to get that bad, and you know it. I wish you'd get that through your thick head. Times have changed since you were a kid."

"Right, Peggy, we never have bad weather now. I guess I should have realized that."

"Don't be so damned sarcastic."

"I'm not being sarcastic. You're being a damn fool."

"I am not."

"You are, but it's nothing new. I know you're going to your precious job, no matter what. But will you at least promise me you'll leave when it gets really bad?"

"If I can, and if it actually gets that bad. But I can't just walk off the job on your whim. I do have work to do, the same as you do on your job."

"I've never said otherwise, Peggy."

It wasn't particularly difficult driving in the rain and fog that morning, and Peggy got to work on time. The fog was gone and the rain abated considerably by the time she parked in the ramp and walked the skyways to her office.

From her fourth floor office, the rain turned to snow never seemed to be any more than light flurries. She gave it little thought through the morning. Then shortly after lunch, Curtis called.

"If you can't leave work right now," he said, a note of urgency in his voice, "don't try to come home at all."

"Where the hell am I supposed to stay if I don't come home?" she asked, letting her irritation with his call show.

"I don't care. Go to a motel. Stay with one of your friends. It doesn't matter. Just please don't try to drive home if you can't do it now. It is really getting bad here. You won't get through if you wait. We closed up shop already, I'm home. The schools and about everything else up here is closed. You know it has to get awful bad before the idiots close the schools."

"I repeat, Curtis. Where am I supposed to stay if I don't come home?"

"I just told you that."

"I have no intention of doing that, so I damn well will be home tonight."

"Please, Peggy, don't be stupid. Either leave now or don't try to come home. I'm not exaggerating about the weather. It's as bad as I've ever seen it. I don't care which you do, but make your decision now."

"I'll be home."

"Are you leaving now?"

"In just a little bit. I have a couple of things I have to finish first."

"Let it go. Whatever it is, you can finish it tomorrow."

"Don't worry. It won't take long. A few minutes one way or the other won't make any difference."

"The way it is right now, Peggy, it actually could."

"Stop worrying. I'll be home shortly."

She hung up before he could argue with her any more.

After she told her boss that she was leaving for the day, Peggy was waylaid by one of her coffee break companions and asked to go for a cup. She checked her watch and accepted the invitation. A few minutes wouldn't matter. They simply couldn't.

And now, she was sure they hadn't. It might be hard to see, and it was cold hanging her head out the window, but she was still moving along okay. That was what was important. She did have the car under control, after all, even if it did sway a lot whenever she hit a snowdrift.

She was a far better driver that Curtis gave her credit, and she was proving it. She was close to home and not having any serious trouble. It was still over an hour before dark, so she would be home before then. Walking the last mile wouldn't matter that much.

She made good time, even if it did take over an hour to finish up her work and if the coffee break had used up another hour. She would just tell Curtis that all that time was used up driving. Then he could gloat with his typical "I told you so" male attitude.

That was okay. She knew inside she could handle this situation without him or his advice. Quite possibly, better than he could. At least, she didn't get upset about a little snow.

She stopped her wandering thoughts then, concentrating on the highway and searching for the turnoff, she knew was just a short distance ahead.

Her glasses iced up, just as the windshield did, so she put them on the dashboard. Normally, she didn't see very well without them, and now with the heavy, blowing snow cutting visibility down to a couple of hundred feet, she couldn't see anything clearly.

She was almost on top of her turnoff before she saw it, and she braked hard to slow her approach. The car slid hard as it turned, and she felt a momentary pride in her driving ability when she maintained control. It made little difference though, because the car stalled as soon as she hit the first high drift on the country road. She was hopelessly stuck.

The drift was so deep she couldn't open the car doors and was forced to climb out the window. Once out, it surprised her how deep the drifts were.

She barely left the car before she remembered the bad weather gear Curtis put in the car trunk that fall. She laughed at him every fall for the last fourteen years, thinking it silly to go to all that effort to clean up the gear and put it in the car. After all, she hadn't needed it in all that time.

Now it didn't seem so silly. She was already cold and realized how much sense his fall ritual made.

She turned back to get the gear, but couldn't see the car. The light was failing and the wind was increasing. She could only see a few feet in any direction.

She followed the tracks she made, but they quickly disappeared. The drifts were increasing in depth. She fell several times as the wind constantly changed directions. It was one time at her back, then blowing into her face.

As darkness set in, she looked around for lights from nearby farms. None of them appeared with the darkness. Stranger still, she hadn't as yet reached her car. Peggy stopped walking and turned in a slow circle, searching for something familiar.

She found nothing. No lights, no car, not even any trees. Nothing but her, the snow, and the howling wind. She was lost and knew it. What happened? How could she get lost here, so close to home? She'd driven over this road, if she was still on the road, hundreds, no, thousands of times.

She was in deep trouble now. Just the kind of trouble Curtis so often warned her about. But how could this happen nowadays? No one was supposed to get caught in a snowstorm. It never snowed that hard.

She was sure it never would. In all the time since she and Curtis left the city and moved to the country where he grew up, she never saw snow like this. She saw blizzards, but nothing like this. Even in the worst weather, she went to work if Curtis helped her get out of the driveway. Of course, he always refused, and sometimes, she was stuck home for two whole days. It took a week before she could be civil to him again. She believed it was stupid of him to make her lose that much work.

Kind of stupid anyway. Almost as stupid as not knowing where the car was.

Peggy's clothes were doing very little to keep her warm. Her hands and feet were already painfully numb and cold. She knew she had to get them warmed up soon or they would freeze. She gave up on the car and turned in the direction she hoped would take her home.

She trudged through the deep snow until she was exhausted, then stopped to rest. Perhaps she shouldn't have taken the time to finish up that last bit of work. But it was important and hadn't taken that long anyway. It hadn't made the difference. Stopping for coffee is what made the difference. She should have skipped it. If she had, she would be home and warm now, instead of out here in the dark, lying in a snowbank, freezing.

It would feel good to get home, to be warm again. If she got home? She wasn't sure she was going in the right direction. If she didn't get there or somewhere soon, she knew she would die. And if she did, she knew she'd done a very stupid thing. Never before had she done anything as stupid as taking the time for coffee.

Peggy pushed herself to her feet and struggled on, determined to get home or find shelter before she rested again.

She thought she saw a light up ahead. It was way up ahead, but it was there. She was certain it was. It had to be. It simply had to. She couldn't die, just because she stopped for a cup of coffee. It would be too much. To die out in the snow and lose everything. Curtis, her two daughters, her home, her life. Everything! And for what? It was just too ridiculous. She could lose it all, just for a cup of coffee.

THE RABBI'S CHICKEN
Bud George

Micky and I walked out of Billy Deal's Polar Grill—well, Billy told us to leave because we were interrupting his card game.

It was a pretty good lunch. I had a hamburger, a corned beef sandwich, some french fries, a cheese burger, and a bowl of chicken soup. Mickey had more or less the same, but in a different order.

"Let's go up to Desnicks and get a chocolate sundae," I suggested.

Mickey said, "No, we have to cross the street here because Zola's over there washing store windows."

"Who cares?" I asked.

Mickey said, "The rabbi's daughter is over there talking to Zola."

We crossed the street.

The rabbi's daughter had a lovely smile. Zola and the lovely rabbi's daughter told us about this crazy chicken guarding the shed and pen behind Greenstein & Post meat market. They said it chased people out of the alley. An attack chicken, they said.

"No way," we both said, being two ex–farm boys. We had studied chickens on the farm. "No such thing as an attack chicken," we both said.

We went up the alley making clucking noises and flapping our arms.

The chicken attacked, wings flapping, white feathers flying, making noises we never heard from any chicken on the farm.

Mickey ran east. I ran west. The chicken went straight, into the side of Max's pickle truck, made a hell of a dent, shook its head, and went after the rabbi's daughter. Zola threw his bucket of window wash on the chicken and on the rabbi's daughter. She looked good wet.

The next day, I dropped the delivery truck at Joey Schwart's garage. I stopped at Brochin's Deli and bought an onion bagel, walked back to the store, and up the alley. I forgot about the chicken, standing in the middle of the alley. The chicken was pawing the dirt just like a brahma bull, ready to attack. I had no place to go, I was trapped. So I threw half the bagel at the chicken. The chicken cocked its head, looked at me, pecked at the bagel, and forgot about me.

The next day, I picked up a plain bagel with cream cheese. The chicken loved its half.

Over the next couple of weeks, I kind of looked forward to sharing a bagel with the chicken and our conversations. About halfway through the third week after meeting the chicken and seeing the rabbi's daughter wet, there was no chicken in the alley.

I went into Greenstein & Post meat market and asked Mister Greenstein what happened to the attack chicken.

"Well," he said, "the rabbi was here this morning to supervise the processing and had a bagel with him. Turns out that crazy chicken had a weakness for bagels. Caught the chicken easily. I sold it to the rabbi's wife this afternoon."

GUARD CAT
Bud George

My grandma Ruth raised chickens. Free-range chickens. They mostly hung out in the apple orchard on hot summer days. As far as I know, she never actually counted them, but seemed to know their numbers were decreasing, and that there were fewer eggs. A few days after this observation, she noticed the neighbor's big dog hanging around.

"The dog is probably stealing the chickens."

What's a person to do? Can't confront your neighbor about a dog that is maybe stealing chickens. Besides, Swedish Lutherans don't confront anybody about anything, as far as I know.

It happened that Grandpa (George) was reading some poultry magazine. I think it was called *Fowl Droppings*, which, by the way, contained all kinds of really useful information, like how to use duck tape. There was no duct tape in 1944. It was duck tape and was meant to be used as a contraceptive for ducks.

Now, at that time, I had no idea what a contraceptive was. But the idea of chasing down some ducks and sticking some tape on them did have some appeal to me back then.

George found an ad in *Fowl Droppings* for guard cats. A buck a pound, with a few at one half price. Missing tails.

"Hey, Ruth," George asked, "how much we got left in egg money?"

"Well, Maybe eighteen or twenty dollars," she answered.

He showed her the ad. They looked at each other with the biggest grins I ever saw.

It took a while, but this big wood crate came. Grandpa ripped the top off with a big crowbar. The cat inside hissed and refused to leave the crate. It stayed in the crate all day.

That night, we had fried chicken. Well, kind of fried. You do not fire free-range laying hens. You first boil them for most of the day, then bread and fry them. This is especially true if you have false teeth.

The cat stayed in the crate until morning, when Grandma Ruth had a great idea. Maybe a revelation. She brought the cat some leftover fried chicken. That cat hopped out of the crate, ate the chicken, drank a half gallon of water, farted, peed on Grandma's shoe, and followed her into the kitchen.

The cat was pretty funny looking. No tail. They named it Bob.

A couple of days later, the dog showed up.

"George, let the cat out." Ruth said.

Bob treed that dog—ran it right up into an apple tree, sat down, and started cleaning its front paws. The cat came in for supper. Fried chicken. The only thing the cat ate was chicken. The dog stayed in the tree.

"This ain't working out," George observed.

A couple of days later, the neighbor came looking for his dog. He was kind of worried the dog got into some kind of mischief I guess.

George and the neighbor and a ladder got the dog out of the tree. The dog was pretty hungry, so Ruth fed it some biscuits with strawberry jam. She gave me one too.

The neighbor said it seemed he was maybe missing a few turkeys, although he never counted them.

Ruth and George smiled sympathetically and told him about Bob, the guard cat. But I don't think they mentioned his diet.

The cat went home with the neighbor, the dog stayed with us.

Grandma gave it another biscuit. We got a fifty-pound bag of dog food. The dog, Pal, liked it just fine.

I did not like it much.

Grandma sold the neighbor quite a few chickens that summer.

The Garage A Hole and Sister

Michael George

Alex found his mother in the kitchen, crying.

"Why are you crying?" he asked.

"It's nothing for you to worry about," she said. "Now go outside and play."

"Are you crying because we had to leave Grandpa's farm and move to this stupid city?" Alex hated the city. It seemed cold and grey, and where he lived, there were big empty fields that scared him with their emptiness. It made no sense to have fields without cows or horses or corn on them. There weren't even any hay stacks.

"Please, Alex," Mom said again, "go outside."

"But, Mom…"

"Now, Alex!"

He knew she wasn't going to answer him, so he went outside. He searched for his brother, Lester, and found him hiding in the lilac bushes across the alley from their house.

"Mom's cryin', Lester," Alex said, "and she won't tell me why. Do you know why she's cryin'?"

"Sister's sick. Moms always cry when sisters get sick."

"Mom don't cry when I get sick."

"Sister's sick is different. I heard Mom tell Grandma, Sister's got polio."

"What's polio?"

"It's a really bad kind of way to get sick."

"But I been sick lots of ways, and Mom's never cried once yet. So why does she got to cry now? It's just 'cause it's Sister sick, I bet."

"Naw, that ain't mostly why. It's mostly 'cause polio's a worse kind of sick than what you or me ever got. I know Mom likes Sister better'n us, cause she's a girl, but that ain't why she's cryin'. It's 'cause polio gets you so you can't walk. It makes yer legs funny too, sometimes. Then it comes and kills you."

"If that polio stuff comes and kills you, does that mean Sister's supposed to die?"

"Naw, Mom told Grandma not."

"But if that polio stuff kills you, then Sister's gonna die."

"No, she ain't."

"Why not? Don't it kill other kids what it gets?"

"Sure it does. But them other kids ain't Sister. You know Mom won't let no stupid polio hurt Sister."

"I guess yer right. She won't. Mom's tough."

But Alex continued to worry, and his concern grew even more when the doctor came, and Mom continued to cry. It wasn't until the funny little white truck came though, with the big red lights spinning on top, that he grew afraid. It took Sister and Mom away.

He wasn't afraid because he was alone. He still had Lester to explain everything he didn't understand. And Grandma was still there. Even outside, on top of the shack he and Lester built, he could smell the pies and biscuits she was baking. No, it was more the fear Mom might not come back. Then, he was sure, the polio stuff would come for him too.

He didn't mind getting sick so much. No one yelled at him then. Not even if he wet the bed. But he was pretty sure he didn't want to die. He was even more afraid of having his legs get funny. How could he climb trees if they did? He just knew if polio caught him without Mom home to be tough, it would all happen to him.

So it was a huge relief when Mom got home. But she told him that he and Lester had to stay in the yard all the time, until Sister came home from the hospital.

"Why do we have to do that?"

"Sister is very sick, and they are afraid you might be too. So they don't want you to play with the other kids because you might make them sick too."

"But I feel not sick, Mom."

"You have to stay in the yard anyway."

"Who said I do?"

"The doctor and the police."

"I hate that mean doctor. Why did the police say such a dumb thing? I thought they was supposed to be nice."

"They are nice. You still have to stay in the yard. Now go find your brother and tell him he has to come home."

"Okay, I'll go find him. Can we go in the alley?"

"No. Now bring Lester home.

"Okay, but he ain't gonna like it. He's gonna hate all them mean people too. We ain't done nothin', so they's just mean."

Alex found Lester in the lilac bushes again, eating green apples.

"Where'd you get them apples, Lester?" Alex asked.

"Swiped 'em from Old Man Foster's tree."

"Can I have one?"

"Just one. I ain't got but ten left."

"Okay. Mom says you got to come home now. We got to stay in the yard all the time until Sister comes home. Else the police is gonna come get us. They's really mean."

"Police ain't mean, they's just kinda dumb sometimes."

"Then how come they's makin' us stay in the yard until Sister comes home, just 'cause she's sick?"

"I bet they ain't. Yer telling me a lie 'cause I got more apples than you."

"I ain't lyin'. If we don't go home, someone's gonna tell them police to take us to jail. They beat you up in jail. I don't want to get beat up, so I'm goin' home. Bye, Lester."

Lester reluctantly left his apples and followed Alex home, even though he didn't really believe he had to stay in the yard. He went in the house and asked Mom about it. When he came back outside, he kicked the back porch and threw a rock at the garage.

"Them dumb police is mean," he said.

"Did Mom say we had to stay in the yard, Lester?"

"Yes, Alex, you stupid dummy. She told me. It ain't fair."

"What should we do, Lester?"

"There ain't nothin' to do in the yard."

"We could play in the shack."

"I don't wanna."

"Let's throw rocks at the garage."

"We ain't got hardly no rocks."

"Maybe we can find some."

"All the good rocks is in the alley."

"We can't go in the alley."

"Let's sneak out there. If you watch out, I'll do it."

Alex watched for the police while Lester got rocks out of the alley. Then Alex saw a black and white car on the street.

"Jiggers, Lester," he yelled, "here comes the police."

They ran at top speed for their shack and huddled in its darkest corner. After no one came, they went back outside.

"Did you get any rocks, Lester?" Alex asked.

"Some, but I'd a got lots more if you didn't yell about them police."

"You told me to yell if I seen 'em and I seen 'em so I yelled."

"We'll throw these at the garage anyway."

They threw all their rocks at the garage, hitting it almost every time.

When they were gone, Alex asked, "What should we do now?"

"Get some more rocks. It's your turn now."

Alex managed to come back with his pockets full of rocks. For the next three days, they continued with their rock game, with just enough interruptions from the police to keep it from getting too boring.

"I'm tired of throwin' rocks," Lester finally decided. "Besides, Mom might see them dents in the garage we been makin'. So let's dig a fort."

They found a spot they thought would make a good fort and started to dig. When it got too deep, Alex jumped in.

"Did you let one, Lester?" he asked.

"No, I didn't."

"It smells like you did. I ain't gonna dig in this hole no more."

"I'll dig in it then."

Alex climbed out of the hole and Lester went in.

"It smells like you pooped in here. Did you?"

"No. I bet it's the hole what stinks."

"Know what, Alex, I bet this is the poop hole what got filled up when the toilet got moved. I ain't diggin' here no more either."

"Do we gotta put all this dirt back in the hole?"

"We better. Mom'll get mad if she knows we dug up the old poop hole."

"Why does it stink when we can't see no poop?"

"Poop always stinks, Alex. Even if something eats it."

They filled the hole.

"What should we do now, Lester?"

"Nothin'. I'm goin' in the house to listen to the Lone Ranger on the radio."

After they listened to all of their afternoon radio programs, they went back outside.

"What should we do now, Lester?" Alex asked again.

"Let's play fireman."

"That ain't no fun, 'less you got a fire."

"Let's make one."

"Where?"

"In the garage."

"No, everyone gets mad when we do that."

"Well, we can't do it in the house. That'd get Mom really mad."

"Let's play cowboys."

"I know, Alex. We can make a fire in the shack. No one can get mad at us for that, it's ours. And they don't go in there anyway."

"Only if we don't let it burn all the way down."

"We won't. The best way to play fireman is to put the fire out."

"That's good 'cause it's fun in there sometimes."

"Yeah," Lester said, smiling. "Like that time Missy Larson was in there with us."

"You wouldn't let me go in there with you that time, Lester."

"Oh, yeah," Lester's smile broadened, "you might not have had so much fun as what I did. Let's make a fire now."

"Okay. But why was it fun in the shack with Missy Larson? She's just a girl."

"I ain't never gonna tell you that, Alex. You might tell Mom."

The inside of the shack was paneled with cardboard. Lester decided it would be the best thing to burn.

"Are we gonna take some off the walls?"

"Naw, it ain't so much fun that way. It'll be more like it's burnin' down if we leave it this way."

"Can't that really make it burn down?"

"Course not. The rest of the shack is wood. Everybody knows cardboard can't make wood burn."

"I didn't know that, Lester."

"Course not. I always got to tell you everything."

But Lester was wrong. The cardboard could light the wood, and they needed to get help from real firemen to put it out. When it was, Lester admitted he was wrong about cardboard. And they agreed about something. The excitement of watching the real firemen was worth the spanking and being put to bed even before it was dark out.

They also felt bad. Only part of their shack still had a roof. So before they fell asleep, they agreed that as soon as Sister came home and they could leave the yard, they would go to the new houses being built and try to find enough stuff to fix the roof.

"Let's make rubber guns, Alex," Lester said when they went out the next morning. "I got some old inner tube left in the garage."

"Naw. When Sister ain't here, there ain't nothin' to shoot at."

"We could shoot at each other."

"That hurts too much."

"There sure ain't nothin' much to do, is there, Alex?"

"Nope. And all 'cause Sister's got polio. I sure wish we could go out of the yard. Then we could go get Missy Carlson and play that game you said was so fun when you played it with her."

"The shack ain't got all its roof no more."

"I forgot."

"I know. We could get them old whiskey bottles we took from the dump out of the garage and play drunks."

"I don't want to, Lester."

"Why not?"

"'Cause the stuff in them bottles gets me sick."

"Yeah, I remember. You threw up last time."

While they were sitting on the steps, trying to decide what to do, Mom came outside.

"I've got good news," she said. "Sissy is coming home today. I'm going to get her now."

"How come she's comin' home?" Alex asked. "Are her legs funny already?"

"Are they, Mom?" Lester asked. "Boy, them doctors sure can do things fast."

"Her legs are fine. Sister is a very lucky girl. She's well now."

Mom left to get Sister.

"Gee whiz," Alex complained. "They made us stay in the yard when Sister had polio just so nobody else could get it. Now Mom says it's lucky to get. I don't understand them grownups much."

"Me neither, Alex."

That afternoon, most of the kids in the neighborhood came over to see if Sister's legs looked funny from polio. Most of them were disappointed that they weren't. But they followed her in a grand parade around the block anyway. Lester and Missy Carlson followed close behind Sister.

Alex was left at the back of the crowd. No one seemed to notice him, as they all tried to stay close to Sister, just in case something still might happen to her legs. Finally, Alex left the group and went home alone.

"What's wrong?" Mom asked when she saw his sad face.

"I wish Sister was still in the hospital."

"Alex, why on earth would you wish that?"

"'Cause when she was there, it was the only time since we lived in this stupid city that Lester wanted to play with me."

A Pillow for Teddy
Michael George

Spencer Thadeus Alexander IV loved his teddy bear. He received it as a gift from an elderly aunt (along with a blanket and a pillow) when he was born. Those three things were the only friends he ever had.

His parents were quite wealthy, and as rich people often do, they had a grave distrust of most other people. Because of that, Spencer saw little of the world outside the big house he lived in for his entire eight years.

His medical needs were taken care of by a pediatrician who made house calls, only to the rich, and then for a considerable sum of money. His schooling was taken care of by a long series of private tutors, instead of the one or two that would be normal for a boy his age. The problem was caused by his obsession with his three friends. Often, when a tutor asked a question pertaining to his studies, Spencer ignored the question and answered with something irrelevant. For instance, "I can't spell that word until after Teddy's nap." After the tutor waited for the end of the nap and asked the question again, Spencer replied, "Teddy told me you should know how to spell it, that kids like me shouldn't have to tell teachers how to spell words. When I grow up, I'll know how to spell and not make kids do it for me."

It was Friday afternoon when Spencer lost his latest tutor. The tutor had given up on his arithmetic and was trying to interest him in his reading lesson.

"Now, Spencer," the tutor instructed, "read the story on page 10 to me."

"I can't," Spencer argued.

"Why not?"

"I'm not supposed to read stuff in that book."

"Why not?" the tutor snapped, his irritation having grown enough to forget about losing his high paying job.

"It's a green book," Spencer explained, hoping to make the tutor angry enough to quit and gain a few days from his detested studies. "Teddy said green books are bad to never read them."

"The color of a book cover has nothing at all to do with its content." The tutor's voice was beginning to rise.

"You're not supposed to yell at me," Spencer whined. "Teddy'll get you if you do."

"That's enough of this nonsense," said the furious tutor. "And it stops now!" He grabbed the teddy bear from Spencer's arms and threw it across the room.

It hit the wall head first, with a loud thump. Spencer grabbed his own head and screamed as if it was his head that hit the wall.

The tutor's first instinct was to comfort the boy, but knowing it was impossible, he prepared himself for what followed. He was packing his briefcase when Spencer's mother rushed into the room.

"What have you done to my son?" she demanded to know.

Spencer wailed the first answer, "He hurt me. He hit my head on the wall."

"I did nothing of the kind," the tutor countered.

Mrs. Alexander gently examined Spencer's head. "You evil man," she growled at the tutor. "He has a huge bump on his head."

"It is most likely, madam, that he got the bump earlier, when he fell off that banister he's so fond of sliding down. But however he got it, it certainly wasn't from me. I haven't touched him."

"He did too," Spencer howled. "He threw me into the wall."

"Did you?" she asked, fire in her eyes.

"Of course not. It was his damned bear that I threw."

"That's the same thing," Spencer cried. "Oooh...my head hurts so much."

"Even if what you say is true," Mrs. Spencer said to the tutor, "we still can't tolerate violence in any form. It doesn't matter what you threw, I have to let you go."

The tutor smiled. "That's fine with me. I prefer to quit anyway. So if you'd be so kind as to write me a check for my time with this intolerable little creature, I will leave immediately."

She frowned at the little creature comment, but said, "Certainly. Come downstairs with me."

The tutor followed her down the winding steps of the old mansion.

"Wait for me there," she said at the bottom of the stairs, pointing into a sitting room there.

The fireplace in the room was lit, and it took the chill out of the late fall air. He chose an old, leather, and oak rocking chair near it to sit down.

As he waited, he studied the stone mantel, with its rough bottom and edges and smooth top. He wondered about the stone mason who carved it and the carpenter who set the wooden beams supporting it. He decided that it would be nice to have a job like theirs. Something a man could do with his hands and never again have to deal with someone's spoiled children.

Mrs. Alexander wasn't in any rush to bring him his check, and his eyes were following the tight joints of the mammoth field stones making up the rest of the fireplace when she returned.

"I'd appreciate it if you'd go out the servant's door," she said, handing him the check.

The tutor was tempted to be defiant and leave by the front door, but went out the way he was directed so he could find Colleen, the Alexander's pretty young maid, to tell her he was leaving.

Colleen was a robust young lady with big, beautiful, blue eyes and an easy laugh. In spite of her large hips and oversized breasts, she carried a glow that made men want to hold her.

The tutor was no exception and was pleased to find her in the kitchen on his way out. She was chewing on a roast chicken leg and didn't notice him creep up behind her. He put his arms around her and kissed the back of her neck.

"Oh, you," she laughed lustily, "you mustn't do that while we're working. You'll have both of us fired."

"There's little chance of that." He kissed her neck again. "I already have been."

Colleen pulled free of his arms.

"What on earth for?" she asked, with a touch of disappointment in her voice.

"That child! His teddy bear, blanket, and pillow, simply became too much. I lost my temper and threw the animal. You'd have thought I hurt the boy, the way he cried."

"You knew you shouldn't touch his teddy, the way he loves the thing."

"It's more than loving a toy. He's obsessed with it, far beyond anything natural."

"All the same…"

"I know, but forget that. I'd like to see you again, if I may? Can I call you when I'm resettled?"

"That would be fine, but tonight," she said with a sly grin, "just the boy and I will be home until very late. You could stop by after I've put him to bed. Around nine or so."

"Are you sure it'll be safe? There's no point in getting you fired too."

"I'm sure it will be. Tonight is the monthly bridge party at the Grovers. The Alexanders never get home much before morning. I think it'll be safe enough."

"I'll be here then."

"Just be sure you come in the back way."

"Of course."

Colleen knew what she wanted, and when she wanted it, so she was careful the rest of the day, to be sure nothing happened to spoil her evening. She gave Spencer everything he asked for, worked hard to ensure the evening meal was perfect, and was careful to not get caught smoking. A habit she indulged in constantly, but one that Mrs. Alexander deplored.

Colleen was calm through the early evening, but a light-headed excitement began as soon as the Alexanders left for the evening. The thought of a man visiting filled her, and she immediately started to get Spencer ready for bed. She wanted him asleep before her company arrived.

Spencer behaved while she bathed him, put on his pajamas, and tucked him in bed. Once he was tucked in, she went down to the kitchen and poured herself a glass of red wine from the Alexander's private stock. She settled down in front of the fireplace in the sitting room.

As she became lost in her thoughts while watching the fire leap and curl, Spencer moved quietly into the room.

"Can me and Teddy have a glass of water?" he asked, startling her. She jumped, spilling wine on the expensive carpeting, leaving a deep red stain that would be difficult, if not impossible, to get out.

"Spencer," she gently scolded him, "don't sneak up on me that way. You made me spill."

"It doesn't matter, Teddy'll clean it up while you get us some water."

"I'm sure he will," Colleen said sarcastically and went for the glass of water.

As soon as Spencer finished his water, she hurried him off to bed again. Five minutes later, he returned.

"Teddy can't sleep without his blanket," Spencer complained. "Will you get it for him, Colleen?"

"What blanket are you talking about?"

"Teddy's blanket. The same one he's always had."

"Do you mean that old rag you're always dragging around with you?"

"It isn't a rag."

"Well, whatever. Where is it?"

"It's in the laundry. Mother said it got washed today, but she forgot to bring it to me.

"If I get it for you, will you stay in bed?"

"I guess so."

The laundry room was in the basement, at the far end. Colleen hated the basement and shivered as she went down the old, narrow stairway. She turned on every light she could find as she walked through damp, chilly basement. The musty smell of the wine cellar filled her senses. Her heart skipped a beat when she heard a rat scurry across the floor of the coal cellar that was empty and unused for years.

She was perspiring and short of breath when she returned to Spencer with his tattered blanket and hurried him up to bed.

"Now, Spencer, I want you to stay in bed," she said while she tucked him again. Then, "God, I hope that's the last time I'll see him tonight," she said to herself as she left his room.

But of course, it wasn't. In a short time, he was downstairs again.

"Teddy needs a new pillowcase for his pillow," Spencer said as he entered the sitting room. "This one doesn't have the right kind of edges." He held up the pillowcase with his right hand and clutched the teddy bear to his chest with his left. "Teddy says we have to have one with straight edges."

"Okay, Spencer," Colleen said, her aggravation showing, "I'll get you another damn pillow case. But if you come down again, you'll make me very angry. This better be the last time."

Her words had little effect on him because he returned a few minutes later.

"Now what do you want?" she yelled when she saw him.

"Teddy was wondering if you saw how good he cleaned up the wine you spilled?"

"Okay, brat, that's enough out of you." She trembled in anger as she grabbed Spencer by the arm, jolting him enough to drop the teddy bear.

"I dropped Teddy," Spencer wailed, "I dropped Teddy. Let me go!" With strength that surprised her, he pulled free and picked up the teddy bear. "You shouldn't make me drop Teddy," he warned. "He might not like it."

"That's just too damn bad. You are going to sleep...or else!"

"If you make me drop him again, I'm going to tell mother about you smoking all the time tonight, when you're putting me to bed," he warned, his voice threatening.

"Go ahead, brat," she answered and, out of spite, flicked ashes from her cigarette onto his bed.

The question Spencer asked when he came down reminded Colleen of the wine stain, and she went to clean it up. She was surprised when she couldn't find it, but she didn't think about it long. It was nearing nine o'clock, and her anticipation was growing.

Spencer's face showed defiance when he came down again. "Me and Teddy are hungry," he boldly demanded, "and we want something to eat."

Colleen reacted harshly. "I've had enough of you, Spencer. Get back to bed!"

"Not until we get something to eat. I want some cookies and milk, and Teddy wants a sandwich."

Colleen grabbed Spencer's arm and squeezed hard. With her free hand, she yanked the teddy bear and threw it to the floor. It landed with its legs doubled in half. Spencer collapsed against her and moaned in pain.

She shook him. "Now stand up. You're not hurt, and you're going back to bed to stay."

"I can't stand. You hurt my legs."

"You damn well better or I really will hurt you."

"But I can't."

She shook him again, then dragged him back upstairs to his bedroom. He asked for his teddy bear.

"This is too much," she said, slapping his behind. "You're going to bed, and you're going to stay there."

"I can't sleep without Teddy. You have to let me have him."

"You'll get nothing."

Colleen picked him up and dropped him hard on his bed. "Now, Spencer, if you get up again, for any reason, you'll be spanked."

She slammed the bedroom door behind her. She could hear his whimpering as she went down the stairs. In her anger, she didn't see the teddy bear as she went into the sitting room. She tripped over it, nearly falling.

Furious, she picked up the teddy bear and pitched it into the roaring flames of the fireplace. The instant it landed, she heard Spencer scream in terror and pain.

"Good Jesus, how did he know what I did?" she said out loud in a quivering voice.

Terrified of what she did, she fished the remains of the teddy bear out of the fire with a poker. Gradually, as she put out the smoldering remains, Spencer's screams abated.

The fear of what she did nearly destroyed her excitement about having company. White and shaken, she sat down to consider the consequences. She didn't consider them long, though, because Spencer soon joined her. She lifted her lowered head slowly and looked at him.

His face was black and his hair and nose were gone. One ear was merely a hole in the side of his head and the other ear hung by a small strand of skin looking like a tattered oak leaf, still on the tree late in winter. His lips were blistered and split over his teeth. His eyes stared from lidless sockets. A pink tongue moved rapidly in and out of his mouth as he spoke.

"Why did you burn me, Colleen?" he asked, his voice weak and hissing like a snake. "Why did you burn me?"

Colleen left her chair, and standing, she was unable to keep her eyes free of his. She opened her mouth to scream, but save the crackle of the fire, silence filled the old mansion.

Bridal Gown

David George

O virgins, o demons, o monsters, o martyrs,
great spirits contemplating reality,
devout lovers, seekers of infinity,
sometimes bursting with cries, sometimes brimming with tears,
Poor sisters, I love you and I weep for you,
For your lonely sorrow, your endless thirst,
And the amphoras of love, overflowing with your hearts!
"Les femmes damnées."

—Beaudelaire, <u>Les Fleurs du Mal</u>

The three-story house had a wrought-iron gate in front with bars curled like lianas; above the gate hung a frosted lamp in the shape of a drooping poppy. A decorative feature held the house in its grasp: along the base of the building crept rusted metal trailing vines with tendrils shooting up the exterior, over a gable and down the other side, ending in twisted iris blossoms and roots. Tall, narrow windows beneath eaves supported by fleur-de-lis brackets resembled eyes shaded in slumber. Inside were dark corridors, hardwood floors inlaid with floral patterns, leafy decorations around doorways and windowsills. Up a winding staircase curved iron railings like swirling foliage; the foliation was repeated on the wallpaper next to the stairway, creating the illusion of a distorted reflection. The upper floor of the house was a tower with stained-glass windows, over-

looking a garden. In the summer, green lawns gave way to tangles of rambling roses, daffodils, snowdrops, bluebells, irises, sunflowers. Creepers cascaded from trellises over serpentine pathways. A fountain cupping a stone flower bud was dry and tinged with moss. A statue executed in some soft stone was badly eroded. Hovering over a reclining figure—a woman?—was another, the crown of its head covered by a laurel wreath, its face seemingly fleshless, due perhaps to the effects of time and weather. Now and then, observant early-morning strollers—carrying a walking stick and wearing perhaps white pants, blue jackets, straw boaters— noted the presence of small pale flowers, their stamen veiled by white filaments, their petals folded down over the stem to form a skirt. If the strollers returned in midmorning, the flowers would be gone.

Doesn't matter if she's too young to play the part. Hey, it's not as if she lacks confidence in her acting skills. Okay, sure, one of the graduate students who tried out might have more life experience and all, especially for the scenes in the play where the main character is ancient, like thirty-five. And speaking of the play, she has her doubts. This is supposedly the world premiere of the translation into English of a Brazilian play...*nobody's ever heard of!* Its title is *Bridal Gown*. She doesn't know and doesn't care what it's called in Spanish? Portuguese? The playwright's name is Something Rodriguez. World premiere. If it's such a big deal, it's really ironic Ms. Simmons would choose someone as young as her for the part. So what? She's not going to let anything get in her way. Not even her suspicion that the director is just trying to get her into bed. Ms. Simmons has a reputation for giving parts to students she detects on her gay radar and wants to shack up with. No way she's going to be put in that position. She'll pick her own partners, thank you. Although right now, since she and Sally broke up, she doesn't feel romantically inclined. Besides, the role is hers; she's going to sink her teeth into it and won't let go.

The character's name is Alaide. Ms. Simmons gave it this weird pronunciation. Like All-ah-EE-jee. What she especially likes about the character, what she identifies with, is that Alaide keeps everyone guessing about *who she really is*. The whole play takes place inside Alaide's disintegrating mind. The character is dying; she's lying on an operating table after having been run over by a car. Alaide flashes back to moments in her life and experiences hallucinations. Memory and fantasy allow her to split into several characters to imagine she's someone besides her boring self, to live lives other than the actual one she's so sick of. The memory part of her mind projects scenes from her adolescence, stormy marriage, love triangle with her sister. In her hallucinations, she fantasies about a prostitute, Madam Clessy. Ms. Simmons says there's a subtext. About Alaide being secretly gay. The patriarchal—she hates that word—society made it impossible to come out of the closet, even for the playwright to talk explicitly about the character's identity. When was this play written anyway? Whatever, the gay subtext works for her.

She's got the Thanksgiving weekend all to herself to prepare for the role. Not coming home for Thanksgiving really pissed off her parents. Ms. Simmons wanted her to come into the theater for some one-on-one sessions to work on emotional memory. She begged off. Said she had a humongous paper due on Monday. Besides, she wants to do it her own way. And she's got a great space to work in. Her friend Babs is caretaker for a residence the university uses as a guest house and for receptions. Bling-bling Babs everyone calls her because of all the baubles bangles beads she wears. Anyway, Babs is going home for Thanksgiving, and they got administrative approval for her to be substitute caretaker from Wednesday night until Monday morning. The best part of the deal is there are no guests this weekend so she's got the place all to herself. She made it a point *not* to tell Ms. Simmons she'll be staying there. It's called Floreale House. She's not sure who that Floreale person was. Seems most of the campus buildings are named after somebody who was famous a long time ago, but nobody knows who they are anymore. It's kind of creepy. Like all these ghosts are floating around and nobody pays them the slightest attention. And speaking of ghosts, Babs said there's a legend according to which a wedding was held at the residence soon after it was built in the early 1900s. The bride died the very night of the wedding, apparently nobody knows exactly how. The cool part is that she was buried in her wedding dress. After that, the family moved out and the house fell into disrepair. They say guests at the residence have actually seen the ghost of the bride descending a winding staircase.

Although she thinks people who actually do believe in ghosts—and UFOs and all that other paranormal crap—ought to have their heads examined, she finds the ghost story simply delicious because it fits in perfectly with the mood of the play. Anyway, the family donated the house to the university some time ago and the administration raised the money to restore it. Babs says it's decorated in art nouveau style. It's way cool. It looks so hand-made. Like all these wacky artists said, let's build ourselves a house. At least that's what she thought last spring, the one time she was there for an awards ceremony honoring the top freshman students. It's just perfect for the play. According to the stage directions, most of the scenes from Alaide's memories and fantasies take place in a turn-of-the-century mansion. She guesses the university's guesthouse will fill the bill just fine. She's going to give herself a new identity for the weekend, a new name. She'll be Flora. Goes with the name of the house. She'll be Flora, the ravishing ghost of Floreale House.

Flora shows up with her backpack full of books, munchies, most importantly, the script. She's also brought a few bottles of wine. Vin de table rouge. She finds it amusing that such a fancy-sounding name just means red table wine. Babs says there's always a key under the mat by the front gate so it's no problem letting herself in. She wipes off the fallen leaves that have stuck to her boots, turns on a light in the entryway, moves down the hall to a winding staircase, climbs up to look for a room. Flora can stay wherever Flora wants. On the second floor is another staircase, this one narrower. It leads to a kind of tower she's seen from the outside but thought was just an architectural detail. A trek up the stairs reveals that the tower contains a bedroom, with a fireplace and stained-glass windows, one depicting a woman with delicate features and poppies in her hair; surrounding her is a circular design filled with buttercups and marigolds. The colors in the window range from pale yellow to dark orange. Etched at the bottom is a name: Sarah Bernhardt. The lamps in the room are also decorated. Are they Tiffany? One has a glass lampshade with a motif repeated all around it: two women holding hands, their hair connected like tendrils or vines. There's even an upright piano in the room. She decides this is where she'll settle in. She drinks wine and studies the script until she has the plot structure down pretty well, although the play is kind of confusing because almost everything happens in Alaide's mind.

Flora decides to think of the script as a kind of fairy tale, to make Alaide, and therefore Flora herself, a princess under a spell. Once upon a time, there was a young woman named Alaide from a high-class family in Rio de Janeiro. It was a long time ago, way back in the 1940s. One dark and gloomy night, Alaide is run over by a car as she crosses the street. As she lies dying on the operating table, she hallucinates about a woman named Madam Clessy. Alaide travels back in time to when she was fifteen, and she discovered Clessy's dairy in the attic of the grand house she lived in with her parents. The diary was written in the early 1900s. The dairy entices Alaide with its forbidden tales of call girls and bordellos. Madam Clessy was a prostitute and madam in Rio's high society. Alaide also remembers finding a scrapbook with news reports about Clessy's murder; she was killed in her wedding dress by her young lover. After that, all Alaide could think about was Clessy, who became her ghost companion, her invisible guide. Lying on the operating table, Alaide's has imaginary conversations with Clessy. A strange man suddenly appears in the midst of one of these conversations and accuses her of murder. Alaide confesses to Madam Clessy her secret desire: to kill her husband, Pedro. In her fantasy, she believes she has carried out the act. Alaide's mind switches to memory. She recalls a violent argument with Pedro; she is convinced that Pedro wishes she were dead so he could marry her sister Lucia. While the doctors in the operating room try desperately to save Alaide's life, she continues to imagine she is having a conversation with Clessy. They talk about Alaide's wedding day, about a mysterious woman whose face is covered by a veil. The mysterious woman turns out to be Alaide's sister, Lucia. Alaide complains that Lucia is trying to steal Pedro from her. As the play goes on, Alaide's memories and fantasies become more and more confused. Madam Clessy's story, her murder at the hands of her young lover, are mixed up with Alaide's wedding, her marriage, the imagined or real conspiracy between Pedro and Lucia to get rid of her. And then, Alaide dies on the operating table. With

Clessy at her side, she observes her accident, her funeral, Lucia and Pedro's wedding. In the final scene, Alaíde's ghost advances toward her sister and widowed husband, reaches out with a bridal bouquet. The lights dim, and there is only moonlight shining on the Alaide's tomb. Blackout.

As she sips her wine, Flora thinks about the play, about the mystery of Alaide's life and death, her strange attraction to Madam Clessy. She thinks about emotional memory, the events in her own life she can draw from to play Alaide, to become Alaide. She remembers her own rebellion at age fifteen, when she came home with her first body piercing—a nose ring—and a small tattoo of a butterfly on her right shoulder. Her old man was furious, threatened to ground her, to have the tattoo artist arrested. She threatened right back: if he did any of that, she would run away from home. Was there anyone like Clessy who fueled her rebellion, who inspired her to break free of the things in her life that stifled her? Maybe Rita Mae Brown and her novel *Rubyfruit Jungle*, about the character Molly Bolt growing up lesbian in a poor Southern family. Except Molly stands up to an intolerant world, and her story pretty much ends up happily ever after, not tragically like Alaide's. Then there's Sylvia Plath, her poems, like the one titled "Daddy" which she copied on a Fathers' Day card for her own pops. She especially remembers the lines, "But they pulled me out of the sack, And they stuck me together with glue. And then I knew what to do. I made a model of you, A man in black with a Meinkampf look." Her old man blew a fuse over that one. Her mother, as usual, just sat in a corner and wept. And there was Sylvia's autobiographical novel *The Bell Jar*. Going crazy, attempting suicide. She could identify with that, for sure. She remembers now her Sylvia Plath games when she was fifteen or sixteen, things like lying on her bed and pretending she was receiving shock therapy, sticking her head in the oven, as if to commit suicide like Sylvia did. And like Sylvia, she was talented: lead in school plays, good grades, offers from the best colleges. Flora begins to feel very tired. Just as she's falling asleep, she imagines she hears organ music coming from downstairs.

She sleeps until noon, gets up, showers. As she towels herself off, she takes in the surroundings. The bathroom is covered in tiles with geometric designs in different colors. On the wall, there are framed posters. In one, a nude woman with long red hair lies on her back. Tiny white flowers are entwined in her hair. Her frame is thin although her stomach is ever so slightly distended. Her body is unlike so many you see nowadays. It's not hard-body athletic nor is it pudgy from eating too much junk food. In fact, the woman could be Flora herself. Another poster, mostly in blue, depicts a woman sitting before a pond filled with swans. Their necks are intertwined like flowers. The woman's blue dress has gauze-like puffy sleeves. Her hands touch her tightly curled black hair. Her skin is pale, her eyes saucer-like, open wide yet dreamy. Flora realizes suddenly that the woman in blue looks like Sally. She runs her hand over the poster, wishes the woman could step out of the poster and lie next to her on the towel. She unfocuses her eyes, allowing the posters to merge. *The woman in blue gets up from the table, kneels down next to the prone red-haired figure, runs her hand along the stomach, breasts, brushes her lips lightly across the other woman's red pubis.* That's enough of that, Flora tells herself. If she spends the whole weekend freaking out over Sally, she won't get a thing done.

Typical of her to fall for her total opposite. She, wild and crazy. Sally, a straight arrow. She remembers their last conversation, Sally's confrontation, her *ultimatum.*

"I'm worried about you. You don't take care of yourself. You're self-destructive."

One thing was certain: she had a short fuse and Sally ignited it.

"Okay, so I'm not an earthy-crunchy lesbo like you. What I eat, drink, smoke, is my business. So just piss off."

"Look," Sally responded, "I'm not trying to turn you into a vegan, but you need help."

"What the hell are you talking about?" she demanded.

"You need help" was Sally's answer. "You should go to the counseling center. If you don't deal with your problems, I'm afraid I can't see you anymore."

She could feel pressure against her temples, a hot flash zapped her brain. "That is the stupidest bunch of crap I've ever heard." She was shouting now.

And Sally was like "You're abusive, too, right now the way you're treating me, that's abusive."

This time, Sally had gone too far. She asked in the most sarcastic voice she could muster, "Abusive? You're calling a gay woman abusive? You been hanging out with those campus evangelicals? Gonna sign their petition to ban gay marriage?"

Sally pleaded, "Stop yelling, you're scaring me. When you drink, you're a different person. Please get some help."

She looked Sally straight in the eye, dead on, and commanded in a slow, cold voice, "It's time for you to leave, now. Out. Make sure to close the door behind you."

After Sally left, she continued the conversation, all by herself alone. She went to college thinking, finally she was out from under her parents' suffocating rules, then she had to deal with more idiotic regulations handed down from the lords above in the deans' office, and now Sally was riding her ass. Fuck that! Enough of Sally. Gotta put these bad memories out of her mind. This is definitely not why she's come to the Floreale House.

Flora returns to the bedroom, opens her backpack, takes out some cheese and a baguette for…she'll call it her brunch. She goes down to the main floor, enters the library, better get her homework out of the way, a stupid essay about bird migration for her biology class. Give me a break! By the time she's finished, it's dark. Saturday night and all alone. Now she can really get into the character.

Flora opens a bottle of wine and fills a glass that she has removed from a cabinet in the dining room. It's heavy. Decorated too. With flowers and leaves etched into the glass. Where to begin? She'll work in what looks to her like the main room. The plaque says, "Louis Sullivan Great Room." Who knows who he was? The room is filled with heavy antique furniture. And there's an organ in one corner. Whatever for? Time to get to work. She'll start with a regression exercise she learned in a drama camp she went to the summer before last, a high school graduation present her parents reluctantly gave her, worried she'd get seduced by some older man. If they only knew… they'd be all up in the Kool-Aid. The irony is that the camp head honcho actually did put the moves on her. The last weekend at camp, he invited her out for a drink.

"Got a fake ID?" he asked.

"Like yeah, obvioso."

Off they went in his jeep to the bar. Mr. Honcho started inching toward her, moving in on her private space.

"I'm really attracted to you, you know, your bee-stung lips, I've never seen bright red hair like yours before, it enflames me, and your green eyes, you're like something out of an old Hollywood movie, like…Maureen O'Hara."

"Maureen who?"

But before he could answer, she gave him the news, "Sorry to rain on your parade—I'm gay."

And he's like "That's no problem. Gay women turn me on. I've always wanted to get it on with a dyke."

Oh, he was way cool, calling her a dyke, like he was so in the know he could use the word to insinuate himself into her world.

"So who do you think you are," she asked him, "Quentin Tarantino?"

"What's Tarantino got to do anything?"

And she's like "You know, Tarantino's so hip he thinks he can use the N word and not offend anyone, just like he was black or something."

He gave her this puzzled look, "What are you talking about?"

She looked straight into his eyes, moved in close, her nose almost touching his. "You Tarzan, me dyke. Tarzan want dyke but dyke no want Tarzan. Dyke want Jane."

He didn't flinch. "You've got a mouth on you. Needs kissing."

She touched her nose to his. "Oh yes, kissy, kissy. Tarzan show dyke path to Jane's tree house."

And she began hooting like an ape, people at the bar staring at them, Mr. Honcho looking like he'd wished he could disappear, she walking away from the bar, repeating, "Me go Jane's tree house," hooting, until she was outside. She walked the five miles back to camp.

Time for the regression exercise. She finishes off her glass of wine, lies on the floor, begins deep breathing. She focuses on the blood flowing through her body. First the feet, then legs, up through the torso, head, letting the blood bring warmth to each area, breathing in a rhythm that follows its flow and the beating of her heart. She imagines herself in the womb. She tries to stop what her camp drama teacher called internal monologue, cease thinking, focus entirely on sensation, the warm flow of her blood, her heartbeat, imagine it is the mother's heart, feel a stirring, a constriction around her, time for birth. Now a newborn infant, the shock of the world, air flowing into her lungs, paralyzing cold surrounding her, then imagine being enfolded in a blanket, the mother's warmth once again. Begin to grow, move through time, explore the environment at one year, two years, continue until age fifteen. Stop there. Let the character inhabit her. She is Alaide in the attic of her family's mansion. She is furious over her parents' strict control of her life. She has found a dusty old diary in a corner of the attic. It is dated 1904. The author is Madam Clessy. As Alaide reads, she discovers she's called "Madam" both because she's French and she runs a house of prostitution. Clessy is also in love with a much younger man, fifteen, the same age as Alaide when she finds the diary. There's something very effeminate about the young man. Is it really a young woman? At any rate, Alaide would like to live a glamorous life like Clessy, break the rules, take on young lovers, stick out her tongue at society, defy her parents and all their rules.

Alaide's fantasies about lovers dissolve into Flora's thoughts about Sally; she begins to fondle herself. She halts the exercise. Oh no, you don't, you're just going to start conjuring up Sally again. The wall clock, decorated with heavy inlaid gold vines and leaves, shows it's ten fifteen. She drinks more wine. How about a bite to eat? Doesn't feel like climbing back up to the tower to rummage through her backpack. Wonders if there's anything in the kitchen. Bling-bling Babs told her, "Keep out of the kitchen, don't touch anything."

Who's to know? She enters the kitchen. It's mammoth. Two stainless steel fridges. Stainless steel everything, sinks, counters. Neato. She opens a refrigerator. Champagne. Ooo-la-la. She checks out a cupboard. Canned paté de foie gras, crackers. Yum. Champagne and paté. Tres chic.

Flora returns to the Sullivan room after her snack, carrying the bottle of champagne. She thinks about Ms. Simmons. The tryout had gone well, the director praising her vocal control. When she read, she identified immediately with Alaide. Ms. Simmons walked about the rehearsal room, gesturing grandly, giving loud instructions, handing out praise and criticism to her and the other actors. Actually, she was the only recipient of the director's praise. Ms. Simmons pranced about in this weird outfit. There was something kind of androgynous about it, that part was cool. But it was a getup from another time, she guessed. Sixties style, maybe? She wore these brown pants, high-waisted, tight around the ass then flaring out in the legs. Her blouse was brown with polka dots. And black and white shoes, oh my god. Ms. Simmons wore the outfit again to the first rehearsal, after she'd selected the cast. She got an idea about the director's clothes. She went on the internet and found Ms. Simmons's outfit: the Katherine Hepburn character in Scorsese's flick *The Aviator*. She can't wait to tell the other kids. So our director doesn't wear clothes, *she wears costumes*! And they're not even original. Let's hope she has some original ideas about directing a play. All right, let's get down to business.

How about working on Alaide's accident? She turns off all the lights to do the breathing exercise again. The room isn't completely dark. There's a clock with an illuminated dial on the wall, night-light by the front door, headlamps from passing cars on the street beyond the grounds. She begins deep breathing. Observe blood flow. Regress to womb. Birth. Move forward in time. Fifteen, twenty, twenty-five, thirty, thirty-five.

Alaide stands at the edge of the street. Where has she been? Where is she going? Why does she want to cross the street? Is she fleeing from someone? A thought crosses her mind. Suicide. Her bossy parents. Lousy marriage to Pedro. Deceitful sister Lucia, trying to steal Pedro. Lights in the distance, car approaching, she walks to the middle of the street, stops, shuts her eyes tight, screeching of brakes, blackness. When she awakens, she's lying on her back, echo of murmuring voices. Is this a hospital? She can't feel her body or move. She has her mind, though. Memories. She recalls a violent argument with Pedro. Accuses him of wanting her dead. So he can marry Lucia. Her rage is overpowering. Pedro has finally fallen asleep. Alaide gets out of bed, takes a poker from the fireplace, raises it over Pedro's sleeping form. Hello? Who's there? Madame Clessy! What are you doing here?

Ma cherie, I've been looking for you. You need some help, n'est-ce pas?

Oh yes, merci, Madame Clessy. I've killed my husband. See his body lying there. Can you help me hide it? If my parents find it, they'll…

Do not worry, ma cherie…

Wait! That's not Pedro's body. It looks like Sally. I'm so sorry. I didn't mean to…No, wait, it's Ms. Simmons. Why is she here? Glass shards cover her body.

Flora's eyes snap open. She sits up. Was she sleeping? Dreaming? If she fell asleep, she screwed up the exercise. The floor is littered with pieces of glass. The champagne! The rose-colored wall next to the fireplace is stained. She can clean up the glass, no problem, but how's she ever going to get those spots out? She finds cleaning equipment in a broom closet and does her best, but that stain isn't going anywhere. The wall clock bell tolls twelve. Midnight. Need a bath, some wine.

Flora admires another poster in the bathroom. Its title, La Samaritaine. It features a woman with flowers in her dark yellow hair, which wraps around her body, a tendril across her thighs. Her gown looks like something from ancient Rome or Greece. Garlands of orange and brown flowers are tied around her waist. This woman could be…Clessy?

Showered, Flora wanders about the house, admiring the objects, paintings, posters. Each bedroom has a theme. There's one all in orange. On a table is a burnt-orange vase, with black trees and…a disembodied heart. That seems out of place. On a wall is a poster with a group of orange-haired women dancing. They wear long yellow dresses. The material is light, fluffy, something that wouldn't restrict their movement. Yellow flowers are woven in their hair. Flora sits in a dark orange chair. Its back is carved in curlicues of vines.

She closes her eyes, concentrates on her breathing. She feels herself regressing immediately. Womb. Birth. Infancy. She shoots forward in age. Eighteen.

Music is playing. Tango. Alaide opens her eyes. She is in a café of some sort. Cabaret? Women with flowing orange hair and yellow dresses are dancing slowly, intimately with each other. What is this place? It is a bordello. One of the women approaches and asks her to dance. The woman holds Alaide tightly, kisses her gently. Alaide knows this woman, but from where? They glide softly about the room, caressing, Alaide closes her eyes, the woman lifts her dress, places a hand between her legs. Someone whispers, but at first, Alaide can't make out what she's saying. Now she hears a single word repeated, Clessy, Clessy. From across the room, another woman laughs, Sally, hey, Sally. Alaide opens her eyes. Her dance partner is…Sally. Alaide clasps her to her breast. Oh, Sally, I've missed you so much. Someone roughly pushes Sally backward, growls, She's mine, pulls Alaide against her body. It is Ms. Simmons. Alaide shoves her away, grabs a vase from a table…

This time, only her reverie is broken. Shit, Flora groans, she almost did it again. Christ, she nearly smashed the vase with the heart. It must be really expensive. Babs would never forgive her, and she'd probably be expelled. She notices her face feels damp. She touches her cheek with her fingertips. It's wet. Has she been crying? She never cried after Sally left *and she never will.* Fuck that! The clock in the Sullivan room tolls twice. Two a.m.

Flora takes a wine break, then resumes the exercise. Breath. Blood. Womb. Birth. Age twenty-five.

There's a figure in a black veil at the top of a winding staircase. Alaide stands at the bottom with a group of women. They're wearing veils, too, humming the wedding march. These women look familiar. Where has she seen them before? In Madame Clessy's bordello. Why are there prostitutes at her wedding? Her wedding? Yes. It's today. Alaide realizes she's wearing a bridal gown. Where's Pedro? Who is that woman at the top of the staircase? Alaide begins to ascend. The women at the bottom are singing something dissonant. The wedding march has become a funeral dirge. She turns around, looks back at them. They tell her Madame Clessy is dead, stabbed in the heart by her young lover. Alaide continues up, approaches the woman in the black veil. Her shadowy face looks like a death mask, a skull. She lifts the veil. It is Lucia, her sister. Lucia smiles brightly. Alaide advances toward her, grips her throat, and squeezes until Lucia falls to the floor, the veil covering her face again. Alaide leans over her, lifts the veil, it is Sally, she opens her arms in an embrace, that's not Sally, it's Ms. Simmons, Alaide recoils, falls backward, sound of glass shattering.

Flora's eyes open wide. Did she screw up again? This is not working out. She has to try harder. Flora realizes she is back in the tower room. How?

Glass shards cover the floor. *She's broken a Tiffany lamp.* Damn.

After Flora, she cleans up; she removes another bottle of wine from her backpack, opens it. The clock strikes five. She feels so dejected. Just when she thinks she's finding the character, Sally or Ms. Simmons intrudes. And she's left champagne stains on a wall, broken a humongously valuable lamp. She feels trapped, no way out of this mess. Let's face it, her life is a mess. If she gets kicked out of school for destroying property it'll go on her record, her parents will never forgive her, they won't pay for any more tuition, she'll be on her own, wandering the streets somewhere, job flipping burgers at MacDonald's. Maybe it's her destiny to become a prostitute. Like Madame Clessy? Dancing in a cabaret? No, a streetwalker, with her luck that's how she'll end up. Her body shivers, she imagines fat old men, their hands slithering over her, pressing fat, squishy lips to her body. An image comes to her from a Sylvia Plath poem about suicide: worms like sticky pearls.

Can she put all of this out of her mind and nail the character once and for all? Yes, *blot out* everything, absolutely everything from her mind. Do the exercise again. Give it all she's got. Concentrate as she's never concentrated before. The hell with the stuff she's broken. The hell with Ms. Simmons, with the university, her parents. To hell with Sally, too. Her eyes fasten on a tiny framed painting she hasn't noticed before. Looks like one of the posters in the bathroom but in miniature. It's done in dark blue. A woman in what looks like a satin dress descends a staircase covered with vines. On the other side of a railing that bisects the stairway, a ghostly mirror image of the woman. Time to begin the exercise.

Flora lies on the cold bricks before the fireplace. Breathe deeply. Listen to the blood flow. Follow its course up the body. Focus on the heart, floating in a warm current of blood. Cool, slow it down. The flow is becoming sluggish, the warmth flees. Stop the heart.

At her moment of death, Alaide envisions a photo album. Baptism. First communion. Debutante ball. Graduation. Wedding. Funeral. A piano plays a dirge. Alaide rests in her coffin, watching the people file past. No one cries, they look at her indifferently. Someone places a bouquet of flowers in her coffin. She hears whispering, Clessy, Clessy. Alaide is wearing her bridal gown, now become her funeral shroud. The visitation has ended, the room is empty. She sits up, climbs out of the coffin. She picks up the bouquet, glides to the head of the winding staircase that leads to the main floor. It is filled with people. An organ plays the wedding march. Pedro and Lucia are getting married. The wedding guests fade from view, only the bride and groom remain. Alaide releases the flowers, the bouquet floats down toward the newlyweds.

A voice penetrates the Floreale House, rolls down the corridor, searches through the rooms, winds up the staircase.

"Hello! Rosa! Are you here?" Loud knocking. "It's me, Babs. I'm here with Sally."

A key is inserted in a lock, the creaking of an iron gate echoes in the entryway.

A voice whispers, "I can't believe you left her alone in this place the whole weekend, Babs."

"I'm sorry, Sally, I didn't know she was…"

"Never mind that. Let's get her out of here."

The two women walk briskly through the corridor.

"What are those flowers strewn all over the place? Look at all the broken glass…Hello. Where are you, Rosa? We know you're here. We need to talk…Hello…Hello! Rosa!"

Two women began ascending a spiral staircase, then froze midway. A presence hovered at the head of the stairs, a silk wedding gown embroidered with pearls, sparkling faintly, phosphorescing with light from some internal source. A veil concealed the face; as if empty, the gown was suspended in the air. Piano music filtered down from a room above, a pause between each dampened note of a nocturne. An organ answered from below, its pipes emitted a murmuring danse macabre. The two women remained transfixed on the staircase, isolated by blue and gold light streaming from behind through a stained-glass window, the backlight obscuring their features. The light dimmed, the outlines faded, then blossomed in the penumbra, pale nocturnal flowers, exhaling an evanescent fragrance, imitations of human form, sighing, withering in the darkness.

THE LEAVER
A CHRISTMAS STORY

Michael George

"It's five past midnight on this Christmas Eve morning," the man on the radio said, in a phony-jumpy-happy voice, "merry Christmas to all." He then interrupted the almost constant stream of carols with a sad love song.

He sat for a moment, wishing he'd left the radio off, then went back to lacing his boots. He concentrated on the lights of the town, shining through the only window in the small room, as they danced in the lightly falling snow.

With his boots laced, he walked over to a small pile of dirty clothes in a corner and, picking them up, tried to decide what to do with them. Shrugging, he threw them on top of the clean clothes in his suitcase.

Stuffing his open hands into his back pockets, he stared at the bed. She slept quietly, her lips turned up in a half smile. Lying on her side, she curled around one of the pillows. Sighing heavily, he trembled, trying to shake off the tightening in his throat.

He stood a moment before walking to the head of the bed. Reaching down and touching her cheek with his fingers, he ran the back of his other hand over her hair. He angrily rubbed his eyes with his shirt sleeve when they moistened.

"Goodbye," he said silently with his lips.

Still angry with himself, he closed the suitcase a little too loudly. He stiffened, not daring to breathe when she turned over. As her breathing returned to normal, he put on his parka, picked up his suitcase, and started out the door. Then, on impulse, he took the keys out of his pocket and set them on the table by the bed, turned, and left.

He felt the snow on his face and hoped it would still be falling like that when he saw the pine trees on the farm again.

On the highway, he stuck out his thumb, and a semi going by stopped.

"Going home for Christmas, son?" the trucker asked when they were back on the highway.

"Yes, sir," Bill North told the trucker, "I'm going to try."

*****

Leaning his suitcase against a snowbank, and watching the semi drive back onto the highway, Bill North stretched out the kinks from the long ride. The first pale-green light of dawn forced its way through the heavily overcast sky and lightly falling snow.

Picking up the suitcase, he walked east, across country, as the last faint sound of the truck died in his ears.

He wondered why the highway was so quiet on Christmas Eve morning. Five years had passed, but he still remembered the heavy Christmas traffic it carried, even this early in the morning. Deciding that everything changes, he let the picture of her head lying so quietly on the pillow, flow through his head. Shaking his head a moment later, he tried to capture some of the excitement he desperately wanted to feel, about being home again.

The new snow gave everything a fresh new white, but wasn't deep enough to make walking difficult.

Making good time, he didn't think about it much when he noticed that none of the fields had been planted in recent years. Ignoring his surroundings until he reached an old farm road he used to ride horses over, he was forced to pay attention to them. Even in the snow, weeds stood high and thick, making walking a definite struggle.

He was sweating when he reached the end of the road where neighbors always planted corn. The few stalks poking through the snow were several years old. Wondering for a moment, why it wasn't planted, he shrugged the question off, when finally, the excitement of being home came alive.

He thought of his parents first, then his brother and sister, their kids, and hoped they would all be home this Christmas. He was running as he topped the last hill before the farm.

It appeared nearly the same as when he had left. The house stood at the top of the hill on the other side of the road below him. The driveway still ran up the hill in front of the house, then back to the cabin he and his brother built many years ago.

The old tractor stood in a patch of weeds near the bean field. Off in the distance, he saw the big stand of pines. What a sight they were, giants standing alone out there.

There was one major change. The farm was surrounded by a six-foot-high chain-link fence. The driveway gate was closed.

Seeing the heavy chain and lock holding the gate closed, Bill slowed his pace crossing the road. Rattling the chain, he knew there wasn't any way for him to open it. He yelled a few times without getting an answer. He tried to see through the windows of the garage near the house, but couldn't tell if there was a car in it or not.

He climbed the fence after throwing his suitcase over it. The house was open and he went in. It was the same as he remembered it. The furniture, books on the shelves, and his mother's china still in the cabinet his father built for her many years before hadn't changed. But it was too perfect. Almost as if no one lived there. No dust anywhere, books in their perfect place, and all the waste baskets were empty. The only things out of place were an open pack of filter cigarettes on the dining room floor and a photograph of his grandfather on the new wide-screen television in the living room.

Picking up the picture, Bill studied it. His grandfather was standing near the farmhouse in front of a late-model car.

"How the hell?" he asked himself. His grandfather died many years ago.

While putting the picture back on the television, he heard a sound behind him. Before he turned around, something jabbed him hard in the back. There was no mistaking what it was. It was both barrels of a shotgun.

It bruised his back as it peeled his shirt loose from his pants. The man holding it told Bill, with a gruff voice, to lie face down on the floor. When he hesitated, the man jabbed him hard again, this time drawing blood.

Bill did as he was told. The last thing he noticed, before the shotgun butt smashed into the back of his head, was the tickle of lint in his nose from the carpeting on the floor.

*****

A yellow sheet, stiff but clean, like the one he was lying on, covered Bill when he woke up. A nurse, her voluminous breasts all but spilling out of the scarlet uniform she wore, was bent over him. The collar of her uniform and the trim on her cap were white. Her name tag said Sheila.

"Where am I?" Bill asked, slurring his words with a rasping voice.

"You're dead," Sheila said.

"Why am I talking then?"

"Because you don't know you're dead."

"Yes, I do. You just told me I was."

"But you question it. Only when you stop questioning will you be aware of death."

"If I'm dead but unaware of it, where am I?"

"In-Between. You are in the In-Between-World."

Bill's mind whirled as he asked, "Is it still Christmas?"

He wasn't able to understand what she told him.

"Of course," she answered. "It will always be Christmas for you."

Smiling, she showed him her perfect teeth. Perfect with the exception of the cuspid teeth on her lower jaw. They rose above the rest of her teeth, with their sharp points sparkling in the dim light.

"Why will it always be Christmas for me?" he asked, as the room began spinning around him.

"Because you left time behind when you left me."

"I didn't leave you," Bill argued, "I've never even seen you before."

"Ah, but you most certainly have. You've seen us all and left us all. We have control now."

Sheila leaned over him and scraped her long sharp teeth across his cheek. She opened the buttons of her uniform, letting her breasts fall free and over him.

"Where is your bra?" Bill asked, gasping for air.

"You know. It's in your pocket."

He struggled to reach his pockets, only to discover he didn't have any clothes on.

"I don't have pockets," he cried.

"But you had pockets," she laughed.

Bill tried pushing her away, but she was too strong. Soon, her breasts cut off his air. He stopped struggling to breathe and closed his eyes.

*****

Tobacco juice dripped from his mouth, falling on the mass of hair growing above his lips and drooping down the sides of them. His face stiffened into a tight smile, displaying his stained teeth, as he helped Bill onto the horse standing there.

"I don't want to ride," Bill complained as he landed in the saddle with a thump.

"It might be you don't," he answered Bill. "But those who leave got to ride."

Then, laughing hard, he dropped the reins and stepped back.

The horse, realizing it was free, leaped high in the air. Bill grabbed the saddle horn with both hands and held on, letting the reins fall to the ground.

The horse pitched and bucked, and soon, blood oozed from the palms of Bill's hands. Sliding through his fingers, it ran freely onto the giant black stallion's neck.

Sparks shot from the stallion's nose, soon turning to fire. Smoke, in thick red clouds, poured from its ears, blinding Bill and choking him.

Tenaciously, Bill clung to the saddle as he was taken into ever higher jumps, with constantly more jarring drops. Higher and higher, they went. Over a house with closed shutters and a crimson roof. Its chimney reached out and scrapped the stirrups away from Bill.

"Ride, you leaver, ride," yelled the man far below. "Ride your way to hell where you left us all."

And Bill rode. His face touched clouds, made of cinders and ash. Over wires sending blue sparks crashing through him, scorching his feet. On through trees with velvet leaves and thorns that shredded the flesh on his arms and legs. On until he was lost.

He flew to the ground, which was an endless cliff covered with snakes and burrs that crawled beneath his fingernails as he clawed the loose sand and rocks for something to stop his fall.

*****

Sheila returned.

"I have something for you," she said, smiling.

Bill averted his eyes.

"I don't want to see your teeth," he protested.

"Why not?" Her smile broadened. "In-Between, we all have beautiful teeth."

"They're ugly."

"It's not good to complain, Bill. Did you enjoy your ride?"

"No! I don't like riding."

"What do you like, Bill?"

"I'd like to go home again. I want to go home."

"You are home. You came home when you left me, just the way you left home five years ago. Why do you always leave, Bill?"

"I didn't, I don't, always leave. I had to go. It was bad. It was hard. I couldn't do it anymore. I was afraid."

"Are you afraid now, Bill?"

"No!" Bill screamed. "No! Yes! Yes! I don't know. Where is my brother? I want to see him. He should be here. He was here when I left."

"You will see him later. But first, your surprise. Are you ready for your surprise, Bill?"

"No, I don't want a surprise."

"You have to have a surprise. It is required."

"Please, no. I won't leave again."

"No, Bill, you will not leave again."

Sheila took Bill's hand. He fought her hard but found himself following her in a slow, floating walk. They walked down a dim corridor, lit by green sulphur fires, then down stairways made from paper thin redwood boards. The courtyard they entered was covered with snow and green moss blossoming with tiny, heart-shaped flowers. Then finally, out onto a street running on to a country road surrounded by fields of giant sunflowers. Birds were frozen in place as they ate the seeds of the plants. Off through the haze, Bill could see a family picking tomatoes from plants pushing their way through snow drifts.

"Now," Sheila said, "you shall love me again."

She pulled him to her.

Bill's hand trembled as he unbuttoned her uniform, one button at a time, from the top, down to her waist. She laughed when he discovered all but the last button closed again.

He stepped away from her. "I can't," he said.

"But you must. It was ordered."

She smiled so he could see her beautiful teeth.

He surrendered as the buttons sharpened, making his fingers bleed. Red with blood, the buttons opened freely. He struggled to breathe as she scraped his neck with her long teeth.

*****

Thunder rolled as lightning filled the sky. Bill dug the shovel into the high snowdrift in front of him. He threw the snow onto the high pile he was making over his head. Most of it fell back, onto his shoulders and head. Turning to water, it ran down his back, only to return to ice when it stopped there.

All feeling left his hands and feet, but he shoveled on in the howling wind. He had to reach the house, where the inside was filled with late Christmas Eve sounds of his family. They laughed and sang carols.

Ever faster, he lifted the shovel, throwing snow against the wind. He was afraid he wouldn't reach the house in time to open his presents. He must be there for what was his.

His feet froze, and he felt his toes break off. One by one, they fell, but still, he shoveled. Then his fingers began falling. He was holding the shovel with the palms of his hands when he reached the house.

He knock on the door. No one answered. He knocked again... harder. Still no answer. He cried out while beating on the door with what was left of his fists.

The door opened slowly, and Bill stepped in. His brother was there.

"I'm glad you came, Bill," he said, closing the door. His smile displayed his beautiful teeth.

"Not you too?" Bill asked. "Are you all now In-Between?"

"Of course," he said. "We've been here since you left."

"Not all," Bill's grandfather rose from his great chair to say. Tobacco juice spilled from his mouth.

"Sheila is here," the brother said.

Bill could see her face, lying alone on a pillow, without a body. He went to her, and her lips turned up into a half smile. Just enough to show her teeth.

Bill screamed.

*****

The truck driver shook Bill awake.

"That must have been one hell of dream you had, son," he said.

Bill shook his head, trying to focus his eyes. "It was a nightmare."

"Well, it's over now. So's your ride. This looks like the spot you said wanted to get off."

"Oh, yeah, thanks a lot for the ride. I appreciate it."

Mack got out of the truck, watched the semi pull back on the highway, while stretching to remove the kinks left from the long ride. The first pale-green light of dawn was forcing its way through the heavily overcast sky and lightly falling snow.

Picking up the suitcase, he headed east, across country, as the last faint echoes of the semi died in his ears.

He wondered why the highway was so quiet on this Christmas Eve morning. Even after five years, he still remembered the heavy Christmas traffic it carried.

But, he thought, *everything changes.*

They Did

Michael George

Martha rushed from the house, letting the door close itself behind her. In a hurry, she ignored the lift and ran to the street. No one of her status ran anymore. Not since the change.

Luke stood proudly beside his car, waiting for her. It was the first time he'd driven it anywhere. Before meeting her, he had no intention of ever driving it. But he desperately wanted to impress this strange young woman, so he took the gamble of driving over nearly forgotten roads, exposing the car's finish to the ugly rays of the sun. Only to show it off for her.

Martha stopped abruptly, running her fingers over the sparkling red finish.

"Oh," she crooned, "it's so beautiful. I've never seen one this old before. What kind is it?"

"It's a Chevrolet," Luke explained, his pride in the car showing. "It's almost a hundred years old."

"Was it built close to the end then?"

"No, they were built for twenty years after this one."

"Are you going to take me for a ride?"

"Well, ah, sure, why not? Where do you want to go?"

"Out to the preserve."

"I don't know, Martha, it's out of the metro zone. I spent a long time rebuilding this car and without any soltomic computers. I don't want to wreck it."

"Oh, it's not that far. I want to go. They've opened some new areas I'd sure like to see."

"But all the roads are really old. They don't even have go-guides."

Martha smiled, brushing her lips across his cheek in a way that seemed to promise more.

"Well," he said, melting, "I'll try it. But only if you'll agree to come back if the roads get too rough."

"We won't hurt your car."

"We might, and I don't want to wreck it. It's too old. There aren't very many left. It was real hard to get a permit for it too. The corpguard doesn't allow many. If I wasn't one of the Allowed, I wouldn't have gotten it. I don't think I can ever get another one."

"You worry too much, Luke. It'll be fine. I've been there on the trolbus."

"Well, I haven't been there. And anyway, the trolbus doesn't need or use roads."

"The road is okay."

"Even if it is, I don't like leaving the metro zone. Those of us who have the privilege of working are requested not to. So I don't."

"You men and your working. You're always so pompous about it. Even when everyone knows that nobody needs to work anymore. Besides, they won't know."

Luke still hesitated, but her gentle fingers on his cheek and light tug on his arm convinced him. He opened the car door and held it while she got in. She slid across the seat to the middle. When he got in, she moved closer, until their thighs and shoulders touched. He smiled when she rested her hand on his knee.

The drive out of the metro zone was easier than Luke had anticipated. Outside the zone, the roadsides were lined with neatly laid out fields, separated with magniplast fences, and tended by diligently working robots.

"I don't like it here," Luke complained. "It's spooky, all this stuff growing."

"I think it's pretty," Martha answered, moving slightly away from him, "even if it isn't beautiful the way it once was, before the change."

"Well, it's sort of pretty, but ah…I'm not used to it yet. I don't think I'd like it the way it was before the change at all. I've seen the allowed flash pics, and it was ugly everywhere out of the metro zone. All those wild *green things* growing. Nothing leveled off with eco-sand. I'm sure glad I never had to drive here then."

"If you want to take me on dates, Luke, you better learn to like it. You're wrong about what it was like before the change. It was more than magniplast and eco-sand then. It was real. Like this car. I like your car, Luke."

"Ah…oh, thank you."

They grew quiet, and Martha looked around at the fields. With the exception of the occasional tree still allowed, she didn't like what she saw. The constant blue of the eco-sand and lab-create crops was boring and almost ugly to her. It didn't, it never could, match the beauty she saw in the disallowed flash pics she'd seen as a child. She wanted to win the war of the flat earth, and her eyes noted the frequent depressions in the fields. She smiled inside at the sight of them, hoping the corp-guard was wrong, and that someday they'd return to the rolling hills and spots of green things growing.

Luke was busy concentrating on the road and Martha's hand, still resting gently on his knee.

They left the car at an empty put-space and walked through a huge magniplast arched gate. A sign overhead read, "The Ancient's Preserve."

"Isn't this beautiful?" Martha said. "I just love it here. There's a church and an old farm, with a barn even. You'll like the old machinery. But I want to see the new part first. The places they just opened."

"What's in them?"

"I don't know all of it, but there's supposed to be a graveyard. I want to see that first."

"A graveyard? I thought they were all moved to the space tombs."

"Most of them were. But they found one still here. I really want to see it."

"Why? Those places were awful. All those dead people. I'd rather go see the machinery. Old machines are the only thing about the ancients I like. And it's more fun to work with them than any of the stuff we use now."

"We can go see the machines after I see the graveyard." She looked him in the eye and smiled. "Okay?"

"Okay," he agreed, wondering what the look in her eyes meant. "But I don't know why they allow this place. We're supposed to forget about what was. The corp-guard always says so. This place should be food fields. They should just keep the machinery."

"They allow it to show us how much better it is now than it was then. But some of us know better."

Martha took his hand. leading him as they followed the paths. They walked the path that took them to the graveyard, behind the ancient wood-framed church. The graveyard itself was still covered with trees, brush, and high weeds. The wild green made a stark contrast to all the neatly tended blue around it.

Luke hesitated before following her, not wanting to get too close to the wild growth. It was better among the trees where brush and weeds thinned. Moving slowly, they stopped often to read the strange names written on stones and markers until they came to a small clearing. A shaft of sunlight reached down through the trees, touching the open ground. Short green grass covered the spot.

"How'd this spot stay like this?" he asked. "There isn't any other short grass in here."

"I don't know, but can't you feel it here?"

"Feel what? It just feels weird. This whole place feels weird."

"It's not weird, Luke. I can really feel it. It's just like Grandmother Mickey said it would be. God, I hope she knows I'm here."

"I wish I knew what you're talking about, Martha. And you shouldn't use that word, God. It could bring the punishment on you."

"To hell with that. Just come."

She led him to a green place, then let go of his hand and walked to the edge of the grass. She sat down and pushed it aside.

"What are you doing?"

"Uncovering a marker."

"Who's marker?"

"My great-grandmother's marker."

"I didn't know she was here."

"Nobody does. You know that I'm not supposed to know anyone here. No one is. That's the policy. If the corp-guard was aware, I'd be brought Before the Wrath."

"I won't tell, Martha, but how?"

"I can't tell you how I know. Only that she can't be moved to the space tombs. No one can ever move her. Can't you feel it, Luke? It's so strong. Why can't you feel what's here, in this place?"

"I feel something, but I don't know what it is." He sat down and read the marker. "I thought you said it was your great-grandmother's grave? There's only one marker, but it's over two graves. Who's in the other grave? Why do they have different names when they have the same marker?"

"She *was* my great-grandmother. He was the man who loved her. Don't you know yet, what you feel from this place?"

"No, I'm not sure what it is. But I think it's okay. It seems peaceful now anyway."

"Look closer, at the top of the marker. See what it says." He leaned closer and read the marker. "What does it say, Luke?"

"It says…ah, they knew love."

"That's what you feel here. Their love. Maybe all love. It still exists. No matter what the corp-guard tells us, there's still love. Isn't it good to know there's still love?"

"I'm not sure. I don't understand. Who was he? He wasn't your great-grandfather, was he?"

"No, he wasn't. He just was the man who loved her. Grandmother Mickey said she'd never seen a love like theirs. It took a long time before they could share it. But when they did, he promised they'd never be apart again, and they haven't been. That's why this grave wasn't moved during the change. He wouldn't let them move it. He still won't. His love is too strong to let them."

"That doesn't make any sense, Martha. How can a dead man stop them from moving graves? The corp-guard can do anything."

"No…no, they can't. They just want you to think they can. What they do is just illusion and lies. Grandmother Mickey said it's always been that way. It's just worse now than before the change.

She said he taught her and Great-grandmother that. A lot of people, even back then, thought he was different, kind of strange, the way he looked at life. The way he lived. But he wasn't. He just danced to the music he made in his head, rather than the music he was expected to hear. I wish I could meet a man like him. It is said that way out, north of the metro zone, far passed the magniplast fences and eco-sand, there are still people like him."

"Oh, Martha, they're the crazy ones, the steaders, who fought the change when it came. They'll all be gone soon anyway, when they're brought Before the Wrath by the corp-guard."

'No, Luke, they'll never be gone. No matter what the corp-guard says, their numbers are growing. Very few have been brought Before the Wrath. And don't call the steaders the crazy ones. We're the crazy ones."

"How can you say that? I'm not crazy. You might be, the way you talk sometimes, but I'm not."

"Yes, you are, because you accept all that's happened. I was too until I came here. Then I remembered what Grandmother Mickey taught me. Now that I've been to this grave, I know what to do. Like they would have done if they lived then, I'm going to join the steaders."

"Martha, now you really do sound crazy. How are you going to get there?

"In your car. It's the only way. Detection devices for outgoing road machines are no longer used at the limits."

"I'm not going with you, and I won't let you take my car."

"You can't stop me. He won't let you. And if you try, you'll receive worse than the Wrath can give you."

"You are crazy."

"No, I'm not. But I'm sorry. I hoped you were the one like him, the one for me. When you told me about the car, I thought you were."

"Why would my car make you think that?"

"Great-grandmother had one like it. I thought it was a sign that it's time for me. She said it would come. She understood so much. She knew what love is. It's too bad you don't. Without it, you're not wholly alive. Not the kind of alive that matters."

"I'm going home, Martha. I know you're crazy now."

"No, you're not. Not until I'm out of metro zone control. You know I can't go home, and that I can't let you talk to anyone until I'm away and safe."

"I don't understand. Why do you want to go? You won't ever be able to return here. I don't see how you can go and never come back when those in the grave are still here?"

"Their spirit will follow me. They know why I must go. This is their place, but they understand why I have to leave it. Grandmother Mickey knows too. If life is going to make sense, we all have to feel their kind of love. You would understand, if you'd been told stories of the kind I was told."

Her last comment startled him, triggering a memory buried so deep in his brain it managed to survive the propaganda drugs he was forced to take to be allowed to work.

"Martha!" he called out as old memories filled his consciousness, "I was told stories like yours. My mother told me them before she was brought early Before the Wrath. About a man like the one next to your great-grandmother. I don't remember who he was, but she knew him when he was very old. She said he was one of the few left who still knew about love. She said he learned it from someone he couldn't be with in his early life. He was different, a good man, but not like others. She said it didn't matter that he was wise because a woman taught him what mattered most. She always cried when she talked about him. When I asked why, she said it was because she never had what he did, but hoped that someday I would. I wish I knew his name."

"Look at the marker, Luke. It's on the marker."

"I don't understand. How do you know it's the same man?"

"I just know. I have for a long time. Grandmother kept a history and taught it to me before all the real history was changed. That's why I was sure the car was a sign."

Luke felt a strange new sensation on his cheeks. He lowered his head and wiped his hand across his eyes. Martha reached out and held him.

"I can feel it all now," he choked, "I can really feel it. We have to go away now, don't we?"

"Yes, as soon as you've looked at the machinery here. It might be needed by the steaders, and you need to tell them what it is. They will know how to get it."

"I'm afraid, you know."

"So am I, Luke, but it doesn't matter. As long as we both can feel this, it will never matter."

"Is it from them?"

"Yes, it is. They knew the deepest love, and they're together forever now. It will guide us to our proper place and the life we have a right to. If we can learn to take of our love as they did theirs, we'll win. They did."

She took his hand, slowly leading him away from the place. A shaft of sunlight followed them, warming their backs as they moved through the trees.

Footprints in the Snow

Bud George

It snowed lightly that day, the last snow of the season, he hoped. It was a long week, with overtime every day, and now he would have the walks and driveway to clear tomorrow, his only day off.

There were footprints leading away from the house, small and nearly drifted full. He entered through the kitchen door and found a note.

"I am not coming back," it said, "I just can't stand to be so totally dominated. I just feel so stifled, I can't stand it. I am a person, a woman, and I have to live my own life. Goodbye."

He turned on no light that night. He sat staring out the window at the new snow, throughout the night and most of the next day. And for the first time since childhood, he cried, hating himself for the mistakes he made and his stupidity and lack of understanding.

Late that afternoon, a Sunday, he rose from his chair and went out to clean the walks and driveway.

He finished the job, rehung the shovel on its nail in the garage, and walked to the house. There was a dog sitting on the back steps. A retriever with a long, winter-thick, dark-red coat. Her ears lifted as he approached, and her tail wagged. Gently, he reached out to pet her. She wore no collar.

He thought she must belong to someone, she looked as though she was well cared for. She was an old lady, the fur on her nose and around her eyes was grey.

He went into the house and she followed. He did nothing to stop her. *I'll keep her,* he thought, *until I find her owner.*

She walked through the house slowly, looking into each room, then returned to the kitchen and watched as he heated a can of chili. He divided the chili equally between two bowls and gave her one. She ate hers quickly and sat beside his chair with her head on his thigh as he ate his.

He let her out the next morning when he left for work. She was sitting on the back steps, waiting for him when he returned. She followed him in, and he prepared them a meal.

Days flowed by, and he did nothing about finding her owner. He enjoyed her undemanding company. He began talking to her as he would a human. He told her about his wife and the note she left, about his job, and about his boyhood.

She seemed to enjoy television. *It was the voices,* he thought, *she likes the sound.*

One night as he was watching an especially funny comedy, she put her paw on his knee. Her mouth was turned up in what had to be a smile, and her body was shaking. *She is laughing,* he thought, *she must understand.*

He became more attentive after that. He paid more attention to the noises she made and her expressions. They developed their communications until they could understand each other completely.

He taught her the alphabet, then how to read. She learned very quickly. She had trouble learning the physical act of turning pages, but she mastered it using her front paws and nose. He taught her what he knew of mathematics. She did an excellent job handling their bill paying and checkbook. Her handwriting was much more legible than his.

She became a good cook, and although he preferred meat well done, she liked hers rare. He did not complain when she prepared it to her taste. He came to depend on her for company, her sense of humor, and advice.

It snowed lightly that day, the first snow of the season. It was beautiful, covering the dirty grey November streets with a white, sparkling carpet.

David George, Bud George, Michael George

There were footprints leading away from the house when he came home from work. They were small and nearly drifted full. He entered through the kitchen door and found a note.

"I am not coming back," it said. "I just can't stand being so totally depended on. I just feel so stifled, I can't stand it. I am a dog, not a person, and I have to be dominated. Goodbye."

THE CARD SHARK
Bud George

I stood just inside the stable door as I watched the man riding in. A man with a definite destination in mind, judging from the way he rode. His eyes straight ahead and his back stiff. He wasn't the usual out of work cowboy or drifter who passed through this town. His clothes saw a lot of dusty miles, but cost him several months' cowhand pay when new. The saddle was as dusty and worn as his clothes, but was beautifully made. It was a pleasure saddle, too light for work, and had far more hand tooling than any cowboy could afford.

And the horse didn't fit the fancy saddle and clothes. It was a big-boned grey, nearly big enough to pull a plow, with good, thick, straight legs and the ugliest oversized head I ever saw.

He stopped the horse a few feet from the door and looked me over with just a moments' pause at the star pinned to my shirt. He was older than I first thought, his hair white where it showed under the dark flat-crowned hat. His face had lines that must have taken sixty years to etch as deep as they were.

He dismounted with the short double-barrel shotgun that was laid across the saddle horn, held loosely in his left hand. The gun was cocked.

He addressed the stable boy who was standing just behind me, "Grain him, give him a little water, and hold him ready."

As the man turned and walked toward the saloon, the stable boy slapped the big grey on the rump to move him toward the water tank. The grey reacted faster than a snake. He let loose with both hind legs and caught the stable boy in the midsection and sent him a good ten feet into the wood stable wall.

The man turned his head and again addressed the stable boy. "Handle him gently, boy. He's a mean son of a bitch." Without another word or glance back, he continued his straight, firm walk to the saloon.

I helped the boy up. He would have some good-sized bruises and was having trouble catching his breath, but wasn't badly hurt.

I followed the man as he stepped through the saloon door and moved quickly off to one side. He stood there, shadowed, and looked around the room. A few regular customers and one card shark, who was winning too regular the few days he was in town, were playing poker at the back table.

The old man's eyes stopped at the card shark, who was sitting with his back to the wall, a navy colt on the table in front of him.

"Jimmy, Jimmy Link," the old man called in a clear voice.

The card shark looked up, puzzled. He didn't seem to recognize the old man.

The old man spoke again. "She's dead, Jimmy. The child she was carrying is dead too. The beating you gave her killed them both."

The card shark turned pale and looked for a place to run, but the old man was between him and the door.

"I'm her daddy, Jimmy. I've come to kill you."

The card shark's knuckles turned white as he gripped the table edge.

"Pick up the gun, Jimmy. You have no place to run, and I'll kill you anyway."

The card shark picked up the colt and fired. He was very fast, and the slug tore the old man's right coat sleeve.

The old man fired with his left hand, from the hip. The shotgun blast tore most of the card shark's gun arm off. The card shark screamed.

"I should leave you like this, like you left her."

The card shark screamed again.

The old man fired once more, still left handed and from the hip. The blast caught the card shark full in the face.

"I'm done with this," the old man said as he handed the shotgun, butt first, to me.

He pushed the door open and walked slowly, bent low now, toward the stable.

The Spider Woman

David George

> *It makes dreams cry.*
> *The sobbing of lost souls*
> *escapes through its round mouth.*
> *And like the tarantula,*
> *it weaves a great star to capture the sighs*
> *that float in its black wooden cistern.*
>
> —Federico García Lorca, "La guitarra"

"Sexual harassment? Is that what you're worried about, Professor Grodason?" She sat in a chair placed near the door across from him, his desk creating an impenetrable barrier. It was late afternoon. Wednesday before Thanksgiving and it felt like summer. The campus was nearly deserted; he hadn't expected any student visitors.

"I prefer the door open, okay?"

She rose from her chair, leaned forward, stretched out her arms, stood on one leg and with the toes of the other leg, she hooked the nearly closed door and pulled it open. Her gangly limbs askew, short spiked black hair, contorted yet agile pantomime summoned an image from—a nursery rhyme? The spider and Little Miss Muffet?

"So if I don't get the grade I want in comp lit, I'm gonna claim you put the moves on me?"

"Being a male professor, there are some things you—"

"So can you tell me how I'm doing in your course?"

He located the grade file and scrolled down to her name. Ragno, Charlotte. "Right now you're in, I'd say, upper C range."

"I don't understand that. I got a B plus on the midterm. I think I got B's on my two papers."

He had been looking forward to time alone in his office, the mass exodus from campus for Thanksgiving break. Concentrating on the spreadsheet displayed on the computer screen allowed his face to remain in a state of cybernetic neutrality. He removed his right hand from the keyboard and brushed back his thinning grey hair.

"You're doing fine in that department. But you've missed, let's see, seven classes so far."

"Seven. No way."

"At least seven."

"I've got this roommate problem. I'm not getting any sleep. She's got a boyfriend. They're up all night, doing the, you know, horizontal mambo. Pardon my French, Professor. And there I am in the other bed, listening to their—"

"Have you talked to the people in the deans' office?"

Elbows resting on his paunch, he folded his arms tightly, an unloving embrace.

"Oh sure. Like they're gonna do something about it. They say we need mediation. So I'm gonna learn to accept our differences? You ever tried to go to sleep when people in the bed next to you are having oral sex? I'm trapped. Where can I go at three in the morning?"

White cotton blouse cut low. Bare midriff. Short pants. Apparently, she'd had a bikini wax. *Tack Gud.* Why was he thinking in Swedish? She spoke with increasing vehemence and the weight of her words pulled her forward, exposing more cleavage and opening her legs. To his chagrin, he had to force his eyes back to their refuge in the computer screen.

"Why are you still on campus, Charlotte?"

"I don't mean to burden you with all my personal problems. See, my parents are getting a divorce. My mom's having an affair with her executive assistant and my dad's hysterical. Nothing to go home to. Thought I'd stick around and catch up on homework."

"Sorry to hear about your family problems. But try to get to class. We're all in class to learn from each other, to give to each other. If you're not there, you've nothing to give."

She leaned back in the chair, crossed her legs. "The state I'm in, I don't have a hell of a lot to give. Anyway, I'm sorry about missing class. I like your course. I'm not just saying that, Professor Grodason. By the way. One of the things I'm gonna be working on over break is that book we're reading. *Kiss of the Spider Man*."

"Spider woman."

"Spider woman, sure. Is that character Valentino? Is he a fairy?"

"You're thinking of Molina. He's the homosexual window dresser. Valentín is the political prisoner."

He imagined a rustling sound coming from the corner in the ceiling behind his bookcase, although he knew that was impossible because she was of course noiseless. Was she was getting hungry?

"What did you want to know about Puig's novel?"

"I'm just, like, I'm having trouble figuring out who's who and what they're talking about. It's just so…different."

"That it is, Charlotte. What did you notice different about the first part of the novel?"

"Well, it's just people talking. You don't know who they are." She sat up straight, attentive.

"And why do you think the author doesn't identify the characters at first?"

"Well, 'cause it has something to do with where they are?"

"And where is that?"

"They're in prison, it's dark." She smiled. "I get it. We're overhearing their conversation."

"So what does that make the reader?"

She thought for a moment. "A prisoner in the next cell! How cool is that? A fly on the wall."

"All good ideas. If you come to class, you'll be able to share them with the other students."

"Just one more question, professor. Is the fairy, the gay gentleman, is he the main character? Is he like, the spider woman?" She modulated her voice with a lugubrious tremolo.

"What do you think?"

"The gay gentleman must be the spider. I think he wants to trap the straight guy in his web, like, get him into the sack."

"That's one way to look at it. But the spider web metaphor is more complex. Valentín, the heterosexual political prisoner, also has reasons to sleep with Molina, to ensnare him in his own web."

She tugged at her shorts, which had become bunched in the crotch area. Her body language led his gaze again to the refuge of the computer screen

"But if he's straight, why would he want to sleep with a fairy?"

He glanced toward the corner behind the shelf. It was past feeding time. He hoped she wouldn't make an appearance now.

"People's motives are never simple. Puig is suggesting that sexual identity may sometimes be fluid. And that people use sex for all kinds of reasons."

"Sounds gross. I could never do something like that."

"Well, you're not trapped in a prison cell either."

"You try spending a few nights with my roommate and her boyfriend."

"So why do you think Valentín would want to sleep with Molina?"

"Well, the political guy feels sorry for him. Or he's grateful because didn't like the fairy, uh, gay gentleman take care of him when he got sick and had the runs? Even cleaned his soiled underpants? Yuk."

"That's part of it. But Valentín also had an agenda."

He was relieved he hadn't yet turned on his office lights. The late afternoon sun created a chiaroscuro that illuminated the two interlocutors but kept the area above his bookcase in shadow. It was time to end this conversation before she appeared and frightened his student.

"You see, Valentín knows he's not going to make it out of the prison alive. He wants Molina to carry a message to his revolutionary group and so he sleeps with him. Valentín takes over the role of the spider woman and ends up luring Molina into his web of political intrigue."

"But what about the actual spider woman herself? I have to confess something. I looked it up on the internet. There's this spider woman character Aurora who kisses the prisoners just before they die."

"That's from the Broadway musical version."

"They made a Broadway musical out of that novel? You're kidding."

"Go figure. There's no Aurora in the novel."

"One more question. Those movies they keep talking about in the book, like the Cat Woman?" Her tongue slithered from her mouth and the stud piercing her tongue clicked against her teeth.

"I'm going to have to cut this off, Charlotte. I really do have to attend to some other business. We can talk again after break."

She stood up, stretched, her arms above her head, left hip slanting at a sharp angle, legs akimbo. Again, he was reminded of a spider.

"Thanks for all the help. I really do appreciate it. Want me to leave the door open?"

"What? Oh, you can close it after you. See you in class next Monday."

"You bet. Watch out for them spider women."

Happy hour. He shut off his computer and turned on the radio. Grosse Point College jazz station. Bill Evan's piano graced the afternoon. "Waltz for Debbie." On the windowsill behind his desk were framed photographs, sentinels keeping watch over the grounds beneath his fifth floor office. He looked out at the campus lawn covered with brown leaves and at the barren trees. He thought his fingers were beginning to resemble the branches. He picked up one of the photographs. His son Max. He brought the photo to his lips. Max's radiance always filled him with wonder and gratitude. And now his son was in college. He wouldn't be home for Thanksgiving. Off on a trip to London.

He opened a drawer in his desk and removed a glass jar, its lid covered with punctures. Breathing holes for a nice fat fly. He seized a pair of tweezers, carefully opened the lid, gently seized the fly, and lifted it from the jar. He stood on a chair next to the bookcase and looked over the top. He plucked a string on a large web and secured the fly in place. It squirmed and beat its wings. He waited about ten seconds before she made her appearance. An orb spider initiated her stalking ritual.

TEEN ANGELS

David George

Once upon a time, you could hot-wire a car with a piece of tinfoil from a cigarette package. But that comes later.

Slumped in a folding chair in the common area behind the row of townhouses, William Bergman took a long swallow from his glass of Inca Cola. The doctor had ordered two weeks of total relaxation, but he couldn't help ruminating about the latest publishing venture he had been forced to abandon at a critical juncture. And he was worried about his condition. An avid cyclist, he had thought himself an exemplar of health for a man of his age, and now this.

He heard a shriek. His first thought that it was one of the cougars that had been spotted in the area recently. Last month, the police had to shoot one out of a tree just down the block because they claimed it endangered the residents in the townhouse development. Cougars in Illinois. Who'd-a thought? But this was not an animal. The piercing cry was human, and words could be discerned clearly. If you understood Spanish, that is. *Boludo, cagón, pendejo, mamón.* Words not intended to complement their target. It had to be his wife, Rosalía. William stood up slowly, still weak from his recent mild heart attack, and shambled to the front of the townhouse. Out in the parking lot was all five feet of Rosalía berating a mountain of a man, who could only be a member of the Bulldogs, the Arena football team headquartered the next block over. William guessed the cause of the dust-up. The football player had parked his black Hummer—vanity license plate, 1-BADDOG—in their designated space and Rosalía had inserted her Probe on its tail, rendering its exit impotent. This dispute had been going on for some time now. The team members used the townhouse parking spots rather than their own lot to avoid the fans and the press, particularly since their recent national championship.

As William approached, a crowd was already gathering. The Bulldog lightly pushed Rosalía and she stumbled backward. If the football player knew whom he was dealing with, William thought, he never would have made physical contact. She aimed a kick at his crotch, which he nimbly pivoted away from, then she sank her teeth into his forearm. He bellowed and tried to shake her off. He grabbed one of her graying Andean braids: "You bitch!"

"*La concha de tu madre*" was her riposte. William considered intervening. In spite of what an outsider in the crowd might think, she needed no succor. She was fearless and injustice, real or imagined, released her from all bonds of restraint.

William admired Rosalía's doggedness; somehow, she had climbed on the Bulldog's back and had him in a chokehold, even with her feet dangling nearly two feet of the ground. The football player swiveled around several times, pried at the fingers, but couldn't shake her. The crowd was steadily increasing. Some were on their cellphones, probably calling the police. A neighbor nudged William.

"Isn't that your wife? Aren't you going to do something?"

He pondered the question. He continued to watch the scene from the sidewalk. He was bemused. He had witnessed his wife in action on countless occasions over the years. At the same time, his excitement was piqued. Excitement not so much for Rosalía's sake but for the memories of his own violent youth the confrontation was dredging up. But that was a long time ago. He decided to move in. He approached the struggling pair just as the Bulldog flipped Rosalía over his back. She landed on William, sending them both crashing to the sidewalk. He felt a weight on his chest. But its source was not external, not the hundred-pound weight of Rosalía. It came from within. He was having severe chest pains. He heard sirens as he blacked out.

He awakened in semi-darkness in what he recognized as a hospital room. In the dim light, he saw Rosalía sleeping in a chair at his bedside. He remembered the fight and the shouting, but how did he end up here? The pain in his chest was dull and insistent. He was comforted by Rosalía's presence. He thought about her sometimes uncontrolled anger but understood its source.

After he graduated from college, he had joined the Peace Corps and was assigned to an educational project in a Peruvian Quechua village. How long ago? He had been in his mid-twenties, Rosalía only eighteen. But she seemed so much older. She had lost her parents to the political violence and had become a village leader, the only woman to hold such a position. At first, she was suspicious of him, thought he was at worst a CIA agent, at best "*un imperialista yanqui.*" But they became unlikely allies. He helped her build a school for the local children and set up a literacy program for the adults. And the most improbable thing was that they fell in love and were married in a traditional Quechua ceremony. Then disaster struck.

The Shining Path guerrillas kidnapped Rosalía, claiming she was an imperialist tool. They demanded a million-dollar ransom. William appealed to the Peace Corps authorities, but she had no formal ties to them. The Peruvian government ignored his pleas; it had bigger fish to fry. Rosalía astounded everyone by escaping, all by herself. She tricked her guard by feigning seduction. He entered her shack, stripped down, and somehow, she managed to garrote him with his own carbine strap. She ran headlong down through the mountain cloud forest. Ragged, covered with scratches, thirsty, half delirious, she showed up in the village at the happiest dawn in William's life. Clearly, the Shining Path would retaliate soon and so William and his Quechua wife hurriedly left the country.

They first moved in with his brother's family in Minneapolis, but it was midwinter and Rosalía discovered genuine fear: she thought her feet would freeze to the sidewalk. William tried to secure an administrative position with the Peace Corps but due to government cutbacks—or so they claimed—there were no openings.

Employment materialized from the unlikeliest of sources: an old college friend got him a job in a Chicago publishing company, editing textbooks for high school and college Spanish language and literature courses. By now, it was summer and Rosalía fell in love with Chicago. She became a community organizer in the Pilsen and Logan Square Latino neighborhoods. Years passed and to their sorrow, no children came along to brighten their lives. Recently, they had moved to the townhouse development in a North Shore Chicago suburb. It had been William's idea. Partly because it would afford him opportunities to bike the myriad paths in the area—but too late for his heart attack—and he was tired of Chicago's parking hassles. The irony of the just transpired parking fiasco did not escape him. William fell asleep again.

When he awoke, he became increasingly agitated in his hospital bed. Where was Rosalía? In jail? No, he remembered she had been with him in the room the first time he came to. She had thoughtfully left his laptop at his bedside. The internet was an infinite and relaxing source of the poems he loved to read—and a closet poet, he secretly imitated them—whether the Beats of his youth or the Latin Americans of his later years, Pablo Neruda, Octavio Paz, even Brazilians like Carlos Drummond de Andrade. He tried to ignore his heart palpitations.

He ruminated about his own reactions. It pained him to admit that he had been useless in the fracas with the Bulldog. He fantasized throwing a left jab and a right hook at the football player. He knew, of course, that he would have ended up in the hospital even without a heart attack, but he was haunted by the chimera of playing Siegfried to his wife's Brünnhilde in an opera of hand-to-hand combat. The details of that rare moment of high drama at townhouse row churned over and over in his martial reveries. He imagined multiple versions of the delusional battle. In the end, he wandered through a hall of mirrors that refracted his distant, violent youth. And he glimpsed a reflection of…what did the gang call that guy? Hair? Yes, that was it. His real name was Bernie Gustafson.

*****

William remembered this: once upon a time you could hot-wire a car with a piece of tinfoil from a cigarette package. And his gang, the Thunderbirds, were the tinfoil kings of North Minneapolis. Willy, as he was called back then, wasn't crazy about stealing cars. He was already on probation for assault and battery (he had punched an assistant football coach who called him a queer because of his greased-back hair). It took two quarts of Hamms from the sky-blue waters beer to quiet his nerves and join the sport the Thunderbirds took such pride in: stealing cars, stripping them, and selling the parts to shady garage owners. But nobody called hard-fisted Willy a chicken. They did, however, nickname him Virge. The tough guy became docile and introverted around the gum-snapping rock-around-the-clock gang girls. The chagrin engendered back then by his inexperience in matters carnal was amplified by the hoods' oft-repeated motto: *Ya gotta get yer cookies if ya wanna be a man.*

The "hoods." Had that once defined his identity? A gangster. The Thunderbirds or T-birds for short. Where did that name originate? From the Ford sports car or from a brand of cheap wine they drank? Hair had nicknames and elaborate rhymed descriptions for the gang members, which now echoed in William's memory. There was Marion Thorsten:

Mack the Maniac
loose as a sack
nose like a hose coiled around back.
Grease in his knuckles
grease under his nails
with a grease monkey, it never fails.
Taking a ride with Mack the Maniac,
go tell your momma, you ain't a-comin' back.

Heinrich Schultz:
Shits for short, he's one big gawky Kraut.
He's strong, he's ugly, he's stout.
He'd crack your jaw long as you set it an inch from his paw.
Step on my blue suede shoes says Shits.
You bet your life ain't worth two bits.

Charles Farly:
Charly Farly's a black Irish dimwit.
Chubbier than a fat ol' sow's big tit.

And William himself:

Big Willy's fist, well, it ain't no thrill.
He'll knock you clear up Blueberry Hill.

Hair, William considered with amusement, would have been a rapper if he'd been born a few decades later.

One thing Bernie never made a rhyme about was William's secret life, which none of the Thunderbirds would ever have imagined. The recollection brought a smile to his face. He read Kerouac, Ginsberg, Ferlinghetti. The Thunderbirds hadn't a clue about the Beats. Literary rebellion would have been as alien to them as trading in their souped-up hotrods for bicycles. Speaking of rods, Mack was top dog in that arena. He drove a souped-up Deuce, a '32 Ford—the car of choice for street drag racers—three-quarter race cams and glass-pack mufflers that made it sound like a Chris-Craft speedboat taking off. The Deuce was dagoed at such a severe angle that even during its perilous acceleration the car looked like it was coming to a sudden stop. Mack's performances with stolen cars terrified even the most brain-dead gang members. He played chicken with semi-trailers on two-lane blacktop highways. Truck drivers, in stark terror, invariably swerved into the wrong lane at the last minute. Once, he forced a milk tanker into a ditch and cackled as he watched it in his rearview mirror topple on its side and skid in a foaming white stream out of sight. His legendary status was cemented, however, when he and Shits hotwired an old Chevy and drove to a dirt road out past Osseo. William recalled the scene as Shits had recounted it. Mack looked at Shits with that lunatic grin and asked, "Let's roll this beater, whadaya say?"

"Why not." said Shits, thinking it was merely a test.

"Hold on," went Mack and steered the car into the ditch at fifty miles an hour. Battered and bruised but in one piece, they hitchhiked back to North Minneapolis. According to Shits, the car turned over at least three times.

"Naw," Mack pshawed, "it was just once. A pussy roll."

But why was he having this reverie? Oh yes, Hair's tale, which began one Friday, on a cold and windy late September night, when the Thunderbirds went for a joy ride. Mack the Maniac was at the wheel, which meant they would all be in for a thrill ride: Shits, Willy, and Charly Farly. The first car they swiped that September night was a new Edsel, which they spotted running unattended in a driveway. Mack sashayed under the back porch light, hopped into the Edsel, backed out to the street, pulled up behind a rusty De Soto. Shits and Charly Farly climbed right into the open De Soto—few people locked their cars in those days, William recalled—and began hotwiring it with tinfoil from a pack of Pall Malls. Willy took the wheel of Mack's Deuce. Soon, Shits and Charly had coaxed the De Sotos's engine to life and they burned rubber. Mack peeled out after them, but when Willy popped the Deuce's clutch, he managed to kill the motor. He heard voices, people shouting. He started the engine again, eased out the clutch, and raced off in pursuit of the others. He didn't have them in his sights, but he was sure they were headed out of the city west on Highway 55 to County Road 18. He caught up to them in the suburb of Golden Valley. Mack and Shits were playing bumper tag. They increased their speed to ninety and continued to ram each other. Willy kept well back of them, in eye contact but out of harm's way. They hung a left on Bass Lake Road and another left on a dirt road leading to the Gustafson family farm, where they stopped to pick up Bernie.

Bernie Gustafson's nickname was Hair because of his long—for those days—blond curly locks. The girls called him ginchy. There were those who had tried calling Bernie "Goldilocks," but they paid for it with a bloody nose, split lip, or black eye. In his own rhymed mockery:

Peabrain hero jocks try calling me Goldilocks.
Pay for it with an eye like a black moldy box.

Hair was only five four, but he had the cold speed of a cobra. William recalled Hair's old man, Stanley Gustafson, a lush. He remembered how Hair had lost his fear of physical violence early on. Son knocked out father with a sneaky right the first time at age twelve. Since then he had sent the Drunk—Hair never called him anything else—to the emergency ward as regular as punching a clock. Mr. Gustafson, as the other kids addressed him out of some vestige of childhood respect, had put Hair in the hospital only once since that epochal knockout. He hit Bernie from behind with a two-by-four. But he took his son's place on the gurney the very next day. What was the name of the farmer's wife, Bernie's stepmother? William couldn't summon it to mind. What he did remember, she was another lush. Hair called her the Bitch. But the other Thunderbirds liked her because about halfway through a bottle of Early Times, she'd let them play with her tits and even jerked them off on occasion. If Bernie knew his stepmother played around with his gang buddies, he never let on.

Hair hopped in the Deuce with Willy. "How they hangin', Virge?"

"You call me Virge, I'll call you Goldilocks. Then I'll shove my knucks down your throat."

Willy, in spite of his six feet two and solid frame, feared Hair would take him up on it. Bernie was as crazy about fighting as Mack was about hotrods. Hair put his hands to his neck and in mock terror shouted, "Help, help, he's gonna kill me, I swear. So where you steal the clunkers, daddyo?"

"North side, where else?"

"That Edsel look prime. Gonna strip it?"

"Well," Willy answered, "Luke pays good money for new stuff to use in his body shop. Don't know how he gets away with it. Midnight auto supply. Shit, I hope he never gets caught. I wonder if he'd rat on us."

Hair spat out the window. "I tol' 'em if he ever do, I gonna kill 'em. He know I mean it."

"Sure, Hair. You kill him. Then you go to a real prison. Not some rinky dink youth camp. They take one look at that curly blond hair. Ream out your asshole before you can say Drunk and Bitch."

"Nah. Wouldn't get caught. Stuff his body in the trunk o' one o' them junkers he keep out back. Weld the fucker shut."

William realized his recollection of that night was becoming increasingly photographic. He remembered the dirt road they had been following turned into a narrow track that came to an end in a grove of young poplars. The three cars did a dance around the trees, then skidded to a stop side by side. Charly Farly and Shits got out of the De Soto, Mack the Maniac jumped in, drove into the trees, sideswiping them, bouncing from one to another like a steelie in a pinball machine. The bumpers soon folded like wishbones. Strips of chrome, flayed skin, hung from the car. Mack paused, raced the engine until it screamed, popped the clutch, and rushed headlong toward a sapling, smashing into it, backing up, hitting it again, until the tree bent low and he drove over it. The exhaust system—headpipe, muffler, tailpipe—was left twisted around a second fallen poplar. The De Soto added a roar to its scream. The fourth time Mack popped the clutch, the universal joint snapped and the car was crippled. Mack found a wrench in the glove box, floored the accelerator, and used the wrench to wedge it in place. He got out with the engine still running at maximum rpm's, removed the jack handle from the trunk, opened the hood, and began smashing the spark plugs. The other Thunderbirds, lips curled and eyes yellowed, descended on the wounded vehicle like barn cats on a mole. Soon, it sagged to its rims, a smoking wreck, windows shattered, and metal crushed. They turned on the Edsel then, removing saleable items: wheels and tires, hubcaps, radio, hood ornament, its distinctive grill—*the car with the cunt in front*, in Hair's words—distributor, carburetor, fuel pump. They pulverized what was left. Sated after the vehicular massacre, they lay on the grass, passing around quart bottles of Hamms, talking about motion pictures, music, modes of dress.

Hair gave his rhymed critique of a movie they had recently seen:

Rebel without a cause and all that jive, anybody played in it still alive?

Ever see that movie, ever see that flick, Dick?

No, you never did, are you some kinda hick?

So how did James Dean and his bright boy gang get those cars up there and make 'em go bang? They rolled over the cliff, Biff, smell the smoke, take a whiff.

How those cars appear from nowhere, teen angel beam them down from way up there?

Where was the tinfoil I'm asking you, Doyle, how you steal jalopies without no toil?

The conversation turned to musical tastes, an area in which they were rigidly doctrinaire. Hair, again:

We don't need no stinking books, we like our music, take a look.

Bo Diddly's bad, Chuck Berry's a cool dad.

Jerry Lee Lewis, Fats Domino, Little Richard drive us mad.

Elvis started good but done turned wimp, Fabian's limp, Ricky Nelson's a simp.

Anyone mention Pat Boone 'round us gets stomped like a shady lady by a pimp.

So what kinda music you like, gimp?

They talked about their attire, which also conformed to a rigid code. The boys with jeans down to the crack of the ass, shirts with cigarettes rolled up inside a sleeve, leather jackets with the gang name lettered in silver studs on the back, black leather boots with steel plates in the toes, hair swept back into a duck tail and plastered with more than "a little dab'll do ya" of Brillcream. And they spoke disparagingly about a rival gang. What were they called? The Breezers. As William mulled over it now, there was something almost preppy in their sinister attire: white nylon windbreakers with a skull and crossbones stitched on back, chinos, white socks, shiny brown loafers with razor blades in the soles. Both gangs, in their commitment to violence, carried brass knuckles. Some guys had switchblade knives; the real crazies carried zip guns. Making a zip gun was a simple affair, as Hair described it:

Break off a car aerial right size bore for a 22 caliber short.

Carve a wood handle, can you do that, sport?

File down a capgun hammer or a just a nail, a rubber band or two.

Then you're in business, skip to my loo.

An hour later, they piled into the Deuce and went in search of trouble. Hair wanted to "offer out this here Breezer punk." Willy's gut was tight; he would be expected to defend the gang's rep and back Hair up if he took on more than he could handle. Mack made it back to North Minneapolis in record time. He hit one hundred and twenty on Highway 55.

They drove to Sandy Ollsen's house. Hair's sullen hostility, which Sandy had interpreted as childlike vulnerability, had awakened her sprouting confusion of sexuality and maternity—at least that was the thought that occurred to William all these years later as he lay in his hospital bed. Got his cookies, Hair claimed, dropped her, but heard she was seeing some Breezer asshole. Maybe the asshole was hanging out at her place 'cause Bernie was itching to duke it out with him.

Parked in front of Sandy's house was a cherry '40 Ford with dual penciltip tailpipes. Mack hit the brakes and fishtailed to a stop inches behind it. He put the headlights on high beam and nudged the Ford's bumper. Two heads rose from below the backrests. One was attached to Sandy. The other craned out the driver's side window and croaked, "Back off, thunderturd."

Hair got out, and as he walked, the gravel splintered beneath his black boots. He stomped on one chrome tailpipe. Then the other. Kicked the trunk lid. Steel toe clanged off the pinstriped metal. Hair zipped open his pants and began pissing on the hood, which produced a thin cloud of vapor. The Breezer stayed put. Hair, penis in hand, moved to the passenger side, sprayed urine through the window. Pee drops sparkled in the beams of the Deuce's headlights. The Thunderbirds heard a scream. Hair went to the driver's side and yelled, "Come on outa there, punk. Too chicken? Not man enough?"

He tried to open the door. It was locked. He lifted his right leg, kicked at the window until it shattered, struck his fist through the jagged opening. When no reaction ensued, he poked his head inside. The Breezer jumped like Jack Flash. Hair jerked his head back from the window of the Ford. He turned toward the Deuce and opened his mouth, but nothing came out. He grabbed his neck as if trying to choke himself, staggered around in a circle, sank to his knees. Willy slipped on his brass knuckles and jumped out of the Deuce. The driver of the Ford got to Bernie quicker and kicked him in the face. Hair toppled over. When Willy reached his friend's side, the Breezer held up a screwdriver dripping blood.

"You want some, too, mo'fucker?"

"Oh Jesus." Willy knelt by Hair's side. "Bernie, man, you okay?"

No response. Crumpled on the street, Hair's body shuddered. Willy heard the Ford burn rubber. The Thunderbirds crowded around. Willy put his face close to his fallen comrade's. He couldn't detect any movement. He lifted an eyelid. The glare from the Deuce's headlights seemed to fade into his buddy's eyeball.

"Someone call an ambulance!" Willy cradled Hair in his arms and rocked him. "Hang in there, babe."

"We'll find the prick," said Mack, "rip off his balls."

"Poke out his eyes," went Shits.

"Tear his veins out," chimed in Charly Farly.

William tried to bring back the feelings he had experienced. Rage, terror, pity? He could recall only the physical sensations. His jaw was clenched so tight that for weeks, opening his mouth was a painful ordeal. And curiously, his joints ached, as if a premonition of the arthritis that would afflict him in middle age.

An ambulance screeched to a halt. The attendants brushed the Thunderbirds aside—the first time they'd ever allowed anyone to push them around—and began to check for vital signs.

"Got a pulse here. Faint. Let's put him on the stretcher."

They loaded Hair into the vehicle. Willy rode along, claiming he was the victim's brother. He felt trapped in an underground pit. The siren's wail seemed muffled, spectral medics hovered over the body. Willy silently sprinkled lines from Ginsberg's "Kaddish" over the stretcher. When they reached emergency, Bernie Gustafson was in critical condition from internal hemorrhaging, the gang would later find out, from a punctured artery. The Breezer's screwdriver had torn into Hair's neck faster than he could recoil from the attack. The mongoose gets the cobra every time.

The Thunderbird gang stood around in the hallway smoking Pall Malls and swapping stories of Hair's prowess in gang fights and daring car thefts; they did not mingle with the victim's family members, wraiths drifting through the hospital's corridors. The Drunk and the Bitch staggered in ten minutes after Bernie Gustafson was pronounced dead at 11:45 that night. His violent end made the headlines of the *Minneapolis Morning Star* the next day; back then, a gang killing was big news. The police caught the killer, no sweat. His name was Dale Swanson. Manslaughter. He was committed to the Hennepin County Youth Camp.

Mack the Maniac, Shits, Charly Farly became teen angels that winter. They got snockered one night, Mack parked the Deuce in the middle of a railroad crossing, turned off the motor, slapped the key on the dashboard. The first one to put the key in the ignition when a train came along would be the chicken, who turned out to be Mack himself when he leaped out of the Deuce just before impact only to be crushed by the car's engine, which the train launched into the air smack on top of his head. Shits and Charly Farly died inside the Deuce, which the train reduced to unrecognizable shards of metal. Enlarged pictures of the dead boys began circling around the school and collected by the girls. The photos became saintly relics, icons, local echoes of the national James Dean cult.

Willy drifted away from the remnants of the Thunderbird gang and hit the books. His lifetime of reading came in handy. His soaring grades stunned his teachers—they'd always written him off as a dead-end JD—and turned his old friends against him. But screw 'em, Willy wanted to go to college. The summer after he graduated from high school, before his freshman year at the University of Minnesota, Willy ran into Dale Swanson falling down drunk at a party. Willy's long dreamed-of payback was in the bank. He grabbed Hair's killer by the shirt front, ripping it as he pulled him up from the sofa where he was slouched. Dale Swanson's eyes were unfocused, he drooled, he swayed like a car without shock absorbers.

"Remember me, punk?"

Swanson seemed to look past him. "Don't know you from Adam. Get yer hands off me or I'll…"

At that point, he began to spasm and ran toward the bathroom. Willy could hear him vomiting.

Ah, the hell with it, he had his fill of punch-outs. Willy turned his back and walked out of the party. There on the street was a '40 Ford with dual penciltip pipes. He opened the door, pissed on the snakeskin upholstery, then walked the two miles home.

*****

Sitting up in his hospital bed, William Bergman began composing a poem on the computer. "Variations on the theme of Ginsberg's 'Howl.'" *I saw the dead minds of my generation destroyed by violence clueless heedless hot-wiring racing through the darkness of urban streets looking for an angry fight unhip teen angels bleeding...*

No, this wasn't Ginsberg's cup of tea. He deleted what he had written. He sat back and thought, *Burroughs? Kerouac?* He heard a murmuring in his head, a stream of consciousness he couldn't quite decipher. It soon became clear that he was hearing the voice of Bernie Gustafson, Hair, dead all those long years. He typed furiously, trying to keep up with the ghostly ventriloquy:

Tell you what this's about by and by, don't flap away, don't fly, big guy.
Stop floatin' around, settle yourself down.
You ain't runnin' with your pack, you sure ain't goin back, Jack.
Still like to go huntin' with the Third herd?
The lion sleeps tonight.
Like to go faster'n a fart in a windstorm, Norm?
Slippin' and a-slidin'?
Fly like a turd from a bird?
Bet you'd take a dump in your pants, Vance.
Still think ya got the balls hot-wire a DeSoto with tinfoil from a pack of Pall Malls?
De Soto, Mamoto.
'Member all those brands how about a Packard, Kaiser, Nash, Studebaker, Hudson, son?
Used to be more makes of cars than all the canals up on Mars.
Don't hover there and whine, don't you snort, I'll give you the real dope, so don't you mope.

Stories From Three Brothers

Willy, good old badass former Tbird done went to college, ain't that absurd?

Heard you was what they call it hippie, some kinda commie, that right, Tommy?

Took some junk LSD, what that be?

Read some fruitcake Beats all we knew was beat the crap out of you and yo momma too daddyo.

Anyhoo, Hair, that's me dumb and pintsized Willy, that's you big and smartwise, we stuck together through all kinda weather.

But I took a screwdriver in the throat, that's all she wrote.

And now I hear you growed a gut, don't know it, but real soon now, your ticker gonna flicker.

But I ain't called you to sing no dirge, so how 'bout sittin' back and havin' a smoke 'fore you croak?

How 'bout a puff, Huff?

Hey, don't you go to sleep on me now, I'm just gettin' to the important part, Bart.

Nowadays I hear they got real badass gangs in north Minneapolis dope pushers crackheads that what they're called?

Got heavy firepower do these drive-by shootings meanin' blow your brains out for kicks.

Tell me, is that the way it is, Dizz?

Lordy, we wouldn't last a minute with those guys splish splash, we be takin' a bath in our own blood faster'n you could say beebopaloola.

Man if there'd been ak47s and uzis in those days, most of us we woulda died one helluva lot sooner, but we sure woulda had some crazy fun.

War daddyo hot time on the old town tonight.

Tbirds too young for Korea, never lived long enough to get their butts shot off in Vietnam.

But we got the glory. Heavenly glory.

It's the truth, Ruth.

You think it's a lie, don't give me the bird, I wouldn't shit you you're my favorite turd.

Me, Charly Farly, Mack the Maniac, Shits, we bought the farm met the reaper.

We been teen angels now, how long's it been?

We're still mean and lean all the angel girls wigglin' their hips wadin' in to kiss our sweet lips.

Those angel girls love my curly dome, Kookie, Kookie, lend me your comb.

But here lemme share some tips like I been told.

Only the innocent die young except for us.

Not what I was taught no use to fuss.

Growed up thinkin' there was just heaven and hell you went to one or the other so they tell.

Fact is you get sent somewheres ain't heaven or hell depends on how you croaked when you croaked.

Got a place for old people, young people, drowned people, burnt-up people, od'd on drugs people, smashed to smithereens in car wrecks, stabbed in the neck in the fifties people like us.

Don't matter, don't ask why, don't you cry.

Bitch and Drunk died in years gone by, bad livers, lungs, bad insides, they ain't hangin' where Hair resides.

They drank all their gin, they're deep in the bin, they'll never kiss Hair's sweet lips again.

And like old Hair says won't be long before you gonna turn up your toes, Mose.

When they kick over your coffin, it's gonna come up snake eyes.

A word to the wise, no you can't join our gang, Wang.

Nothin' personal, they don't allow it there's a place you gotta find with your own kind.

You still see yourself wearin' those Tbird threads gettin' your hair greased up, Pup?

Don't be a dip, Flip.

They don't let you be somethin' different from what you is just because you done passed away like they say on that final rainy day.

That's the way the cookie decomposes, Moses.

Anyhoo see you 'round, daddyo, got me a date with Peggy Sue, so don't be blue, just keep your cool, Fool.

William Bergman fell asleep at the keyboard as the sun poked its bloodshot eye over the horizon. Slumped in his bed, he awoke suddenly. What time was it? Where was Rosalía? The computer screen was blank. He checked his files but was unable to find Hair's monologue. He felt a chill, a tightness in his chest, a dull pain in his left arm.

Willie the Lump and Eloise
Bud George

She told him, "Roger, I'm taking my break now."

He glanced up from his work on the grill. "Okay, Eloise."

Eloise poured herself a cup of coffee and slid into a booth at the rear of the small cafe. The evening paper, under a half-full ash tray, was lying open on the table. Bored and tired, she scanned the page. The words, "Tell them Willie the Lump is still here," caught her attention. She read the article through, and the memories came flooding back.

Christ, Willie was still there. Willie the gentle, easygoing, quiet man. Willie was against the strike. The line speedups, the inhumane work rules, even the spying television cameras hadn't seemed to bother Willie. He just shrugged his shoulders, said the hell with it, and went on with it.

Six months. It was six months, and Willie was still there. The newspaper photo showed him as a big bearded bear of a man that he was. He was in his beat-up old parka with a wool hat pulled over his ears.

"Eloise, get off your ass," Roger called her back to work.

She finished her shift in a daze, unable to concentrate. Her mind was on Willie, the factory, the strike, and her part in it. She set it off. It was a hot summer day, another line speedup, and the plant inspector was behind her. She was thirsty, but the latest work rules said you could only get a drink on your break. The inspector moved so close behind her that she could feel him, feel his body heat. The machine clatter, her machine and those around her, became a roar. The inspector moved closer and touched her.

"Enough! Enough! Get away from me, you son of a bitch."

The inspector laughed, and she spun around, slamming her elbow into his soft gut. He dropped his clipboard and backed up, open mouthed and clutching his stomach with both hands.

"Get away from me, you son of a bitch," she repeated, then thought, *Well, that does it.* But she was calm.

Eloise turned and shut off her machine. She walked slowly to the water fountain, passing the plant manager's glass windowed office on the way. She held up her middle finger for him, then got her cool drink of water, and started for the only exit that wasn't locked. She again passed the manager's office. He was standing in the open doorway.

"Get out," he ordered.

She stopped, turned to face him, and he stepped back.

"Get out, you bitch," he demanded now.

She slammed his office door with all the force in her, smiling with pleasure when the glass in it shattered. The splinters hit the manager, causing him to jump back and fall over a chair.

Eloise slowly walked to the exit. As she touched the door, the sounds in the factory began changing. The noise level dropped as one by one, the machine operators were shutting down. One by one, they followed her out the door, gathering at the plant's entry gate. One hundred and sixty-eight people. Willie was the last one out.

Eloise was still thinking about it when she left the cafe. Without a conscious plan, she walked the familiar streets to the plant.

"Have you got another sign, Willie?" she asked when she got there. He smiled and handed his to her.

They stood in the cold, early morning light and watched as the day shift shuffled through the entry gate, talking. Only a few mumbled a greeting in Willie's direction. Fewer still spoke to her.

Eloise and Willie spent the day walking to keep warm. Back and forth past the gate, talking. She tried to explain why she left, why she hadn't stuck it out.

"It's okay," he said, not seeming to care. "I understand."

Eloise returned to the plant again the next morning and was surprised to find several people there, all holding picket signs and pacing back and forth past the gate.

The strike grew slowly this time, but the number of strikers grew each day.

An article was printed in the local paper telling of the striker's grievances, as stated by Willie the Lump and Eloise.

Organizers were sent from the regional union headquarters. After long hours of talks, a contract was negotiated.

A new local union was formed.

Elections were held.

Willie was nominated for office of president.

"Give us Willie," the workers yelled. "Willie the Lump won the victory for us. Hey, Willie, give us a speech. Come on, Willie. We want to hear from Willie the Lump."

Willie rose and walked slowly, amid the cheers and applause, to the speaker's platform. He pushed the microphone aside and held up his hand for quiet. Gradually, the cheers died down.

"I can't," Willie said. His voice grew stronger. "I won't accept this or any other nomination. I am leaving. This strike, this fight, is over. I won, but I never meant to win for you. I fought and I won, for myself."

Willie left the platform, walking slowly, his shoulders held back and his head up, to the exit. At the door, he turned.

"Goodbye, Eloise," he said.

THE BULL
Bud George

"Mind if I sit in?" the kid asked.

The three cowboys at the table with me stopped their mostly good-natured kidding, and thought it over for a long moment. Then, almost as one, a shrug, a half smile, and a nod of the head, they gave their okay.

Hell, he didn't even look like no cowboy. He was skinny, not lean-hard nor big in the shoulders like most bull riders. And his hat was too goddamn big. And he wore plastic-framed glasses that slid down his nose.

I dealt a hand.

"Kid, it looks like you must of fell of a bicycle or something," a cowboy said.

Respect, I thought, coming from a rodeo cowboy. They wouldn't kid him if he wasn't accepted.

"You want us three genuine professional rodeo cowboys to sign that pretty new cast what you got all over your leg?" another cowboy asked the kid.

"He ain't got time for that," I pointed out, "'cause by the time he teaches you all how to write, the leg'll be healed up."

"It's not going to heal. I can't ride no more bulls. Give me two," the kid answered matter-of-factly.

The kid hung on to the end and lost the hand. His face was too easy to read, and I knew he was running a bluff. He rode the same way.

I followed the rodeo. I made my living from it. With cards now and a while ago from riding the bulls. The bulls plain scare me now. The cards are easy, an easy living. I can control them completely. I've never took the cowboys for too much, and sometimes, when one of them's broke, I feed him enough cards to walk away with a small stake.

I dealt another hand. "Kid, what are you gonna do now?"

"Go home, I guess. Farm maybe. But first, I want to buy a bull."

The kid hung on again and lost, so I dealt him a hand he could win with. He had me interested now, or curious anyway.

"Buttermilk?" a cowboy asked.

"Yeah," the kid answered.

"The hell you say," another cowboy commented. The thin cowboy just laughed.

The kid was in the game for money, and he sure as hell didn't have any. He hadn't rode a winner but two or three times this season.

I don't know what happened to the kid. He did all right his first season, better than most, and he went home with a pretty good stake. But this year, he drew Buttermilk twice in a row. He got thrown just out of the chute both times.

Buttermilk was a mean son of a bitch. No one had ever ridden him. He was the last bull I ever tried to ride, and he made a fulltime card player out of me.

After the first couple of times riding him, the kid went a little crazy. He was scared of the bull, and it showed, but at the same time, he wanted to ride that son of a bitch again. When he didn't draw Buttermilk, he'd trade another cowboy for him.

It was tough to let the kid win without taking the three cowboys for more than I normally would, the way he played every hand down to the end. Stubborn.

He got himself thrown off that bull nineteen times this season. It got so the announcers were telling the crowds how many times he'd tried and lost. The crowds loved it, cheering all the time for the bull.

I let the kid win a few more hands, when most of the money was mine. Then he bought a round of drinks.

Today was number twenty. Then he rode that mean son of a bitch. He didn't make no money at it, but I don't think he cared about the money anyhow.

I dealt the three cowboys good-enough hands so they would about break even, then lost a big one to the kid.

When he rode that bull today, he came off way before the bell, but his hand was still on the rope. Stuck maybe, but I don't think so. I think he was still hanging on. When the pickup man came in close, the kid grabbed his saddle horn and somehow got back on the bull.

That stopped old Buttermilk. I guess he just couldn't believe it. Then he started bucking, twisting, jumping harder than I'd ever seen any bull do. Twice more, he threw the kid, and twice more, he got back on. I ain't so sure how. The crowd was going nuts about then, standing and cheering the kid finally. But that old bull, he was really going crazy.

Old Buttermilk used up about everything he had and then some, I think. Finally, he just stood there shaking, his legs spread, and his tongue out, with nothing left.

When the pickup man brought the kid in, I could see the white bone sticking out of his torn jeans.

"He done it the first time he come off," the pickup man told me.

The kid had a pretty good stake, it was late, the game was over, and I had barely enough money left to make it to the next rodeo to try to win back part of my money.

"Kid," one of the cowboys asked, "why the hell do you want that broke-down bull?"

"'Cause my daddy taught me," the kid answered him, "never leave a man with nothing."

Hell, he couldn't have been more than ten when I told him that.

It Was Unfortunate

Michael George

The old wooden boat's paint was cracked and peeling, and it constantly took on water as the three horse outboard pushed it through the channel.

Aaron Brown ignored the land around them. Reeds and rushes brushed his face when the boat moved too close to the shore, and ducks played hide and seek with it, but he paid no attention. His eyes were locked on the girl at the back of the boat, as he busied himself with his rod and reel and pint of whiskey held tightly between his knees.

The early morning light was beginning to push its way through the heavy fog, as a light breeze interrupted the perfect calm, filling the air while they crossed the lake behind them.

"How far is it to the next lake, Dad?" the girl named Kris asked.

"I'm not sure," he answered.

"I thought you came up here all the time when you were younger?"

"I did, but it's been years since the last time I was here with your uncle Jay and Grandpa Tom."

"Why did you stop coming?"

"It wasn't the same after Dad…Grandpa Tom drowned."

"How did Grandpa drown? No one ever told me?"

"We don't know for sure. He was out alone, over in the lake where we're going. Jay and I didn't want to go with him so early that day. I don't know why, we usually did. It was a nice day too. Some fishermen found his body floating near his boat."

"But you don't know how he got in the water."

"No. According to the autopsy, he died of drowning. He didn't have a heart attack or anything like that."

"Didn't he know how to swim?"

"He was a good swimmer. He might have panicked from the shock of the cold water when he fell in."

Suddenly, Aaron felt a short but strong tug on his fishing line, followed by a constant pull.

"Shut off the motor, Kris," he told her, "I have a bite."

As Kris shut off the motor and tipped it out of the water, Aaron gently set the whisky bottle on the boat floor. He never used any finesse when fishing and cranked as hard and fast on his fishing reel to land the fish. Kris was ready with the landing net and brought the fish into the boat.

"It's a good-sized fish, Dad. What kind is it?"

"A northern. It must weigh five, six pounds. Pretty good for the first catch of the day."

Aaron put the fish on a stringer, tied the stringer to the boat, and dropped the fish in the lake. After taking a sip from his bottle, he asked, "When are you going to start fishing, Kris?"

"Maybe when we get to the next lake. I'm afraid I'll run the boat into the weeds if I fish when we're in this channel."

"I'll run the boat if you want to fish now."

"No, I'd rather run the boat."

"Some of the best fishing is here, in the channel."

"I'll wait anyway."

Even though Aaron was right about the fishing, Kris continued to run the boat. He caught three more fish, all as big as the first, before they were out of the channel.

The lake was choppy when they left it. Aaron directed Kris toward a small but sheltered bay a short distance away. He brought his line in, and she turned the throttle on full. The small motor wasn't near powerful enough to lift the bow of the boat, so they plowed their way through the waves, rather than riding the tops of them.

It was calm in the bay, so Kris readied her fishing gear after stopping the boat. They trolled around the bay, just outside the weed beds. After twice around the bay without a catch, they crossed the lake to an island near the middle. Again, Kris slowed the boat, and they fished as they went around the island.

Near the bottom end of the island, Aaron pointed out an outcropping of rocks. "There's where Grandpa drowned."

The vegetation ended near the spot Aaron pointed at, and a narrow peninsula made up entirely of rocks, jutted about three hundred yards into the lake. The rocks made Kris nervous, and she didn't turn the boat until she was way out into the lake. That far from the island put them in the high waves, and as the boat turned broadside to them, it nearly capsized.

As the first wave hit them, the round bottom boat listed heavily to one side and took on water. Aaron violently shifted his weight in the opposite direction to steady it. As he did, Kris turned the throttle on full, and they nearly went over in the other direction. Several inches of water sloshed around in the bottom of the boat by the time Kris steadied it and was heading into the waves again.

"I'm sorry, Dad," she said, visibly shaken. "I didn't realize the waves were so high."

"Don't worry about it, Kris. It could happen to anyone."

"Do you think that might be what happened to Grandpa?"

"It's possible, I guess. But I doubt it. He fished this lake too many times to let it fool him that way."

"But you just said it could happen to anyone. If it couldn't have happened to Grandpa, why did you say that? Or did you just mean anyone stupid, like me and my mom."

"I sure didn't say you're stupid. I meant it could happen if you don't know the lake. Your grandpa did know the lake. About as well as a person could."

"Okay, I see what you meant. You do think Mom is stupid though, don't you?"

"No. What give you that idea?"

"She said you did. She said that before you got divorced, you always treated her like she was stupid."

"Did I? I don't remember. Maybe I did."

"How could you not remember?"

"It's been a long time."

"Is your new wife really better?"

"Better is the wrong word. More compatible is more accurate."

"How come you stayed away so long? I'd almost forgotten all about you when you finally showed up last year."

"I didn't do it on purpose." Aaron furrowed his brow and sipped his whiskey. "I guess I just never got around to seeing you until then."

"Were you really that busy with your wife and other kids?"

"No, I wasn't. I just never got around to doing it. But let's not talk about such unpleasant things today."

"Fine, we won't talk about it anymore," Kris said, her disappointment showing.

Pretending he didn't notice, Aaron forced his face into a grin. "When you can, Kris, beach the boat. I want to tip it over to empty out the water."

"Okay, Dad."

Heavy brush grew to the water's edge after they were around the rocky outcropping of rocks, so they continued around the island. They fished another mile of shoreline before the found a sandy beach. It was another quarter mile before there was a break in the weed beds large enough to maneuver through.

Aaron drank from his bottle and watched his pretty young daughter wander up the beach after the boat was emptied of water. The bottle was empty and Aaron was sleeping when Kris returned. He didn't respond when she tried to wake him. After an hour, he still didn't respond, so she tried to get him in the boat. His two hundred pounds was far too much for her to handle.

"Damn," she swore in anger.

She kicked the sand as she paced around the sleeping Aaron. She felt like leaving him and going back to the cabin alone. She hated drinking, and here was her father. Drunk! He didn't even drink that much. Only a pint. She drank that much at a party once and didn't get very drunk. So why should he pass out? She didn't understand why he did something like this, especially so early in the morning.

Kris wasn't going to leave him there, but she wasn't going to sit there and wait for him either. It was just too boring. So she pushed the boat out into the water and went for a ride. She was going around the upper end of the island when he woke up.

His head throbbed and his mouth tasted and felt like it was full of sand. He staggered when he tried to stand.

"My liver must be shot to hell," he mumbled to himself. "It has to be, the way I've been passing out lately."

He stood, breathing heavily a moment, before he realized Kris and the boat were gone. He didn't blame her for leaving and decided to take a walk while she was gone. He never considered the fact she might not return.

He soon reached a small creek, running into the lake. It was too deep to wade across and he didn't feel like swimming, so he followed it upstream. He'd never seen the creek before, so he was curious as to where it went.

Walking was easy to start, with wide stretches of sand along the creek banks. It continued to be easy as the banks became grassy and was manageable even as they became rocky slopes. He would have turned around when the path turned sharply upward, but his curiosity pushed him forward.

Quickly, his breath turned to prickling gasps, his legs to lead, and his mind to a bleary weariness. Even so, he managed to reach the summit, then collapsed. His throat burned, pain scorched his lungs, and terror of additional movement raked through his knotted legs. Far below, in a deep ravine, the land laughed and swallowed the creek.

Pushing himself to his feet, as soon as his lungs subsided to mildly racking sobs, he continued his walk. Crossing the hill to the other side of the ravine, he saw Kris come around the lower side of the island, near the outcropping of rocks. He watched her make the turn out in the lake and felt a momentary sense of pride when she did it perfectly.

Then he hurried, wanting to get down to the beach before she got there. The path rapidly narrowed as he went down, then moved to the edge of the ravine. Had he not been in such a hurry to meet Kris at the beach, he would have turned around and gone down the way he came up. Instead, even though heights terrified him, he continued down.

The going was difficult and dangerous on the path's steep descent. It was rock strewn with occasional small climbs of brush blocking it. He didn't get far before he heard Kris pass by on the lake.

He felt a momentary panic, fearing she would leave him there, but quickly became sure she wouldn't leave without at least a minimal search for him. And even if she did leave then, it would only to get help.

But he didn't want her to go for help. If she did, it would mean having to explain to his wife why he was up there. It would be constant complaints from her and the inevitable fight. They always fought when he drank and often when he didn't. He was constantly exhausted from the guilt trips she sent him on. A weariness suddenly swept over him.

Bone tired and numb, his head pounding and trying to split open, he argued with the guilt. Arguing fiercely and ignoring the obstacles in his way, he hurried his descent.

He heard the gurgle of the creek and the slap of the waves on the beach as he slipped and his feet left the narrow ledge the path had become.

Thoughts of his father, daughter, wife, ex-wife, and his drinking ran through his mind. The guilt. It was his. He let his father go fishing alone. And die. Alone. He ignored his daughter…left her alone. He was guilty. He drank. But the guilt would soon be all…

It was unfortunate, however, that Aaron hit his face on a rock on the way down, for no one was ever able to see his smile.

COLD HOTEL LOBBY

Michael George

He stood in the cold hotel lobby, shivering, as he checked his watch for the third time in minutes. His stomach tightened as he realized how late she was. He tried to tell himself she would show up and felt the terror of knowing she might not.

He walked around the lobby, his hands in his pockets, trying to find a spot without a draft. Every time he found a place, the automatic doors opened, and the cold hit him again. After three trips around the lobby, he gave up and stood near the door.

Checking his watch again, he decided she wasn't coming and headed out the door. He ran into a rich lady in a fur coat, wearing too much perfume, changed his mind, and decided to give her a little more time.

He walked to the magazine rack, picked one out, and tried to read. First, his eyes blurred, then her face covered the page, and he felt a familiar emptiness he carried since the first time he ever saw her, and she penetrated so deeply into his life.

Because reading was futile, he gave up the magazine and went back to the door. He was focused on the rush hour crowds passing by outside, when she finally appeared on the sidewalk, walking toward him.

He began sweating, his hands shook, and he could feel his face warm as he watched her approach. He was smiling when she reached him. She looked tired and distracted. His smile faded.

"I'm sorry I'm so late," she said, "It's been a long day and I had to work late. I won't be able to make it tonight. It's already too late." She tried to smile, but failed miserably. "Maybe some other time, we'll have the chance."

"Don't you even have time for one drink?"

"No, not tonight. He called me at work. He's already angry." She turned to go. "Maybe some other time," she said as she walked away.

He watched her go, thinking he would ask her again next week, even while knowing inside, somewhere, that he never would.

From This Moment On

David George

Act I: *You're in Trouble Now, Darlene*

Scene 1.
Small cottage outside Middlebury, May, Liv at age fifty. In the background, an iPad broadcasts Louis Armstrong's rendition of "Ain't Misbehavin'." Liv Malmgren sits at a small fold-out table while water boils for tea. She never tires of the view the expansive kitchen windows afford her. Grassy slope leading down to a pond where green-blue wood ducks flock. Lambs like grounded clouds in a field beyond the pond. View to the west of the Adirondacks, east to the Green Mountains, and in her mind's eye, the White Mountains of New Hampshire.

She stands up to stretch, then wanders into the living room to admire once again a new charcoal drawing she acquired at a charity auction in Rutland last week. Liv paid only a hundred dollars; she feels like a thief in the night. Its execution is so accomplished, its linen matting and minimalist frame—cherry wood?—so professional, it belongs in a museum. The drawing depicts a group of people seated on the ground beneath a tree. There's an aura of stillness. More than that, the kind of stillness following a noisy celebration? The canopy dominates the upper third of the space, the people's faces shaded into invisibility. They sit in small groups. Families? Sweethearts? The background, rolling landscape sparsely populated by trees, suggests a rural setting. Grove? Orchard? What draws the eye into the piece is a figure slightly off center, a woman, the only member of the group standing, directly facing the viewer. There are flowers strewn at her feet, but since the drawing is charcoal, it is difficult to identify them. Roses? There are moments Liv senses the woman making eye contact with her. At times, the facial expression seems triumphant, other times mournful. Liv discerns doubt and regret in that countenance. The woman is asking something. When Liv bid for the piece, the question was, where am I going? But now it is, where have I been, what am I waiting for? *I must be patient till the heavens look with an aspect more favorable. I am not prone to weeping, but I have that honorable grief lodged here which burns worse than tears drown.* Hermione from *Winter's Tale*?

The kettle's train whistle breaks in and she hurries to the stove. Liv pours steaming water into a blue Rorstrand teacup. Dubious family legend has it that her great-great-grandmother transported the cup from Sweden to Minnesota in the 1860s. She fishes a bag out of the porcelain pot where she stores her haphazard collection of teas. She returns to the table and plops the bag into the teacup. Chamomile. Hadn't she had chucked their entire supply? After rehearsal, Paulo and Liv drank chamomile. Each and every night, he repeated the same joke: *nella camomilla, la veritá.* In chamomile, truth. She hadn't thought it clever the first time she heard it. *La veritá*, she ejected Paulo from the cottage after she caught him in bed with Frankie.

Just now, a gaggle of Canada geese has come blustering into the pond, disturbing the tranquil colloquium of the wood ducks. The geese honk in disordered formation about the pond. The ducks form a tight gabbling circle.

<u>Scene 2.</u>
Green Mountain Players, Middlebury. *Biederman and the Firebugs* by Max Frisch. Liv in the role of Mrs. Biederman. They are into the second week of the run. Mr. and Mrs. Biederman are huddled stage left anxiously jabbering away about the arsonists hiding in their attic. A moment of suspense, Liv and the actor playing Mr. Biederman so far

have been unable to project. They almost achieved it last night, but then some cretin's cellphone went off in the audience. Now, however, they begin to feed off each other for the first time, a shared emotional memory. Tension coils through the auditorium. They are isolated under a single spot. Leko for tight focus, with a gobo projecting a spider web effect. Green gel for estrangement.

Suddenly, out of the corner of her eye, Liv sees a shadow move down the aisle and up to the stage. A voice from the balcony rings out: *Oh boy, Darlene, yer in trouble now.* Mr. and Mrs. Biederman continue their dialogue, but faster and faster, lines spurting from their lips, as the shadow stands no more than two feet away, watching them without saying a word. Another shadow glides down the aisle and onto the stage. Mr. and Mrs. Biederman fall silent. The second shadow, a thin man, goatee, balding, forties, takes Darlene by the arm, stops stage center, faces the audience, shrugs, smiles, leads her away.

Whose idea was it to invite the mentally challenged residents of a halfway house? One of whom obviously was Darlene; she wanted a close-up view of those strange people in funny costumes. It was the director's idea, of course. Last week, he bussed in a group of ex-convicts from Burlington. Liv simply adored performing before an auditorium filled with rapists and armed robbers. The director. Mr. Socially Responsible. Mr. One Must Be Generous in Life as in Acting. Mr. Thou Shalt Not Covet Thy Neighbor's Stuff. And isn't there supposed to be one about not coveting thy neighbor's love pal? The director. Frankie St. Paul.

Act II: *Hecate vs. the Bat*

<u>Scene 1</u>.
Apartment overlooking Salem harbor, November, Liv at age forty-four. On an iPod connected to Bose speakers in the background, Ella Fitzgerald sings "Bewitched, Bothered, and Bewildered." Water in a teapot bubbles and boils. Liv takes the pot off the burner and pours water into a blue cup. She randomly takes a tea bag from a porcelain jar and dips it into the water. Earl Grey. She carries the cup around her living room as she straightens the paintings covering the

walls, rearranges objects. On the north wall is a print she recently purchased in a Salem gallery. It's mostly black with figures emerging in light brown. There's a head of a man—or woman?—cloaked in a hood, with some sort of winged animal emerging from the forehead. An owl, a bat? The piece is brooding, full of portents. *Come, dear, let's not get melodramatic.* She looks over what she thinks of as her memory pictures, proscenium frames through which she views scenes from her life, her triumphs and regrets. On the west wall, a jazz band. On the south wall, a primitive portrait from Rio. On the east wall, another Brazilian painting: a multicolored fish swimming in a sea of green with Jackson Pollock splatters. Barely noticeable among the larger pieces in her collection on the north wall, a Pop Art VW and a small abstract with eddies of colors, mostly blue and yellow.

An off-white stressed table under the windows on the east wall is bare, so as not to obstruct her view of the harbor. Liv rests the teacup on the table, sits down. *And how are you this morning, Liv Malmgren? Just dandy, thank you. Forty something, a swell age to be doing Lady Macbeth. Put that in your teacup and scald your throat with it, Paul. Don't want to sit around and mope now, do we?* She had thought they were companions well suited to each other. She gave Paul moral support when his career as an investment consultant suffered a setback after the dot.com bubble burst. He helped her with scripts, reading the other parts as she memorized her lines. But she sent him packing after he returned home in his cups from a night out to commiserate with his fellow investment mourners. Paul produced a spiraling soliloquy: Liv was wasting her life as an actress and why didn't she get a real job? He tried to win her back by FedExing a dozen roses. Probably cut and stripped of thorns by some exploited teenage girl in a flower factory in Colombia. She chucked them in the trash. What's done is done. All's well that ends well.

She observes the late autumn scenery. Sheets of rain sweep across the water. Wind gusts bend the already barren trees. Will her fingers one day resemble those twisted, knotted branches? The weather has driven away the mourning doves that alight on her small balcony each morning to visit her bird feeder. She notices a schooner in the harbor rolling in the waves. It wasn't there yesterday. Schooner or tall ship? What's the difference? She wonders if that's the sort of ship her ancestors sailed from Sweden. There's someone out there by the wharf. A woman? She's wearing a long dark cape. She bends down then straightens up, over and over. Is she tugging at something? There is a fence running the length of the wharf built, she thinks, from old ship's timbers. The woman's cape seems to be snagged on one of the timbers. She pulls and pulls as the rain pours down on her. Liv suspects it's her imagination telling her that the woman's movements are becoming increasingly frantic.

Scene 2.
Salem Globe Stage. Shakespeare's *Macbeth*. Liv in the role of Lady Macbeth. The director is Baine Ekdahl, a Minnesota Svenska like herself. Quite the coincidence. As background music, Baine has chosen Arvo Part's "Tabula Rasa." Baine explains that the haunting sound fits the play, but he has other reasons. Many AIDS patients listen to the piece, for them it is angels' music.

Lady Macduff asks, *Are you saying AIDS is some kinda subtext?*

Baine replies, *that's what I'm saying. Think about it. The untimely deaths, Macbeth's tragic fate. Not to mention Lady Macbeth's dementia, the blood she can never wash off her hands. The curse, the curse...*

One of the Murderers interrupts, *The audience'll never make the connection.*

A Weird Sister chimes in, *Even if you put it in the program notes, they'd never buy it.*

Though Liv is skeptical, for her, the music sets just the right tone.

The wardrobe is a collective creation. The actors have pieced together their costumes from fragments of clothing found in thrift shops around town. A pair of long johns dyed black serves as tights, a woman's stitch fedora with the band removed and a feather stuck in it masks Macbeth's identity when he visits the witches. Liv has put together a dark purple velvet dress and a cloak from an old rain cape she deconstructed.

The woman who designed the set has come up with a splendid idea. The whole cast and crew have pitched in on set construction. They traveled all over Massachusetts looking for abandoned farmhouses, removing assorted pieces of grayish-brown weather-beaten wood for the set. They built it on two levels, with a narrow connecting stairway stage right. They didn't have enough wood for the entire set, so they used packing crates to fill in the holes, staining them to match the color of the old boards they collected. The look is not exactly the medieval castle of Shakespeare's play. But its aura of timelessness establishes the perfect mood for the piece.

Liv has prepared carefully for this role. She uses Pierre as her source of emotional memory when she berates Macbeth, questioning his manhood over his reluctance to murder King Duncan. It has been difficult to find the motivation to carry out the assassination. Is there a murderer lurking somewhere in a dark corner of her psyche? Then she remembers New York, finds her murderer. For her grief and madness, she takes a cue from Baine. She imagines herself an AIDS patient in the last stages of the disease, her life cut short, waiting for nothing but death, her mind submerged in dementia.

The production has made quite a splash. Most of the performances are sold out. Tonight, there's a critic from the *New York Times* in the audience. Liv waits backstage for her mad scene, "out, out damn spot." She's spooked tonight. Not only did Macbeth lose control and bean one of the other actors with a heavy wooden mug in the middle of Banquo's ghost scene, but during the boil and bubble conjuring on the second-level platform, a real bat flew out of nowhere and hovered over the witches.

It's time for her soliloquy. Okay, that's her cue. She has to enter upstage left at the upper level—hope that bat doesn't reappear—cross the platform to the rickety stairway stage right, make her way down with nothing to hang on to. She begins her descent to the lower level. She hears a tearing sound. Her cloak is stuck on something. She halts halfway down. She tugs and tugs again. It won't budge. It's snagged on one of those packing crates. She pulls harder, and the box tips precariously. She picks up the crate with her cloak stuck to it and makes her way to the lower level. She does the entire scene carrying the box around the stage. There are a few titters from the audience but mostly silence which continues after she exits until the next scene begins. Backstage, she collapses, weeping into arms of the set designer, Paulina.

David George, Bud George, Michael George

Act III: *Oh, What Was That?*

Scene 1.
Apartment near the north bank of the Charles River in Cambridge, July, Liv at age thirty-seven. A CD player in the background broadcasts Coleman Hawkins playing "Just One of Those Things" on the sax. Liv drinks her morning tea—Kousmichoff—and looks out across the river toward Boston's Back Bay neighborhood. Wish she could afford to live there. But all good things come to those who wait. She'll get there some day. And after all, she was lucky to find an affordable apartment this close to MIT. She admires the new painting she found in a garage sale in Bedford. When she saw it depicted a traditional jazz band, she just had to have it. The players are in a semicircle blowing soprano sax, clarinet, cornet, another instrument she can't identify. Trombone, perhaps? It's semi-abstract in black and white tones. She'd say the style is cubist although the date, which she can barely make out, is 1962. *How are we feeling today, dear? On the mend.* Her biological clock has been ticking, but Pavel showed no interest. He moved out…how long's it been? A month? When he brought his cousin Masha home and suggested a menage-a-trois, she gave him the heave-ho.

She looks through her bay windows and watches sea birds circle about in the summer morning light. Gulls and what are those black birds with the long neck and orange throat? Cormorants? They swirl around at the river's edge a block from her apartment. Someone is feeding them. Looks like a girl in a white dress. Liv opens a window and listens to the birds' cries. She hears a loud bang—from what source?—and the birds scatter, disappearing from view. Except for a single gull, which flies directly toward her window then up over the roof of her apartment building. When she looks down, the girl in white is gone.

Scene 2.
Chekhov's *The Seagull*, Cambridge Repertory Theater. Liv in the role of Arkadina. The director, Liza, has put together a lush production. The set is so elegant, with real Persian rugs, antique lamps

and clocks, genuine Russian empire sofa and dining set, mahogany writing desk for Trigorin, étagères with a Tiffany vase containing a single rose and tiny crystal seagulls. The audience can't really see the glass menagerie, but Liza's attention to detail inspires the actors and makes the nineteenth-century drawing room feel lived in. Word has it that Liza mooched the stuff in the set from a rich Boston banker who has the hots for her.

Speaking of the set, Liv has been chewing up the scenery as Arkadina. She loves playing this languid, world-weary sophisticate, tired of waiting for her life to come into clear focus. She uses the distress her breakup with Pavel has caused as emotional memory for Arkadina's *chagrin d'amour* over Trigorin's affair with Nina, played by a freshly minted graduate of the Yale Drama School. The Nina character is stunning in her white muslin dress. Liza says it's actually modeled after a French gown she saw in the Metropolitan Museum in New York. Seated on the grass outside the theater before performances, nestled in her costume's gauze and ribbons, the actress playing Nina repeats the line of her epiphany over and over again, *I'm a seagull, I'm a seagull*. Arkadina's own costume is a dream, green silk dress with bateau neckline, which favors what someone—who?—once termed her "reedy" figure.

Tonight's performance has gone well. Third act and the audience seems to be still with them. Liv is waiting for the gunshot that will cue her startled line. She is preparing herself, using what Liza calls unexpected expectancy. Countdown, five, four, three, two, one…no gunshot. The actors look at each other, quickly try to improvise some stage business to fill the gap. Liv panics, with a sweeping gesture knocks over the vase and its rose, then blurts out her line.

"Oh, what was that?"

Her startled cry is entirely authentic. Then comes the loud bang of a firearm. The audience laughs. And she still has to do the scene that will reveal the origin of the gunshot: Dr. Dorn will take her aside, inform her that her son, his play a failure and his love for Nina unrequited, has committed suicide. She does her best to make it through the scene to the end of the play. After the curtain call—lukewarm applause—she storms backstage and confronts Pavel, responsible for sound effects. Hey, he says, sorry, shit happens. It's just one of those things.

Act IV: *There's Our Cue, Let's Go*

Scene 1.
Apartment in South Minneapolis, overlooking the Mississippi River, October, Liv at age thirty-one. Liv is listening to a Miles Davis LP, "Kind of Blue." His band swinging like trapeze artists, according to the album liner notes. She prefers more traditional stuff, but Miles Davis is an exception to the rule. "Kind of Blue" goes well with this golden moon tea she's discovered recently. She's also recently acquired two paintings, given to her by a friend who bought them in Brazil. The first is a tropical fish in dazzling blues, greens, reds, yellows, purples. The second her friend purchased from a street vendor in Rio. It's black, white, with a little green. In the background are swirls… clouds? In the foreground, a black woman holds an elongated object that looked to her at first like the top of a complicated lamp. But her friend explained it's a fire balloon. Apparently, the people down there make paper balloons, somehow light a fire inside them, and they float off into the night sky. Sounds dangerous but probably looks lovely. People here would be flooding the phone lines with reports of UFO sightings. What if there were one big enough to carry a person? You could go flying high, high above the earth, soaring above a great fire. Higher than you can go on the grass she's been smoking lately. Up, up in the sky in my beautiful balloon. What would happen when the flame went out? Would you fall back to the earth like Icarus?

She took up marijuana after New York. It was the perfect antidote. New York's ancient history, sure. But she felt so diminished afterward. Most of the time, she certain she's shaken the experience, but the memories sneak up on her. She does think about cutting down. But there are other disappointments. Pol is one. They shared, in his words, a love of life but a lust for theater. Not to mention how much fun it was getting high together. Added to the fact that Liv trusted him implicitly. But she gave Pol the boot when he ripped off her entire stash of Colombian red to smoke with another actress, extending his list of lusts.

Back in Minneapolis, where she grew up. Her Swedish roots and all that. How do you say high in Swedish? Something freaky like hög. How about fly? Flyga, or some such. At least she's got a theater gig and a nice place with a view of the Mississippi. From her living room window, she can see all kinds of cool birds flying past now that fall migrating season is in full swing. Flocks of them follow the course of the river and sometimes veer close to her window. Liv has hung a bird feeder outside so she can observe them more closely. It's especially a kick when she's stoned. She's purchased a *Birds of North America* book and can identify some. Wood thrush. Willow flycatcher. Ruby-throated warbler. Let's smoke some weed and fly off with our fine-feathered ruby-throated friends.

Scene 2.
Minneapolis Ensemble Troupe. *Everyman*, anonymous medieval mystery play. Liv in the role of Death. The theater is located in a church the group rents from a Methodist Reform congregation. The church members hold their services in the basement, having foregone the vanity of the church with its high starry ceiling, stained-glass rose window, hand-carved wooden pews with contoured seats, balcony with curved ornamental iron rails. She has run into some of the congregants at cast parties. They smoke dope, too. And they're into wife swapping. The minister put the moves on her once. She told him to go fly a kite. During rehearsals, the actors sometimes hear the church members in the basement where they sit on the bare floor and hold their call-and-response services.

The minister will say, *We are sinners.*

The congregants respond in unison, *We are sinners.* It goes on: *We are guilty of lust, we are guilty of greed, classism, racism.*

Liv's thought is *Get a life.*

The Ensemble director, Todd Peterson, decided to put on the play with the actors doing sign language and speaking simultaneously. He got funding from some state agency to do his bit for the hearing impaired. *Kept the bread all for himself,* she bets. The cast has had lessons in signing, and they've become pretty proficient. The one actor who turned out to be a fluent signer is up on a platform dressed like a mime. She signs the whole play and without any direction from Todd has added brilliant movement and facial expressions. She's the best thing about the play; the groups that come in from the school of the deaf fall in love with her. Liv has trouble remembering the signs what with all the joints she's been tokin'. Todd has given her a non-signing role as one of the allegorical figures, Death. There are other allegorical characters Todd has positioned all over the theater, making terrific use of the space. Through an opening in the starry ceiling, the actor playing Knowledge descends on a rope thirty feet down to the stage. Good Deeds climbs up and down a ladder leading from the main floor to the balcony.

The theater is about half-full. On a platform stage right, Liv awaits the cue for her entrance as Death, holding a trapeze. She has to swing in a wide arc that takes her to another platform stage left. It's a tricky maneuver. She's a little nervous; this is the first time she's smoked pot before a performance. She has to swing six times to be positioned properly so she can meet face to face with Everyman on the opposite platform. The idea is to begin seated on the trapeze, then after the fourth arc hang by her knees, after the fifth by her hands, reach the platform facing Everyman, whose arms encircle her waist. To the audience, it looks like Everyman embracing Death. Its practical purpose is to stabilize her landing on the platform, after which they climb down to the stage together. Everyman always appears at the last second. During some performances, he stands in the dark and is suddenly illuminated by a red-gelled Leko placed directly above his head. At other times, he steps into the light at the precise instant of Death's approach. *There's our cue, let's go.* She launches herself from the platform. She could swing like this forever, basking in the orange light of a follow spot, watching the colors of the stage lights change as she passes under them, pink for warmth, magenta for passion, blue for cool, kind of blue, birds fly over the rainbow. How many times has she crossed the stage? Three? Four? *Ooops*. Better execute the hang by the knees maneuver. Then by the hands. She nears the platform, prepares to land in the arms of Everyman. Where is he? Her feet touch the platform, she topples backward. Liv feels the shock of a violent collision, she falls into darkness.

Morning. Liv wakes up in a hospital bed. Her head is throbbing, her back aches. Someone walks in. The doctor. He tells her she's a lucky young lady. She's suffered a concussion. Falling into the orchestra pit like that, she could have ended up paralyzed. There's someone outside waiting to see her. The doctor exits, another man enters, cradling a bouquet of roses. It is the actor who plays the role of Everyman. *I'm so sorry, Liv.* She looks at him wistfully. *Oh, Pol...*

Act V: *Break a Leg*

<u>Scene 1.</u>
Apartment in Brooklyn Heights, restricted view. March, Liv at age twenty-eight. A tape deck plays the Duke Ellington Orchestra's rendition of "Take the A Train." Liv sips her wild cherry tea. She's actually got a shot at an acting gig in New York. She sings, *New York, New York, what a wonderful town.* Does that song mention Brooklyn? No matter. Through her bedroom window—if she cranes her neck—she can see the suspension cables of the Brooklyn Bridge. *Hooooooeeeeey. And now presenting Liv Malgrem, distinguished New York actress who first made her name...* She looks around her garden apartment. Euphemism for basement room. Place needs some decorating. She can't decide if she should hang the yellow Pop Art wooden cutout of a VW bug that Pablo gave her last year when she interned at the New England Academy of Theatre. Pablo the rascal. Another intern, Trudy, asked her why Pablo kept saying "very well, very well" to her all the time. Not *MUY bien.* It's *MI bien.* My darling. But when Liv found out Trudy had become Pablo's other darling, she told him *adiós*.

Looking out her basement window, she sees people walking by. Just legs, really. Bare legs. Brown, yellow, white, black, hairy, shaved. Covered legs. Denim, corduroy, khaki, cotton. A neighborhood kid plays by himself in front of her building. He hits a ball against the brick facade over and over again. The other residents complain, but Liv doesn't mind. He's probably lonely, waiting for something to happen in his life. One rainy day, he paces back and forth through a large puddle that has formed in front of her window, tapping the ground, splashing water with a bat. A pigeon lands on the sidewalk and the boy swings at it, barely missing the bird which then flies off.

Scene 2.
Cherry Lane Theatre, East Village. Sam Shephard's *True West*. Liv in the role of Mother. Gary Sinise as the straight arrow Austin, John Malkovich as his criminal brother Lee. Liv worries she's much too young to be playing the Mother, even with deep lines etched by makeup, gray wig, stiff-jointed movement she's learned observing elderly women in New York's tea rooms. She is intrigued by an aspect of those women; they all seem to have paused, waiting for something. Not death, too trite. But that one last exciting moment or man, adventure, something, to appear, one final antidote to regret.

Liv isn't about to turn down a chance like this. The actress who'd been playing the role went back to the Steppenwolf in Chicago, where this production originated. The understudy broke her arm in rehearsal when Malkovich wrestled her to the floor, something definitely not in the script. Malkovich is such a wild man, so unpredictable, something different every night. Liv is terrified of him. She is a last-minute replacement. A friend of hers from college, Irene Petersburg, has an in with the producer. Another actress also has a shot at the role. Today's their competition. The rival did the matinee performance. Liv thought she was just so-so. She's certain she can outdo her tonight.

The evening performance is underway. Liv watches the play from the wings as she waits for her entrance. It's Malkovich's golf club scene. His character, the one with the shady past, has sold a film script, he's into the Hollywood scene now. The golf club is the perfect prop to suggest a future of country clubs, celebrity tournaments. But Malkovich likes to improvise, keep the other actors on their toes. Tonight, he grabs the golf club, breaks a beer bottle with it, swings at Sinise, stopping a few inches from his face, then taps his eyeglasses. Oh, oh, here comes her cue. Break a leg. Bad choice of cliché. She walks into the set, a kitchen in a suburban California home, carrying a suitcase. She's about to utter her first line when Malkovich smashes her suitcase with the golf club. Liv blanks, she can't remember her lines. Malkovich and Sinise improvise around her. She makes up some stage business, cleaning up the mess her sons Lee and Austin have left in the kitchen. The audience probably thinks it's all in the script. Her time to exit finally arrives; she leaves the stage with dread in her heart. Now she's crying in the green room. On the table where she's slumped lies a box of roses. Intended for her? A cruel joke? The director approaches, sorry but he has no choice but to give the role to the other actress, wishes her good luck, leaves. Liv tears off her costume, puts on her jeans and leather jacket, scrubs off the makeup, sweeps up the roses, exits through the back stage door of the Cherry Lane, hurls the flowers toward a Dumpster, runs through the Village to the subway, jumps on the A train, gets off at 125th Street, consoles herself in a bar, drinking manhattans and listening to a swing band.

Act VI: *The Great Godot*

Scene 1.
Apartment in Middlebury overlooking the waterfall in the center of town, May, Liv at age twenty-two. An 8-track tape plays Sarah Vaughan singing Cole Porter's "From This Moment On." Liv shares the apartment with two other theater majors, Sandy Wohling and Pavol Aernoudts. Sandy and Pavol are lovers, but he's been giving Liv these glances. He's always yammering about her classic profile and her reedy shape. Whatever that's supposed to mean. He calls her green eyes hazel. Claims she's the only real natural blond around. As if he would know. Says she looks like Ingrid Bergman in *Casablanca*. Doesn't she wish. He keeps trying to give her this weird little blue and yellow painting he did, it's just splotches, but she refuses his offer. Liv drinks her rosehip tea as she gazes through her bedroom window down at the stream below the waterfall. There are swans out there swimming and flapping all over the place. It's like they're doing this mating dance. Or celebration. Anyway, it's a scene filled with joy and promise.

David George, Bud George, Michael George

Scene 2.
Middlebury College Theater. *Waiting for Godot*. Liv in the role of Lucky. Annabel Lloyd, the professor directing the play, has cast women to play the all-male characters in Beckett's work. Liv got her part when she did this improv the prof really dug. She walked across the stage, picked up a boot just lying there, stuck her nose right smack inside it, took a super whiff, smiled with pleasure, dropped the boot, exited the stage, tap dancing shuffle off to Buffalo. They have discussed the play extensively in rehearsal. What are the characters waiting for and why? Who is Godot? God? Hope? A way out of the characters' endless misery and regret? The director suggests they all decide internally what they're waiting for, what Godot represents, then use that as their secret motivation. They should connect it with something in their own lives. Dr. Lloyd calls it emotional memory. It's a way for them—and the audience—to believe in the truth of the characters. Having the actors keep it secret gives them the chance to discover, to surprise each other on stage. Liv makes her character Lucky a kind of Charlie Chaplin or Stan Laurel type, happy-go-lucky in the midst of bleak surroundings. Her character is waiting for the Great Godot, a famous director who will come to offer her a starring role on Broadway. Lucky's sunny optimism is unshakeable.

Now it's opening night, the performance sold out, standing room only. The audience has been chuckling and clapping at Liv's comic bits. Her loose-jointed movement, every pratfall, every double-take gets a laugh. The play is almost over. She wishes the last act would never end. The actors freeze as the lights dim. They clasp hands in the dark. Lights back on, curtain call, actors line up downstage, take a step forward one by one, bow. Thunderous applause. When Liv takes her bow, the audience rewards her with a standing ovation. *Broadway, here I come and then off to London's West End*, she thinks. *Audiences clapping, cheering me on. This is what my life will be. From this moment on.*

Flying Naked

Bud George

I know that you are gonna say, "Dirty old man." Well yes, of course, but that is not what happened here. My cousin called and asked me if I ever thought about flying naked.

"No," I said, "I did have a dream where I forgot to put on my pants. Pretty embarrassing."

"Well, yes," she said, "be at the airport Friday at nine a.m. We'll fly someplace warm, naked."

"Okay," I said. It was probably some big joke, but what the hell, it was February in Minneapolis and 4 degrees.

There were a couple of big MTC busses in front of the terminal, with signs saying "Flying Naked" taped on the sides. I climbed aboard. My cousin was at the door, naked. She gave me a cardboard box and said, "Undress."

My, my, I thought. I had not seen my cousin in that state of undress since that time in the haymow, when we were maybe ten or eleven. She certainly had filled out.

So anyway, where was I? Oh yes, on a bus naked with a bunch of naked people. And my naked cousin. All kinds of naked people, big, small, young, old, and they seemed to be pretty relaxed, so what could I do? I relaxed.

The walk from the bus to the airplane was a little cold, and I think people in the terminal found our group pretty interesting.

Check-in was very quick. As I was looking for my seat, coming toward me was a lady. I recognized Minnesota's favorite senator. As we passed each other, neither of us being what would be considered small or petite, we turned sideways to pass. A close brush with politics, but not unpleasant.

Our pilot and copilot did their welcome aboard and have a nice flight, standing facing us in the front of the airplane.

They were both dressed (or rather undressed) for the occasion, except of course, for their pilot hats, and gold wings taped, I think, to their chests or whatever. Our pilot was a slim, forty-something lady and a true redhead. Our copilot was a guy in his thirties with a big grin and stuff.

The flight was pretty smooth, with just a little turbulence. Some lady did spill her tea.

"Oh, oh," I heard.

"Where did my tea go?" she asked.

"I have no idea," her seatmate said. "Maybe it will show up when you stand."

We landed in San Francisco with real nice weather. The sun was warmer, by quite a ways, than the four degrees we had left. The idea had been to refuel, rest a little, and fly back home that evening.

But! (I hesitate to use that word among naked people, although it may be spelled differently in some cases.) Yes, but (not butt) there was some problem with the airplane that would take some time to repair.

Okay, no clothes, no money, no credit cards, no nothing. This could have been really boring, but (is that the right one?) it was not. Our favorite senator rounded up a group of naked people and with a borrowed cell phone arranged a limo tour of the city. Fun! Until we got that flat tire near the Golden Gate Park. We had no spare.

The driver had an amazing command of four-letter words (although I didn't hear a butt among them) and a load of naked passengers. The car became a little warm and boring.

So we got out of the limo to enjoy the weather and walk a little. I guess a passerby called the cops, who (or whom, it's like I'm never sure) arrived.

They said or asked, "What the hell is this? Please get dressed."

"Our clothes are in Minnesota," we said. "We flew in naked."

Then the cops asked us for IDs. They were becoming a little impatient. To calm the situation, one of my fellow passengers showed them a tattoo on her…well…anyway, it didn't work. But our favorite senator negotiated the use of a cell phone. She called someone named Arnold. Arnold had a really loud laugh. Shortly, a couple of big black hummers showed up.

We finished our tour of the lovely city, parks, museums, and especially Coit Tower's incredible view. I was standing directly behind our favorite senator.

The flight home went well, although the bus company lost our clothes. Getting home from the airport was difficult and cold.

Would I do it again?

I don't know.

What can you tell me about San Diego?

THE SCARECROW

Michael George

The scarecrow danced on the lyrics and melody of an old song. Wind flapped its coattails and ruffled its hair. It laughed and waved its arms, saluting the poverty-stricken spirit playing the piano.

The scarecrow moved its dancing feet along the paths of wayward children and defeated dreams. Incomplete houses, like the incomplete sentences of unfinished stories, are the signposts and music choosing the direction and beat.

The scarecrow stopped and trembled halfway at the sight of the giant tree, the high bridge with the rope hanging from the branch, and the deep river far below. The rope was looped at one end and the river filthy with sewage and chemical waste. Its water ran white.

The scarecrow danced on, stumbling often. It sometimes dragged a leg from the pain of ancient fears and new inabilities. Its hope went back to school, searching for some kind of truth.

*****

"How are you now, Johnny?" Kate asked me. "I mean, how are you really?"

"I'm okay, I guess," I answered her, automatically, mechanically. "I'm about the same as ever."

"No, Johnny, you're not okay." She looked at me with the kind of concern that looked genuine. "You haven't been okay for quite a while. You're so distant from me, and indifferent. Cold almost. Why? What's wrong?"

"Nothing's wrong. At least, nothing new. Nothing that you don't already know about." I said it without looking at her. I didn't feel like discussing what was in my head with anyone. And I was watching *Ironside* on her new wide-screen television.

I enjoyed her new television. I decided that if I ever had enough money, I'd buy one like it, or maybe even bigger. But that was a big if, given that I wasn't now, and hadn't for a long time, worked a regular job. I couldn't even afford one of the really cheap televisions that still used a picture tube.

"I wish you'd tell me how you are though, Johnny," she said, taking my hand. "Is there a reason you won't? You've always told me when something was wrong before."

"I'm not sure, Kate, except I don't want to push off any of my problems on you or anyone else."

"There is something wrong, isn't there? You're not okay." She pulled my hand, trying to make me face her, and direct my attention away from the television. "Tell me, Johnny, tell me how you really are."

I moved my eyes from the television, but still didn't look her in the eye.

"Are you really sure you want to talk about it?" I asked, beginning to feel very tired after being awake so long.

"Yes, I'm sure."

"Well, I'm not." I felt my pulse quicken with the irritation I felt lately whenever anyone asked me how I was.

"I think we should talk about it, Johnny," Kate said with half a smile. "I really think we should."

"Okay, Kate," I said, giving up and deciding to tell her how I felt. "I'm in bad shape right now. Everything's so lousy. Just so damn lousy."

Kate's hand tightened on mine. A tear trickled in the corner of her eye and stayed there. I wiped it off with my free hand, slipped the hand to the back of her head, and pulled her mouth to meet mine.

We held the kiss for a long time. Breaking it, I quickly turned my head around the room, looking for someone not there. We were alone in the apartment, but I had the feeling someone was about to enter, unannounced.

Finished with their search, my eyes found Kate's face again.

"What's bothering you so much?" she asked.

Giving her a blank stare, I tried pulling out one of the things bothering me, from the tangled thoughts in my head. Finally, when nothing specific broke loose, I said, "Everything."

"I wouldn't mind you telling me a few details," she said, smiling at my confusion.

I sighed, turning my head back to the television. The lady detective working for *Ironside* was crying and thinking about quitting the police force because she killed someone in the line of duty. I wondered why she was so upset, with life being so damn cheap. Especially on television.

Kate pressed my hand and kissed me again.

"Johnny, please, is it me that's so wrong? I know I've been awful hard on you lately. Is that it?"

"You haven't been hard on me, Kate. You're always good. I've said this many times, but you've given me things no one else could. You gave me the confidence to try. What we are has nothing to do with what's wrong."

"Please then, please tell me what it is."

"I don't know if I can or if I want to."

"I'm sure it'll help if you talk about it. You've always said talking helps."

"Maybe, but I still don't want to bother you about it. You can't do a damn thing about it anyway."

"I know the only thing I can do is listen. I can do that though. And that's all you need anyway. Someone who'll listen. So tell me. I'll worry more if you don't than if you do."

I didn't want to tell her about the decision I'd already made. It wouldn't do any good to tell her.

"I love you, Kate," I said, stalling.

"I love you too, Johnny. But that's not what's wrong."

"No, it isn't," I agreed, knowing she wouldn't quit until I talked. "I don't want to talk because I hate it when I seem weak to you."

"You're not weak, Johnny. You never have been. You're actually the strongest of us. You always do what you have to do. That's more than the rest of us can say."

Kate's a fine lady. She says nice things.

Ironside ended, and the lady detective was still on the police force.

I kissed Kate and my hand found her breasts. It was nice. I always loved the feel of her breasts. So full and heavy in my hand. She responded to my touch. Something rare in my life, where someone recoiled from my touch, as if it was distasteful.

That never happened with Kate. If she was in the mood, it showed. If not, she simply said no. She put her hand over mine and increased the pressure of its caresses. I opened her robe and moved my hand inside. I quickly looked around the room. Except for us, it was empty.

"You're avoiding it, Johnny," she said as soon as I stopped kissing her.

I tried kissing her again.

She pushed me away. "Don't use this to avoid it."

"Okay," I agreed, knowing it was my only choice.

I turned to see Maxwell Smart doing something ridiculous. It was getting late. The sun would soon be up. Everything is supposed to look different in the morning. It never does. Not better…anyway.

My hand was still on her breasts, and I moved it again. She sighed a familiar small soft sigh. I knew she liked it.

She said, "I love it when you do that, Johnny." She was quiet for a moment, then said, "Why have you been staying away from me?"

"I was trying to avoid having to talk to you." I said, and for the first time in a while, I felt the stirring of desire. But I told her, "I don't want you to be concerned about my stupid problems. They're mostly in my head anyway."

The stirrings were growing stronger. It felt good to lose the empty numbness dulling me lately.

Kate spoke again. As she did, I could see the sadness in her eyes.

"I've worried a lot more about you, Johnny, then I would have if you come around the way you used to."

I decided then that I owed it to her to explain what I'd been going through.

*****

The scarecrow was stopped by the dizziness and sharp pain tramping through and splattering its brains. The field it always worked was supplied with new crows. The corn had grown too high to see over.

It could see the senselessness of it. To continue the struggle while trying to do work it no longer could, continuing the attempt at finishing what it never quite accomplished. Its spirit, like the sharing of the corn, was gone.

It cried out for someone to answer…to listen. It needed new shoes, so it could dance again. Or better, to have dreams again that stirred the music so it could dance as of old. In bare feet.

*****

Kate sat through my dialogue quietly. Her eyes were moist, close to tears.

"You wouldn't do that, would you, Johnny?" she asked as I finished.

"I'm not sure, Kate. I've been awful close a few times." I watched the deep sadness on her face and in her eyes as I talked. It told me I should have stayed away, that I shouldn't have said anything. I didn't belong there anyway. Now, if the time came, she would blame herself. I wondered how I could be so stupid. Why did I always do the wrong thing? Maybe soon, it wouldn't happen again. That, and the unwarranted self-pity I felt so often. The world was full of failures. Who was I to feel unique about it?

Maxwell Smart wasn't on television any longer. I had no idea what he'd accomplished in his half hour. But I suspect, like myself, he'd done very little in his time.

The Monkeys were on. I enjoyed them without having to focus on them. I knew it would be great to have some of their zaniness for a while.

Kate laughed at something they did. I smiled at her change of mood. It was like her, to have it change so quickly. I kissed her, wanting to make love with her.

"I'm sorry, Johnny," she said, moving out of my arms. "You can't start anything now. We haven't got time."

I looked at my watch, and seeing the time, I noticed the first hint of sunrise.

"Let me hold you anyway. Just for a few minutes. Please."

"You'll only get frustrated, and so will I."

"I'd rather go home frustrated than go home with nothing."

She smiled. "Okay."

I took her in my arms and kissed her. My hand dropped down to the hem of her robe and under it. I touched her knee. Her legs parted slightly, and I moved my hand.

Kate is a very volatile lady. In a short time, she wasn't frustrated.

"That helps, doesn't it?" I asked her.

"It helped me, but it didn't do you a damn bit of good."

"It does me a lot of good, Kate. We shared something wonderful and more important, I did something right."

"But now you're going to be miserable," she said, looking concerned again.

I knew she'd agree if I asked, but the apartment looked and felt crowded in the new morning light. It wouldn't...couldn't be satisfying. We would be too nervous and hurried. I stood to leave her.

"It's okay, Kate. I'm satisfied now."

"How could you be?"

"Because I love you, and I'm always satisfied when we share. You give me so much, Kate. And always, you make me believe in myself again. Now, I feel like I can hang in there. At least for a while. You made me believe I have another chance.

"Oh, I hope so, Johnny. I surely do hope so."

And for a change, so did I.

David George, Bud George, Michael George

*****

The scarecrow left the field. He found another smaller field with fewer crows and shorter corn. He bought new shoe laces, a book of dreams, and a shotgun. He knew the shotgun would be of help, one way or the other.

Back in Time

Michael George

I woke up to the sound of the rain beating against the bedroom window in an uneven tempo. Dark clouds hung low in the sky, making them appear darker and heavier than they were. I felt old and depressed as I headed for the bathroom.

"Why didn't you turn off your side of the blanket?" my wife, Nora, complained. I ignored her.

The shower helped open my eyes, but did little for my plugged sinuses and lungs that no longer got enough air. Toweling dry, I again told myself to quit smoking. Shaving, I nicked myself with the razor below my left ear. That was about the way the day should start, I decided, trying to stop the flow of blood with some tissue.

Back in the bedroom, Nora had laid out dress pants, my faded beige sport coat, and of all things, a white shirt, on the bed. I dug out the tie and cufflinks from the bottom of a dresser drawer.

As always, I was well ahead of Nora. After drinking a cup of instant coffee, I went out to start the car. The hard rain was now a steady drizzle. The car started, then fizzled to a stop. The motor was cranking over for about the fiftieth time, and I was cursing the Ford Motor Company when Nora joined me.

As usual, she intelligently asked, "Now what's wrong?"

"How the hell would I know?" I bitched back. "I ain't no mechanic."

"I already know that," she said, her voice emphasizing my ineptness. "So what are you going to do? If we don't leave soon, we'll be late. You know they are counting on you. I better call someone, to get us a ride."

"Not yet!" I said, leaving the car. I went around to the front and opened the hood. "Try it," I directed Nora.

"What?"

"Try it."

"Try what"

"The car! *Try to start the car!*"

"Why?" she asked, giving me her "don't be a fool" look. "You don't really hope to fix it, do you?"

"For god's sake, Nora, will you please try to start the damn thing."

She sighed and got in the car.

I looked at the maze of steel, wires, and funny rubber hoses as the motor rapidly turned over without firing. Just as I was about to slam the hood shut, I noticed a faint blue spark from one of the wires.

"Stop a minute," I yelled at Nora. Unbelievably, she heard me and did.

The wire was loose, and I tightened it down. I gave Nora the smuggest look I could produce when we were finally on our way.

The drizzle continued as I made my way from on freeway after another, trying to leave the city behind us.

We were well beyond the city, on a state highway I remembered well from my youth, when I realized what beautiful fall day we were having. Leaves were at their peak of color. I wondered how life had gotten to the point that this was the first time I noticed them. And on this day, of all days.

We made good time, so I stopped in the last small town for two cups of takeout coffee. It was reassuring when they sold it in old-fashioned paper cups, rather than the usual Styrofoam. Life wasn't yet a hundred percent gone to hell.

"Is it much farther now?" Nora asked as we left the town. Her question broke the constant silence we held since leaving home.

"No, not much," I answered. I sipped the coffee. "Not much at all." My tone left it clear that I didn't want to talk.

The gravel road leading to the church hadn't changed since I last saw it. Only a few new houses here and there. But it was the very familiar last curve in the road that brought back the memories and the terrifying reason we were there. I was suddenly weak and empty. An uncomfortable twisting grew in my gut.

The small white church sat at the base of a hill, with the graveyard spread out behind it. Even before we got to the church, I could see the new open hole.

The road in front of the church was filled with cars, as was the limited parking space. I drove past the church and to end of a long line of cars before I parked.

Even in the constant drizzle, several small groups of men stood out in front of the church, talking as they waited for the last moment before going inside.

"Let's go inside now," Nora insisted when I stopped outside.

"Go ahead," I told her, "I'm going to wait here."

"I don't want to go in alone."

"You might as well. You'll be sitting alone anyway." I pointed to the church hall. "Or you could go in there. That's where most of the women are."

"Oh, damn," she said, before picking up m glare. She shrugged and left. "I'll see you after then."

While waiting, I talked to some of the older farmers who remembered me from my frequent visits there when I was a kid. We talked about the kind of year they had, the harvest they were in the middle of, and a little bit of what I was doing now. All of us avoided the reason for being there.

Finally, six of us were asked to come inside, given our instructions, and escorted to the front of the still nearly empty church. Mercifully, they closed the coffin as soon as we sat down. Moments later, people filed inside. The immediate family came in last.

When the service started, I tried to shut it off and the world out, hoping to insulate myself from any more pain. All I accomplished was to force my mind back in time. And to remember who was lying there and who we once were.

There wasn't much we hadn't done together. We were friends from childhood, growing up in the same neighborhood. Summers back then were spent on his grandfather's farm, not far from the church. We worked the fields together and, when we could, fished and hunted. We even went to church.

Older, we chased the same girls. We fought over one once, although I no longer remember her name. We got married and settled down less than a year apart. The restlessness in our marriages hit us about the same time. I don't remember which of us cheated on our wife first, but we quickly became adept at covering for each other. We cheated differently though. I wandered from woman to woman, while he stayed with the same one. I eventually got to know her well, and it was easy to understand why he stayed with her. So it was hard to understand why they recently broke it off. Almost as hard to understand as the reason I was where I was. Why hadn't he talked to me about it or anything else worthwhile lately?

I was in a fog when the service ended, but it still surprised me how light the coffin felt when we carried it out to the gravesite. He wasn't a small man.

The sun was out, with only a few wispy white clouds left in the sky. The recent rain sparkled on the dazzling array of brilliant colors, as it dripped from the leaves of trees dotting the cemetery. Maples were dressed in bright red and gold, and the oaks were a deep scarlet. Normally, they were the last to change color, but some of the elms were still green.

The gravesite was a short way up the hill. I backed away from the rest of the group when the graveside service started. I was feeling terribly sorry for myself and ready to cry when I saw her.

She stood alone at the top of the hill behind us. Her always short blond hair was longer now. She wore it in pigtails, the way she wore it when they met. She wore jeans and a sweater I helped him pick out for her Christmas present just two years ago. Her hands were in her back pockets and she stared at her foot, pushing leaves around on the ground. I didn't know if she was crying, but I hoped not.

After the service, we went into the church hall for lunch. They served thin sandwiches and weak, lukewarm coffee. Nora ate with gusto but worried over my lack of appetite as I half-heartedly chewed a sandwich, hoping I could swallow it.

I finally gave up and got rid of it in the restroom. On the way back to our table, I stopped to chat with a local neighbor woman. She was a pretty lady still, and I remembered the time I managed to kiss her. I was about fourteen. Nora very quickly joined our conversation.

We paid our respects to his family, then left immediately after. It startled me to feel a sudden heat as we stepped out of the church hall. It was a considerable change from the morning chill.

As we walked to the car, I looked once more to the grave, then to the top of the hill.

Kate was gone.

Time Stopped

Michael George

Nora stood when the call came to board her plane. She turned to me, the exasperation still on her face. I felt her heavy sigh, more than heard it.

"I still don't think it's fair that you're not coming," she complained. "There's really no reason why you couldn't."

"Please, Nora," I answered, "we've been through this all week. If you don't want to go, fine. Let's turn in your ticket and go home, but don't nag anymore about it. I'm not going. I can't get away from work right now, and you know it. I've worked too hard to get this job, and it's too important to me to put it in jeopardy, just to see a big city I know I won't like. So get on the plane, or let's go home."

"You're always this way about everything I want to do. You could go."

"The plane is waiting for you, Nora." I kissed her cheek.

"Goodbye then," she said, and as she turned away. "Maybe I just won't come back."

"You will," I said, knowing that I would never get that lucky.

I waited until she was through the door to the plane and left. She expected me to wait there until the plane took off, but I didn't see much sense in it. And we'd broken so many promises to each other over the years that one more wouldn't matter.

I escaped from the airport terminal as fast as I could. I even had the correct change ready when I left the parking lot. As soon as I was away from the airport and on the freeway, I looked for an exit. I was almost out of gas. With Nora gone for a week, my world was almost hassle free. I didn't want to create a new one by running out of gas.

As I approached the third exit, I could see a huge Getty Oil sign pushed high in the air. I left the freeway. The station was crowded, and to get to the only open pump on the self-service island, I had to squeeze between the station and an oversized camper.

I instantly hated the woman pumping gas into the camper. I always hated anyone who owned things like that. It seemed as though I'd worked hard all my life and had damn little to show for it. Sure, I had three-bedroom rambler in one of the nice suburbs, a good-looking wife with more clothes than she could ever wear, a new car, and the pickup I was driving. But right then, it would have been awful easy to give them all up for a camper half that size. As long as I had a place to go in it.

I lifted the hose from the pump with regular gas and took the gas cap off the truck.

"Hello, Tom," she said. "How've you been?"

I had the nozzle in the tank before I realized the woman at the camper was talking to me. I looked up at the familiar face, and tried to put a name on it. Even with the changes in her face and hair, I knew her. I knew her well. But where the hell was the goddamn name? She smiled.

"You don't even remember me." She continued to smile.

Her voice. This time I was listening.

"Kate?"

Jesus, but it all came flooding back. The goddamn hill. The goddamn hill I never climbed. Why the hell didn't I go up there? Why didn't I call her? Why had I never been back? Why, Johnny?

"That's right, Kate," she said, her smile gone. "Sorry I said anything." She turned away.

"Kate," I screamed. "Kate."

I ran to her, grabbed her shoulders and spun her around. When I kissed her, everything I'd felt and tried to bury for the past eight years went into it. I could feel some of the same passion flow out of her.

"That's better," she said, laughing. "You do remember."

"A lot more than I thought I did," I said.

"That's good. I don't think I'd want you to forget it. I know I don't want to. Not ever. We should talk. Go finish your truck. We'll go to my house. It's close."

I followed Kate out of the station. In three short blocks, she stopped in front of a not very fancy story and a half. It was one of thousands built during the fifties. We went inside. The living room was bare. With the exception of a card table, two chairs, and a few dirty dishes in the sink, the kitchen was empty too.

"Excuse the way this place looks,' she said, "but I'm going to be out of here Monday."

"Where're you moving?"

"Into the camper and on the road. I don't have any real definite plans. I'm just going to head west. I don't know when or where I'll stop."

"Are you really?"

"I sure am."

"I envy you. That was my dream when I was young."

"It was Johnny's dream too."

"Yeah, it was. It was all his. Not mine. He used to fill me with it. I was never as good with dreams as he was. I don't think I even know how anymore."

"Why not?"

"I don't know. Maybe I'm just too old now."

"Maybe it's because you never followed them."

"Maybe," I said, wanting to change the subject. "So tell me how you've been. It's been a long time. I heard you got married."

"I did. It didn't last. There was too much of you and Jonny still inside me."

"Me?"

"Don't play those stupid games. Yes, there was too much of you. There was always too much of you. And you know damn good and well there was."

"No, I didn't. I never know that." Goddamn that hill. Damn everything. Why don't people ever tell each other anything? We never say what we mean. Almost never anyway. But this time. "I didn't know. I love you, Kate. For a long time before Johnny died, I loved you. I think I still do."

"You're still married though."

"Yeah."

"You didn't call."

"I know. You didn't call either."

"I didn't think it was my place to do the calling."

"Were you crying, that day on the hill?"

"What the hell are you talking about?"

"That day on the hill. Johnny's funeral. When you were up on the hill alone. Were you crying?"

"Why are you asking me that now?"

"Because I thought you were, and it still bothers me. I almost went up there. Right now, it bothers me even more than it did then, that I didn't."

"It bothers me too. I waited for you."

"You were gone when we came out."

"I was there, but you came out with Nora. I left after you did. I was lonely for a long time…"

"So was I."

"Were you now? Who for?"

"You, Johnny, just lonely. It was an empty time."

"You had Nora. It's more than I had."

"Nobody has Nora. Least of all me. It really was a lonely, empty time. I felt so guilty."

"What about?"

"Johnny. About what happened to Johnny."

"That took a special kind of conceit. What happened to Johnny was his own doing, not ours."

"But he was my best friend. I should have known. I should have stopped him."

"You couldn't have stopped him. No one could. Best friend or not. I couldn't and I knew and I was his lover. I was closer to him than anyone. But I didn't blame myself. I don't have that kind of conceit. You shouldn't either."

"But don't you think that I, you…we might have had something to do with it?"

"There you go again. No. Those last few months, we weren't that important to him."

"Why then? Why would he do it?"

"Just once, you should come out and say it. Why did he kill himself?"

"Okay. Why did he kill himself? I've never understood. Why? He had so much going for him. He had you."

"I don't know all the reasons, but basically, he just couldn't handle life. He couldn't take being a failure."

"But he wasn't! He…"

"I know, but he didn't think so, didn't believe it. And in the end, he was right. He did fail."

"How can you say that? He was good at everything he ever wanted to do."

"Everything except living. And he failed us. He shouldn't have left us that way."

"I…I guess you're right about that. Are you really going to leave on Monday?"

"Sure, why?"

"I just put Nora on a plane. She's going to be gone for a week. I thought it would be nice if we could spend some time together."

"Not that way, Tom"

"Hey, Kate, I didn't mean it that way. I'm not looking for that."

"What are you looking for?"

"Nothing, I haven't looked for anything for a long time."

"Why not? What's the matter with you?"

"I decided that if I was going to be married, I should act like it."

"Sex wasn't the only thing I was referring to."

"That's the main thing though, isn't it?"

"No, Tom. And you know that better than I do."

"Yes, I guess I do. And I think I should go. You must have a lot of getting ready to do."

"I've been getting ready for this for eight years. I don't have anything left to do. Why don't you sit down, and I'll make us breakfast. Unless there's something you have to do."

"I was going to go into the office today, but there's no rush. Breakfast sounds good, if it isn't too much trouble."

"It's not."

I watched as she pulled her last remnants of food out of her battered refrigerator. Her expert hands moved swiftly as she put together two plates of ham, eggs, and toast. They were followed by wine glasses and a bottle from the cupboard.

"Johnny bought this," she said as she opened the wine. "It's supposed to be some kind of vintage or something. He said I shouldn't use it unless it was a special occasion. I think seeing you for the last time is special occasion enough."

I didn't answer her. I was afraid she was right. The wine was good and went down easy. Johnny always knew good wines. Our plates were empty as Kate poured the last of it into our glasses before either of us spoke again

"So," she said, "you work in an office now?"

"Yeah. I got tired of hearing Nora complaining about money and I broke down and got a decent job."

"Do you like it?"

"No."

"Why do it then?"

"The money."

"It's that important?"

"I guess." I finished my wine.

"Would you like another glass? I've got another bottle. It's not as good but…"

"I better not. Any more, and I won't get anything done today."

She shrugged. "Okay."

Our eyes met. That damn hill. I shrugged.

"Fill it up please," I said, smiling.

She returned the smile as she poured. Then we talked. Through the morning and into the afternoon. It didn't take long before the eight years were gone, and I knew her again. I didn't want her to go wherever it was that she was going. I said so.

"Come with me," she said.

"I can't."

"You mean, Tom, that you won't. Can't is not a real word. Not this time."

"Yes, it is, and you know it. I've got too many obligations. I can't just walk away like that."

"I suppose not."

She left her chair, walked over to mine, leaned over, and kissed me.

I stood, kissed her, then held her in my arms. Somehow, we drifted into the living room. I kissed her again and again, and we were lying on the carpeted floor. When I moved my hands, she pushed them off and rolled away from me.

"Not here and not now," she said.

"I'm sorry," I said.

"Don't be."

"But I am. I shouldn't have done that."

"Yes, dammit, you should have. Just not here."

"Do you want to go in the bedroom?"

"No! I think it's time for you to go now."

I knew how stupid my question was, but I didn't think there was anything I could do about it. I got up and walked to the door

"Goodbye, Kate," I said, opening it.

"Tom," she called, "wait."

She flowed into my arms and we kissed.

"Now go," she said, "but don't forget, I'll be leaving Monday."

The door was quickly closed behind me. I drove home in a daze. Our house was twice the size of Kate's, and Nora's decorating looked professional, but it didn't seem like much when I went in. I drank a double shot of scotch over a couple of ice cubes. I couldn't taste it. I had two more and went to bed.

I was up before sunrise. I spent the day with a scotch in my hand, wandering around from room to room in the house, in the garage, and out in the yard, admiring all the things Nora and I owned. I tried to find something that I really cared about. I didn't. I was numb drunk when I fell in bed.

The sun in my eyes woke me. I rolled over and tried to focus on the clock. I was late for work. I thought of Kate. What the hell did I care about work? But knew I should call them and tell them I wasn't going in. I decided hell with it anyway.

I knew Kate would be gone, but I drove by her house. I didn't know what to do. I started driving. I had to get out of the city. Anywhere, it didn't matter. I drove for over an hour before I realized where I was going, however indirect. It wasn't until I got out of the truck by the church that my stomach started to roll in slow circles. When I got to Johnny's grave, the tears came. I sat down, staring at the small flat stone, just above his head. What a waste it all was. What a goddamn pathetic waste. Time stopped as I sat there, wondering how I ever came to be such a fool.

I didn't see the camper until I started down. Something made me turn around and look to the top of the hill. She stood there alone, pushing last year's dead leaves around with her foot. Her hair was in pigtails, the way she used to wear it when they were together. Her hands were in her back pockets. I started back up.

"I'll have to go back to the house to get my things," I said when I reached her.

"Tomorrow, maybe," she said, taking my hand. "Right now, let's go home."

We walked down the hill to the camper together.

Books by Michael George

Horses Lemons And Pretty Girls
Finding Peri Gray
Of Rain Barrels And Bridges

The Refuge Series
Why A Refuge
Bridge To No Good
Grass Was Greener
To Save The Refuge

Bud George

I am a high school dropout, expelled weeks before graduation.

Married at eighteen; it lasted fifty-eight years. There are four children, seven grandchildren, and four great-grandchildren.

I worked from age thirteen—truck farms, grocery stores, roadside produce markets, supermarket produce manager, security guard, computer operator, construction laborer, union carpenter, and state licensed contractor.

I inquired about a GED test about sixty-two years after not graduating. Nope. No paper test, computer only. I am computer illiterate.

Michael George

Michael is a retired carpenter with a varied working background—operated and programmed the old main frame computers, managed a 24/7 service station, managed a dairy farm, owned and operated a furniture building company, and even picked potatoes with Mexican migrant farm workers. He has been married for over fifty years, had five children, with only three still living, and has countless grandchildren and great-grandchildren.

David George

In my younger days, I worked as a farm laborer, house painter, janitor, and carpenter's helper. I fell in love with theater and worked for many years as an actor and director. That love competed with another: foreign languages and international travel. With many stops and starts, I eventually completed my PhD and became a college professor. Though teaching was my true calling, I also published scholarly books and essays, as well as literary translations. In my spare time, I wrote short stories, some of which appear in *Stories By Three Brothers*. Now retired, I'm working on my first novel. I've been married for thirty-plus years and that union produced my pride and joy, a son, whose brilliance keeps the darkness at bay.

Lightning Source UK Ltd.
Milton Keynes UK
UKHW020536081020
371109UK00001B/7/J